Bury him darkly

Having sold up her employment agency in New York, Philipa Lowe is returning home to England on the QE2. She need never work again, but already she is finding herself bored. This is eased when she meets Bella Fields, better known as the TV star Roma Felucci, who is at least intriguing. There is an underlying tension about Bella, which Philipa cannot analyse. Is she in flight from something – perhaps her husband, Jay? Or does she feel threatened by what is to face her in England?

Bella declares she is returning to her home town after ten years in the States, merely to see the old house again. This seems innocuous enough, but, if this is the only expectation, why is she picked up by the police on disembarking at Southampton?

Philipa pursues her to Horseley Green, to find that Bella was wanted for questioning. When she is released, Philipa manages to discover from her the basis of it all. Bella's father disappeared ten years ago, and there was suspicion that he had been killed.

Later, Philipa is present when proof of a death is uncovered. But to whom did the second skull belong?

BURY HIM DARKLY

Roger Ormerod

Constable · London

First published in Great Britain 1991
by Constable & Company Limited
3 The Lanchesters, 162 Fulham Palace Road
London W6 9ER
Copyright © Roger Ormerod 1991
The right of Roger Ormerod to be
identified as the author of this work
has been asserted by him in accordance
with the Copyright, Designs and Patents Act 1988
ISBN 0 09 470880 0
Set in Linotron Palatino by
CentraCet, Cambridge
Printed in Great Britain by
St Edmundsbury Press Limited,
Bury St Edmunds, Suffolk

A CIP catalogue record for this book
is available from the British Library

1

I was going home. That was what I kept telling myself – you're going home, Philipa. Home being England. And I was doing it in style, in the leisurely and luxurious manner that befitted a woman with decidedly independent means. So why wasn't I happy? I'd deliberately chosen the QE2 rather than fly, simply so that I could savour over a longer period the feeling of release, and anticipate the joy of home-coming. Yet I found myself restless and unsettled. New York does that to you. You either hate it or you love it, and I'd lived there long enough to grow into loving it. I could not shake my mind free from the fact that I was leaving, not returning to, something.

Get it down to basics, and that was really the trouble. There I was, able to settle into genteel retirement, and me only in the thirties, damn it all. I'd worked all my life. Worked hard. Now I didn't need to, and I was already bored half out of my mind. And I couldn't imagine anything interesting waiting for me in England. Well . . . there was Detective Inspector Oliver Simpson, but I wasn't sure what his reaction would be. Enigmatic, that was Oliver.

I had a luxury single cabin on the boat deck, which meant I was only a step away from miles of promenade deck and acres of space for deck chairs and general relaxation. But it was October, and the weather wasn't all that marvellous, so that only the hearty few of us ventured into the open and the very fresh sea air that first morning. It was there that I met her, tramping towards me at a slight list against the wind, one hand clamped on a wide-brimmed hat, which was ridiculously unwieldy out there, head down, and with some sort of wide beach slacks or culottes flapping around her legs. The dark mirror glasses were surely superfluous as there'd been no sign of the sun since we'd sailed from New York.

As we approached she seemed to notice me only at the last possible second. A gust of wind nearly took the hat from her hand, clamping it over her face, and she seemed to stagger. I stepped sideways, but all the same we nearly collided.

'Stupid woman,' I heard her mutter.

Then she was past me, and I was left to stare after her, wondering whether she would be able to remain on her feet. She couldn't have been drunk, as it was pre-breakfast-time. But the spike-heeled shoes certainly wouldn't have been much help.

And yet I'd had the distinct impression, the previous evening, that those same mirror glasses had been viewing me from a discreet distance, and more than once.

So naturally I kept my eyes busy after that, searching her out. It was something to do. That shows how derelict my mind had become, that I couldn't find anything better. I'd go mad, I realized, without some objective in my life.

She was there for breakfast in the Columbia Restaurant, with a table all to herself in a corner, like someone hiding behind her dark glasses, yet in a manner guaranteed to draw attention. She had changed into something very casual but elegant, and clearly expensive.

Only gradually did it impress itself on me that I was not the only one finding interest in her. She was very beautiful, and thus would attract attention, but this was a murmurous and distinct attention, though of course, in the Columbia, dignified and subdued. But people did turn in their seats; they did whisper to each other and glance again. They were doing it at my own table. I didn't dare to seek out her identity, not wishing to seem a fool, so, as we'd already met, so to speak, I took my second cup of coffee over to her table, sat in the spare chair, and asked, 'D'you mind if I join you?'

She stared intently at me. I was reflected in miniature twice in her lenses, both smiling. Her expression was completely blank, but nothing, not even the immobility, could detract from the perfection of her face. Usually there's a tiny flaw, the eyes too close or too slanted, the nose not in proportion, the mouth too wide, too small, or too prim. But no, she had every item correctly placed and in absolutely perfect proportions. I'd have gone for

6

a lighter make-up myself, though. Looking closer, I could see that what was visible around her eyes had been over-treated, and the lipstick applied too generously. Her hair was a golden brown, not so far from my own hair colour, which resembles copper wire and usually looks like a tight tangle. Hers was perfectly styled, sweeping down behind her ears, and with a hint of fringe over her wide brows.

I had plenty of time to absorb all this, because she took a long while deciding how best to tell me to bugger off. Then she whipped off the glasses and blinked. I'd been correct about the eyes. Too much eye-shadow. But they were a clear and intelligent grey.

'Is it dyed?' she asked.

'What . . .'

'Your hair.'

I laughed. 'No. It's how it is. It's like copper wire, and I can't do anything about it.'

'Remarkable. And the eyes?'

'Pardon? What about my eyes?'

'You're not wearing coloured contact lenses?'

This was all very strange, even slightly insulting. 'Of course not. They're naturally brown.'

'Which', she observed, 'goes darker when you're angry.'

'Is it surprising . . .'

'Sorry. I was being too personal.'

Then, as though to close the incident, she made a move to replace the glasses. I said, 'I wouldn't, you know. Too much shading makes your irises shy, and then they won't close down and you lose your distance vision.'

'How clever of you. But I need them.'

'Weak eyes?'

'No. Protection. I'm hoping not to be recognized.'

'They draw attention,' I assured her. 'And you have been.'

'Is that so?'

'Everybody seems to know you.'

She raised her eyebrows. The lips twitched, almost into a smile. 'You nearly persuade me that you don't.'

I grinned at her, then pursed my lips and shook my head.

'You don't?' She leaned back in her chair, forward again. Then she hissed, 'Roma Felucci.'

7

'Ah!' I said.

'You still . . .'

'I'm sorry. But as you said, I'm stupid.'

'As I said . . . oh, I see. I didn't mean you, I meant me. Those ridiculous shoes! Sorry. My apologies.'

'It's quite all right. But tell me – who *are* you?'

'Jesus! Where have you been? Don't you watch the telly?'

'I've been in New York for the past few years, working fifteen hours a day. No, I never had the time nor the patience to watch the box. I don't even own one.'

'Well . . .' she said. 'I never thought I'd meet such a person. Haven't you even heard of *Colossus*? That's our show. *Colossus*.'

'Never heard of it.'

'Ha!' she barked mirthlessly. Then she put her head back and really laughed, a spendidly fluent peel of joy. Heads lifted all over the place. 'Oh, I *am* glad I met you. Jay would be shocked, but he's got no sense of anything but his own importance.'

'Jay?' I asked politely.

'My husband. Jay Messenger. Male lead in the series.'

'But you're Roma – '

'My film name, that is. My professional name.' She leaned forward so I did too. She wished to confide. Her accent had been middle-west with a touch of Irish, but abruptly it became very English, Shropshire English. 'I'm Bella Fields, really. Bella Messenger . . . for now. The bastard. Never mind that. D'you want my autograph?'

'No, thank you.'

'Good. Then let's get out of here.'

That was the beginning of our friendship, if it can be so described. Relationship, perhaps. Suddenly I found myself very popular. The eager fans of Roma Felucci seemed reluctant to approach her. She adopted an icy reserve, which I felt was a deliberate barrier, but that was before I got to know the fiery and unpredictable bitch she portrayed on the screen. Perhaps it wasn't entirely an act. Whatever the reason, she was avoided by everyone but me. So I was the one to be approached, and I spent a fair part of my time fending off their eager enquiries. As this is somewhat dampening to the ego, I soon discovered I was happier with Roma than without.

She seemed indifferent to my reason for seeking her company,

8

but not displeased. We did not reach the relaxed and cheerful relationship that required only the casual remark, 'See you at the Theatre Bar', to arrange the next meeting. I would look around, there she would be, alone and with a space around her, and I would fill it. Her eyes possibly lit up at my approach, but I couldn't tell. I wondered whether she slept in those damned mirror glasses.

It is not surprising that I began to feel protective towards her, as I reckoned I was the elder by a year or two. She seemed so lost and remote. It was even difficult to extract from her the reason for this journey.

'Going back home,' she said, when I gently pressed the point. 'A week or two, just to see the old place. It's been ten years. Sure to be that. Who's counting? God knows what it's like now. It was nearly falling down then. One of those square, red-brick old dumps they used to build, about six bedrooms and a huge kitchen with an old range. And we . . .'

At that, she seemed to recollect herself and put her glass to her lips to silence them. We were in the Yacht Club Bar at the time, me on gin and lime and she on bourbon on the rocks. I waited. Nothing more.

'Where?' I asked.

'What?'

'This house. Where is it?'

'On the edge of town.'

'Which is?'

She raised her chin. 'What's it to you? I hated the place.'

'But all the same you're going back. Didn't you mention Shropshire?'

She flicked her glass with a long finger-nail, provoking a ting. The note was that of an empty glass. I called them in.

'I did not,' she said confidently.

'Perhaps it was the accent,' I conceded.

She cocked her head at me. A note of approval entered her voice. 'You've got a good ear. It's Shropshire, yes. Nearly in Wales. Horseley Green. Know it?'

'Not forty miles from Penley, my own home town.'

'Well! Small world.' She was losing interest.

'And a touch of Irish,' I said.

9

'It's still there?' I might have been using it as a criticism, the way she was suddenly on the defensive.

'Shouldn't it be?'

She shrugged. Every gesture was overdone. 'Doesn't matter. I'm the wild Irish-American bitch in the series. I left it in.'

'The accent?'

'Sure, the accent. I got that in Dublin.' As though she'd found it in a shop. 'I was there two years. Theatre mostly, before a tiny part in a film. With Jay. I'd met him a couple of years before that, when I'd got a bit part on the stage. At the Alex, that was, in Birmingham. Brum. You ever been there?'

'Birmingham, yes. The Alex, no. I've never been much of a theatre-goer.' I sensed a loss of interest, which usually came when we weren't talking about herself. 'You were saying – about your husband? Jay, isn't it?'

'Dear Jay! He saw me on the stage in Dublin, and he remembered me, and got me a bit part in a film. Isn't that marvellous! He was in Ireland making one of those wild-Irish-boy films. That was him. The wild Irish boy! Christ, he was over forty at that time. You couldn't tell, though. *I* couldn't tell. I'd be . . . what?. . . just over twenty. And in the film we were supposed to be young lovers! Jesus! The fake! That's what he was, and always has been. Every couple of years he goes to a clinic and has a year chopped off his face. You never see the real Jay. Nobody does. Except his wife, and that's me.'

'That was where you married him?' I asked. 'In Ireland?'

'Oh no. He came back for me. Now ain't that romantic!' Her disgust slipped her into the vernacular. 'Flew over to take me to the States. And I've been there since.'

I did some mental calculations that she would now be about thirty. She looked much more mature, I thought. Certainly you'd take her for older than me. The first mirror I came across, I checked. Yes. Perhaps I was older, but I thought I looked the younger.

At that stage I decided she was in flight from her husband, going back to pre-Jay days. She seemed in flight from something, though I got no further than that at the time. Her tension was probably part of her personality.

I told her a little about myself. This was on the third morning, with the weather brighter and the breeze no more than a light one. I caught up with her on the promenade deck. As usual, she was elegant, slim, walking purposefully with a straight back. She grunted a greeting, not quite rejection. So I told her about my years in New York, as partner in an enterprise that found important jobs for top executive types. On my partner's death I'd decided to sell out and return to England. Already, I confided, I wasn't sure I'd done the right thing. I couldn't remove from my mind the memory of the parting from Marietta, my secretary, tearful in each other's arms. How long would she take to forget me?

Roma's first comment on this review of my life was probably coloured by five years of *Colossus* scripts. 'You've got a man waiting for you,' she decided.

'I'm not sure. There's hardly anybody I know, though there's a policeman . . . I'm not certain of his interest.'

'Then forget him, darlin',' she advised. 'You'll never be sure. I've been married eight years to that bastard, Jay, and I still don't know.'

'You think he might follow you?'

'I'll kill the friggin' louse if he does.'

'I'll keep an eyes on the newspapers,' I assured her. 'Star of *Colossus* Found Dead in Ditch.'

I said it lightly, even laughed to soften the mood, but she merely glanced at me and tossed her head. Their marriage must have throbbed with tension.

By the evening of the third day at sea I'd officially switched tables to be more often with her. I felt I still hadn't learned why she was returning to England. It was just that it seemed to be a matter of self-esteem that I should solve this small mystery. It was in my blood, digging into people's lives and aspirations. Already I was feeling more relaxed and confident, probing the enigma of Roma Felucci.

'Do they know?' I asked, over the main course, the fillet of pork medallions.

'Who?'

'Your company, bosses, whatever. The *Colossus* people. Do they know where you are and where you're heading?'

'I doubt it.' She peered at her plate. 'I took a month off.'

'They can spare you, can they? You as the lead – and it's a weekly show, I gather.'

11

The medallions bored her; she was easily bored. She thrust her plate aside, banging her elbows on the table and cupping her chin. Her eyes were bright. I'd managed to persuade her to discard the shades.

'You're nosy, d'you know that?'

'I was just thinking the same.'

'I don't understand your interest.'

'It passes the time, and your life's a damned sight more glamorous than mine.'

She lit a cigarette, whipped it from her lips sideways, blew smoke upwards. I hate people smoking between courses. 'Glamorous? Hah! Funny. It's just a grind. You've seen the show – no, you said you hadn't. Right. We work ahead. Have to. There were eight weeks in hand, eight shows on tape, and we were easy. So we all had a month off. It'll be back to the grindstone, a script stuck in my fist, and we'll be shooting the first scene a quarter of an hour later. We improvise a bit. Have to.'

'Yes,' I said. 'I suppose so.'

Twice she had said, 'Have to'. There was clearly a tight regimen involved, Hurry, hurry. No time to sit and ponder.

The waiter came to collect the plates. She chose the cheesecake with the hot blueberries, I the strawberries and ice cream. She seemed not to worry about her figure, ate whatever she fancied, and yet remained slim and shapely. Burned it all off, I suppose, with her simmering internal aggression, which was never too far from the surface.

'This *Colossus*,' she said, 'it's a chain of hotels. All over the States. We shoot it all in the studio in New Jersey, and they fill in with shots of other cities. It's mostly office set and boardroom set, and my bedroom. I'm the boss of *Colossus*, since my father died. That was dear old Joss Delavere. He really did die – on the set. They had to write me in as the new boss, so it got me the starring role. Jay was livid. It gave me top billing. Over him. Livid, he was. Fuming. It was worth it, just to see his face. In the show he's the trouble-shooter, travelling to all the hotels where things're happening, though he doesn't actually go anywhere. It's all done in the studio. We have rows. In the script, I mean. Flaming fights. People love it. Then we go back to our own flat and have our own flaming rows.'

She popped in the final blueberry. Her lips were purple. She

12

distorted them into a grimace. I gathered that even the old house, falling down or not, would be a welcome change. Crumbling masonry for crumbling marriage. But perhaps not. She seemed concerned more about what she was going to face at Horseley Green than what she was fleeing from.

This seemed to be confirmed the following morning. It was our last day at sea, and we were due to dock at 1 p.m., GMT. From breakfast onwards she seemed more tense, more often to be found standing at the prow than at the stern. We had entered the Channel.

I tested it out, still probing. 'What happens if you don't get back in time?' I asked.

I had slipped quietly to her side at the rail. Perhaps she hadn't realized. Her head whipped round, and abruptly there was dark fear in those grey eyes, at once disappearing. She did one of her elaborate shrugs.

'They'll write me out of the script. Should be easy,' she told me sourly, the wind whipping at the silk scarf she had round her neck. 'The last episode we've taped . . . oh, there was all the drama and emotion you could wish for. I'd got a lover, you see. In the script. Am I making myself clear?' she demanded.

'Indeed you are. As the boss-lady you'd have packs of lovers.'

She eyed me suspiciously, then tossed her head. 'As long as you understand. My lover . . . he'd just been found dead in his burnt-out auto at the bottom of a cliff. That gave me a good long hysterical scene . . .'

'Top of the drawer acting,' I put in.

'What?'

'I thought – it would take all your acting ability, you being hysterical.'

'Oh? Explain yourself.'

'You told me. This character you play, she's all fire and brimstone. *She* would never indulge in hysteria.'

'But she would! She *would*. You don't understand her at all. In business she's cold and tough, a fighter. But underneath she's all emotion, all warmth and love, and . . . and . . .'

'Sex?'

'Yes, damn you.'

'I can imagine. Which was what it'd been with this character

13

in the burnt-out car! Yes, I see it now. Of *course* you'd be hysterical. I would myself.'

'Will you *please* try to separate the character from the actor!'

I grinned at her. 'That'd be for you, Roma.' And I wasn't sure how far the character had taken possession of the woman, or I'd have called her Bella. 'But you were saying: that last episode in the series . . .'

It was several seconds before she dragged her eyes from mine. Perhaps I'd hit too close. Then at last, 'You're so blasted difficult to talk to, Philipa Lowe. We're talking about acting, here. Acting.'

'So tell me. You had a splendid hysterical scene – '

'Then I got in my own auto and drove at an insane speed to the cliff where he'd died, and the show closed with the credits running over a shot of my Cadillac driving straight at the cliff edge.'

'Dramatic,' I said. Corny, I thought. 'And so?'

'What the hell does that mean?'

'And so . . .what happens next?'

'How would *I* know? Use your intelligence, if you've got any. I'll get back and grab a script, and then I'll know.'

'Guess,' I suggested. 'For poor, stupid Philipa.'

Once more there was a hint of her smile. We were for the moment tuned to the same wavelength. 'I'd scream to a skidding halt a yard from the cliff edge, and bury my face in my hands. Tears for him, my lost lover, and tears for myself because I hadn't had the guts to follow him over the cliff, and because I hadn't loved him enough for that, after all . . . and then, head high, a sniff, an expression of firm resolution. *Colossus* needs me, broken heart and all . . . and a close-up of my hand engaging reverse. Fade. For God's sake, woman, use your imagination!'

'And you'd convey all that without dialogue?'

'Of course. Why not?'

'Clever you. And the alternative, if you don't get back in time?'

'Hah!' She loved to use her bark of derision. 'They simply write me out. There'd be a funeral. Mine. They wouldn't need me for it. And a new head for *Colossus*. Probably that bastard, Jay Messenger.'

14

'What a fascinating life it is, this acting business.'

'It's tooth and nail,' she said bitterly. 'Damn it all, look at the time. I'll have to go and pack. What about you?'

My turn to shrug. 'All done. I like to watch the coast getting closer.'

Then she walked away. There'd been no exchange of addresses; neither of us could offer one. There had been no expressions of mutual affection, even muted, no sorrow that we might never see each other again.

Disembarking, I saw nothing of her. I was far too busy to look for her, anyway. The Customs people were very thorough, and the luggage search was comprehensive, and though I wasn't too heavily encumbered with cases – most of my stuff was coming over as freight – I was caught by a specially suspicious official, who ransacked every item I had. Perhaps I looked like a smuggler.

When I eventually fought myself free I reckoned I'd be lucky to find a taxi. But there was one at the kerb. I assumed it was a taxi, because there was Bella/Roma just getting in, though it seemed unusual that the driver should be helping her into the rear seat, with a hand on her arm. Then I saw that the driver was still sitting behind the wheel, and that the one with his hand on her arm was using a fair amount of force.

I abandoned my trolley and began to run. 'Heh!' I shouted. Flashes of thought skittered through my mind. Kidnap! A rival TV company, crippling the opposition! 'Hey, you there!' I cried.

For a second the man looked round. His hand flashed inside his jacket. It couldn't be, I thought, couldn't be! And it wasn't. His hand emerged holding a leather folder. He flicked it open with one finger, and waved it beneath my nose. I recognized it as an identity card of some kind.

'Police,' he said severely. 'Keep out of this, ma'am, if you please.'

Then he was thrusting her inside, and she managed no more than one quick glance back at me. The door slammed and they pulled away. No screaming tyres. This wasn't television, it was for real. And all I could remember was the look in Bella's eyes. She was an expert at conveying emotion without dialogue.

'Help me,' the eyes had said. 'Help me.'

I felt her mirror glasses crunch beneath my feet.

15

2

For a few moments there was panic. My mind wouldn't focus, couldn't accept it. Half an hour on British soil and she'd been picked up by the police! But why should I care? We were shipboard acquaintances, and these relationships normally remain transient. 'We'll keep in touch.' But nobody ever does. Yet I recalled her peculiar unease. She had been expecting something. I wasn't sure that I wanted to become involved.

I went back to where I'd left my luggage trolley, secured a taxi without too long a wait, and directed him to the police station. It made a change for him, no doubt.

'Police?' he asked.

'Please.'

He dropped me outside, and a young copper in uniform helped me into Reception with my stuff. 'Come to stay, have you?' he asked. I couldn't work up a smile.

Neither could the desk sergeant, a bluff and experienced officer who'd seen it all, and wasn't impressed by my contribution.

'Not us,' he told me.

'Well, who then?' I demanded. 'You ought to realize – I *have* to know. He said he was from the police, but how can I be sure? It might have been a kidnapping. You never know.'

'Important, is she?'

'She's the star of *Colossus*,' I said in an awed voice, and he reached for a phone, whispered and nodded, and replaced it.

'It's quite in order, ma'am,' he said. 'It *was* the police. Official.'

'Then can I see her?'

'Not us. They were from Shropshire. Their case – their men.'

I stared blankly at him. 'Their case? What case?'

'Don't ask me,' he said. 'Must be important, though, or they'd have asked us to pick her up.'

'Ah!' I said. 'Yes.' My mind felt like cotton wool. 'Where can I hire a car, d'you think?'

'Just down the road.' He gestured. 'Coupla hundred yards.'

I looked round helplessly at my clutter of luggage, three suitcases and a bulky canvas thing with shoulder straps. 'Can I leave this lot here?'

Straight-faced he said, 'Might get 'em pinched.'

I sighed. Funny-man. But my constable was right behind me. 'I'll help you, miss.'

He led the way with one case in each hand and one under his arm. I struggled after him, hunching a shoulder to keep the straps on. Two hundred yards, the sergeant had said. It seemed more like half a mile.

The constable dumped his load in front of the hire office. I thanked him. 'It's been a pleasure.' He saluted, just like the old-time coppers, and departed. A young man with a bright future, but perhaps not in the police.

I signed for a neat little Rover 213, after I'd assured the young lady I could drive on the left. Was my accent becoming American, I wondered? But my driving licence is British, so everything was legal. I loaded my luggage on to the back seat, consulted the map they supplied, and got going. It had begun to rain. Fortunately, I could do the whole trip without using motorways, which are bad enough in dry weather and pure misery when it's wet. By this time I was hungry, having missed lunch, so I called in at a fast-food production line, swallowed something I couldn't recognize, and pushed on.

It turned out to be about a hundred and eighty miles to Shrewsbury, over two hundred when I found Horseley Green, which was barely more than a tiny dot on the map. But it rated more than that, a sprawl of a town in a green and lush valley. Hence the name, I supposed. I halted on the rise, looking down on it, the view not very clear because the light was going and because the rain was now a fine drizzle. Probably it had been, and still might be, a marketing centre, but on the outer reaches there were buildings that had to be factories, they were so ugly and graceless. I drove down, slowly now, eyes busy to get the general atmosphere. Yes, factories, one of those battery hen places I detest, and an agricultural machinery distribution point, a tannery, and a fertilizer manufacturer. One would know they were there when the wind was right. On the far edge of the town a large building crowded the slope, with a ghostly tall chimney puffing gloomy grey smoke into the mist.

I began to wonder whether I'd made a mistake. Perhaps they hadn't brought her here, but to Shrewsbury, or to regional HQ, which wouldn't necessarily be in the county town. But I had to start from somewhere. Slowly, I drove into the town centre.

There was, in fact, a Green with its pond, fed and drained by a tiny stream that ran in a culvert under the main street. They treasured their Green; it was surrounded by an iron, spiked fence. The town centre was large enough to boast a Sainsbury's, a Woolworth's and a small arcade. They didn't seem to offer a car park, though, as far as I could see, and the police station was along a side street with a cobbled surface. The street-lights, which were now lit, were affixed to the walls.

I parked directly in front. Let them chase me off or tow it away – I was tired and niggly, looking for a fight. This wasn't the homecoming I'd anticipated.

The building was an ungainly three-storey red brick monstrosity, sprawling and untidy, possibly built originally as an important town house by one of the local dignitaries. There was a blue lamp at the head of half a dozen wide steps, POLICE on a sign over the double doors, which were wide open and welcoming. Big enough to be run by a superintendent, I decided from my purely vicarious experience, my father having retired as a chief superintendent. They'd possibly brought here here, so the related incident or incidents had occurred in this town.

Straightening my shoulders, I marched up the steps.

A tiled hallway, my heels echoing into a lofty ceiling, a smell of disinfectant, and a long bench along one wall, polished by thousands of fidgeting bottoms. Facing this there was a wide counter, with nothing on it except a bell. Behind it, at a table against a side wall, a uniformed constable was leaning forward to stare at a VDU, and wearing headphones larger then his ears. I banged the button on top of the bell. Paused. Did it again. Its ting didn't penetrate the headphones, but a burly station sergeant entered through a side doorway, wiping his hands on a dirty old towel.

18

'Well, madam?' he asked. 'In a hurry, are we?'

No, I wasn't, I realized. It was after six o'clock, but I was prepared to argue for hours. I was tired, but my brain was bouncing around with stimulation and an empty stomach.

'Have you got a woman called Roma Felucci here?' I asked quietly.

'And who are you, ma'am?' he asked.

I told him. Philipa Lowe. Arrived on the QE2 that very day. That was to clue him in on my interest, but he was unimpressed. He held up a hand while he wrote it all down.

'What was that name again?' he asked.

'Roma Felucci.' I spelled it for him.

He wrote it down, lifted his head. 'Not to my knowledge,' he told me, going back a few questions.

'Star of *Colossus*.'

He wrote it down. 'What's that?'

'A television soap.'

'Is it?' I hoped he could spell soap.

'You'd perhaps know her here as Bella Fields. Or Bella Messenger. Or Isabella, I suppose. Or any permutation of those.'

He wrote it down, heavily ponderous, a great masculine lout who was having his bit of fun with the helpless and agitated female.

'And your interest, may I ask?'

I told him again that we'd met on the QE2. 'And as soon as she set foot on British soil,' I said tersely, 'she was apprehended, kidnapped, arrested, whatever you'd like to call it, by two men purporting to be police officers in the performance of their duties. Write it down,' I told him sharply. 'Or call your superior. It shouldn't be difficult to locate one.'

He stared at me. The point of his pencil snapped off. I said, 'Now look what you've done.'

He went to a corner and used a phone, whispering with his eyes on me, while the young constable turned and winked. He could hear well enough. Inside two minutes the sergeant was back. 'Inspector Connaught will be down. If you'd care to take a seat . . .'

Then he lost interest in me, and I simply stood there, not intending to sit because it had been almost an instruction, not

19

intending to walk back and forth and betray my tension. It was becoming clear that I'd intruded into something of importance, even possibly of unpleasantness.

Then suddenly, quietly, he stood before me, a man in his fifties, I guessed. Inspector Connaught. Arnold, I discovered later. This was one of your sleek ones, dapper, slim, smartly dressed in a grey suit and a red tie, his moustache beautifully trimmed, as though he counted the hairs each side of the parting, his hair light brown, abundant and professionally styled. A woman's man, this one was, you could see it in his eyes. He expected a reaction, to detect something sparking between us. As it might have done, if his mouth hadn't ruined the impact, his lips too moist and with the hint of a sarcastic quirk in the corners.

'What can I do for you?' he asked, no inflexion in it.

Patiently, I went through it again, staring into his sexy brown eyes and not offering anything. 'Roma Felucci', I said, 'or Bella Fields or Bella Messenger. Is she here?'

'We have an Isabella Fields, yes.' He was eyeing me now with intense interest.

'Is she under arrest?'

'No. There's no crime to level at her.'

'Then what the hell . . .'

'She is being questioned,' he said soothingly.

'Is it permissible to tell me what about?'

He smiled at my controlled patience. 'Perhaps you'd better ask her about that yourself.'

'You're releasing her?'

'We ought to be through in half an hour or so. We keep getting the same answers.'

I hesitated, then looked away from him so that I could concentrate. 'Is there a decent hotel here?' I asked.

'You could try the Crown. Very sedate. You'd like it, though the beer's lousy.'

'Then I'll register there and be right back. All right?'

He smiled. One eyebrow twitched. 'Is that your car outside? Yes? Then turn her around, and go back to the main street, turn right, and it's on your left, just before you reach the castle.'

'I am much obliged,' I assured him politely, formally.

The castle was no more than the crumbling remains of a keep

and a bit of collapsing wall. What could they expect, building a defensive stronghold in the bottom of a valley? Sheep were grazing on the grass in the courtyard. The Crown wasn't impressive, but the inside was soothing and restful. They didn't waste much money on light bulbs. I registered for a double room overlooking the street, and was told there was a small car park at the rear. Later, I discovered it was better described as a yard. There wasn't a lift, and I'd never get all my stuff up those stairs, so I slipped the receptionist a quid and he did it for me. He was young and strong, and the way he reacted to my smile meant I'd wasted my money. He'd have taken them up a mountain for me.

I took the Rover back to the station, because that was where Bella's luggage would be. She was pacing up and down in front of the desk, looking *distraite* and severe, a caged tigress searching for somebody to bite.

'Oh, it's you,' she said. 'They said somebody . . .' She finished it with a gesture, impatient and graceless. I might have been her maid.

We took her stuff out to the car. You'd have thought she was moving home, not just sneaking a month off. 'Here?' she asked, surveying the hotel. 'The Imperial's better.' Then she forgot it. 'I need a bath, a shower. Something. They made me feel filthy . . .'

He was there, eagerly, my receptionist. One look at her . . . oh, *he* knew her. At once.

'This way, Miss Felucci.' And he led the way up the stairs.

She looked round the room. The receptionist slid out, feeling the sudden chill. She stared at the twin beds.

'What's this?' she demanded. 'I don't want a double room.'

'I thought – '

'Please don't make decisions for me.'

I gestured to the phone. 'Ring down and tell them. They'll find you something more suitable. But I thought you'd want a bit of company.'

In fact, I'd wanted to keep an eye on her, and a shared room seemed to be the obvious way. Friendship didn't enter into it. I wasn't yet certain of my own feelings on this matter. It was she who'd seemed to be in need of a friend – but she didn't encourage this sentiment.

21

'Why did you follow me here?' she demanded.

I shrugged. 'You seemed to be in trouble.'

'Nobody asked you.'

'Nobody had the time. I had to make a decision.'

She pouted, dismissing the decision. 'It's none of your damned business.'

'I'm interested. You seemed to need help.' I was still being very gentle with her, determined not be be insulted into retreat.

'You? Who're you to help?' she demanded, crossing quickly to the window and looking out. 'Nobody asked you,' she repeated.

But I could remember that expression in her eyes. 'I had the idea we were friends,' I suggested quietly. 'At least, I've got a shoulder you can cry on.'

She whirled on me. 'Cry? Who wants to friggin' cry? I need to strangle somebody, kick a door down, smash something.'

'It's not in the script.'

'Then tell me how they knew!' she challenged. 'They were waiting. I haven't been in England for ten years. But they were waiting. Some bastard tipped 'em off. If it was Jay, I'll kill him. I swear it.' She thrust a cigarette between her lips, snapped the lighter at it, and nearly choked herself trying to speak at the same time. 'After ten bleedin' years!' she gasped.

'So it must be important.'

'What?'

'That the police still wanted you. That's what makes it important.'

'For questioning. *Questioning*.'

'It must matter to them, though.'

'Yeah – to them. *They* call it murder. They can't even prove he's dead, though.'

'Who?' I almost breathed it. We were getting to basics.

'My father. Where's the blasted bathroom?'

'That door there.'

She flung a small case on to the right-hand bed and ransacked it for what she wanted, drifting underwear all over the floor. Then she marched into the bathroom.

'No bloody shower!' she shouted.

'Have a good soak then. And hurry it up. I want a bath, too.'

I heard the water flowing. 'Ye gods, it's brown!' she howled.

22

'It'll run clear.' I went to stand in the doorway. Stripped, she demonstrated the fact that she needed no artificial aids for her figure. Slim, perfectly proportioned, beautiful. Why is it that some people have the lot? It just is not fair! She settled herself in for a good old soak, as I'd suggested, so it soon became clear that I'd have to wait a long while for my turn. She was a wallower. We would be too late for dinner downstairs, and I was starving. But I waited, and I listened, because the water soothed her and the fury soaked out of her, and she gave me the facts I'd been dying for. Threw them at me. Discarded facts.

'My mother died,' she told me, 'when I was about four. There were two of us, me and my sister Tonia, two years younger than me. I say mom died. I still don't know. We were little kids . . . I suppose my father didn't know what to tell us. Said she'd gone away, then later, when I was about twelve, he changed it to died. But I'd heard. You know, around the town. She'd gone away with a man. But it doesn't sound right, does it? A mother leaving two little girls! No. I didn't know what to think.'

It didn't sound right to me, either. I said, 'So it was your father who brought you up?'

'If you can call it that. Oh, it's all right when you're little, but he was . . . well, funny. You know. With girls. The odd pat on the behind that was close to a squeeze, and touching, touching . . . Hell, I've lost the soap. Where's the bloody soap?'

Oh God, I thought. Not that! 'And as you got older?' I prompted.

She seemed to answer a different question. 'He was one of these easy-going types. Always good for a laugh, my father was. Good old Rowley, they called him. Rowland, really. Rowland Fields. He thought he could get away with anything if he made a joke out of it, and usually he did. Like when we were older, me and Tonia. I was seventeen, she fifteen. We shared a double bedroom. Great friends. I hear that's rare with two sisters. Supposed to fight like cat and dog. Jealousy or something.'

She stepped delicately from the bath, wrapping herself in a huge towel. 'You can have the bath, now,' she said grandly.

'Thank you.' But the transition didn't really suit me. I'd had control of the situation, standing in the bathroom doorway, but now the control would be hers. Yet now she was launched, swooping down the slipway of her memory, and nothing was going to stop her. She stood and watched as I stripped down. As a sister of a sister she would be used to it. Not I. The embarrassment was there.

'You've got a good figure,' she said. I couldn't decide whether she was condescending. 'Why the hell don't you dress for it?'

'I'm not out to make an impression.'

'Make the best of what you've got,' she advised. 'And you've got it, kiddo.'

Kiddo! I stepped into the water, which was now running clear, averting my face to hide my reaction. She was treating me as her kid sister, blast her. The bath was old-fashioned, huge, perched on four legs. The hotel supplied bath oil, but Bella had used most of it.

'Shared a room, you said,' I prompted.

'Well yes. Did I? Yes, I did. You know, two girls together, we romped a bit, had fun. But father, he used to come bursting in. Didn't matter if we were in the rude. He'd just shout out, "Hello, girls. In the pink I see," and try to get his hands on you. All fun, of course. Good, clean fun. But it wasn't so funny for us.'

'You could've put a bolt on the door.'

'We did. You can bet your life on that. But he had it off. Said he wasn't having any secrets in *his* house. But a girl's got secrets. He was a filthy pig, no getting away from it. We hated him.'

'I can understand that,' I said, just to keep her going. I'd met them, covering their leery attitude with a veneer of snide joviality. Great fun, girls, let's see you laughing.

She walked away into the room, but she didn't stop talking. Perhaps she didn't want to face me with this part of it. 'I came home one day. Growing up by then, we were – I could fend him off. He knew he had to watch for my knee. Tonia was more scared. Like a rabbit. I walked into our room and his hands were all over her. Swine! I near brained him with a vase. That kept him away for a while. It seemed to make up our minds for us. We'd been talking about walking out on him, you see. I'd been doing some acting, and Tonia wanted to be a model or something, and that room of ours got to feel like a prison. We couldn't ever be alone in it – had to stay together.'

She was back at the bathroom door now. The water was

24

cooling. She leaned on the door frame, a cigarette between her fingers, lounging, floozy-like. One of her poses. I realized, now, why she'd objected to the double room. It brought back unwelcome memories, with me as the surrogate sister.

'Not much chance for either of you in this town,' I suggested.

'It's a dead hole, no getting away from that. You finished?'

'About. So you both left him, I suppose.'

'The other way round,' she told me casually. 'He went first. What time's dinner?'

'About two hours ago.'

She threw back her head and laughed. 'We'll have to go out on the town.' Abruptly she seemed years younger.

'In what way', I asked, towelling briskly, 'do you mean? The other way round, you said. He went first.'

'Oh . . . him! Yeah. Well, we'd told him – it'd come to that point – told him it was him or us. Said we'd kill him. There were so many other things involved, you'd never believe. He was out and around with half the women in this dump, but we weren't supposed to have men friends. So we made the situation clear. And he went. Probably with a woman.'

'Went?'

'Here one day, not the next. It was like heaven. The police thought we'd done him in,' she said casually.

'But Roma . . . Bella . . . a grown man can disappear if he likes. It's not a police matter. So why are we talking about murder?'

'Do we have to go on nattering about him?'

'They were waiting for you at Southampton. Why?'

'Drop it, shall we?'

'Why?' I repeated, following her into the room. 'Why was murder suspected?'

'Because,' she said, staring me in the eyes, 'he left with nothing. Took no clothes, no money, and his bank account wasn't touched. He hadn't taken anything to drive in, and he had a choice. Had a garage – did I tell you that? No? Well, he did. But he didn't take a car, didn't catch a bus, didn't take a train from the station. Just went. Phutt! Like that.'

'I see.'

But she seemed to dismiss it from her mind, pouncing on one of her cases, throwing it beside the other on the bed and foraging in it for what she wanted. I noticed that she'd instinctively chosen the right-hand bed, as though this had been so when she'd shared with her sister, Tonia.

'We'll go to Fletcher's,' she told me, her mood suddenly changing. Years seemed to have fallen from her. She was a teenager, rushing to throw something on for a date.

'Famous, Fletcher's is.' She straightened, holding a T-shirt against her ample chest. I Love George Bush, it declared. 'Fish and chips,' she said. 'A restaurant. Don't wear your sable jacket.'

'Haven't got one. You wearing those jeans, are you?'

On the face of it they looked tatty old things, but when she'd fought her way into them I realized they'd been tailored for her. That and the T-shirt, and (having glanced out of the window and checked it was still raining) a short and possibly waterproof jacket, and she was ready, an eager and sparkling young woman, all set for a great adventure.

'I can't match that lot,' I said, hunting for my oldest slacks.

She was doing something to her face, standing in front of the mirror set in the door of the ancient wardrobe. I was slipping on a jumper and my anorak. It would be cold outside. When she turned she was eighteen again, and all in a few seconds. I'd have expected her to spend hours on make-up, but . . . a deep red lipstick, too much eye-shadow, a touch to her eyelashes, and there she was, a bubbling teenager going out for a meal at a fish and chip restaurant, and it was suddenly the highlight of her dreary life. She bounced with immature excitement.

'A headscarf,' she suggested. 'Your hair will be ruined.'

Not mine. Nothing would budge it. But she flung a silk square over her own hair and tied it beneath her chin. She'd gone back a dozen years, physically and emotionally. We clattered down the marble staircase, clattered through the lobby and into the drizzle and mist of the main street, almost deserted now, the lamps dim, the shops with mesh-protected windows. She took my arm. We were Bella and Tonia, walking the tired streets. Almost instinctively, I checked. A shadow followed us on the opposite pavement.

'Three weeks we stayed on,' she told me, apparently picking up the thread of her story. 'They warned us not to leave the district. Questioning. When they found anything to question us about, and they didn't find much. So there we were, hanging

26

about, wasting time, when I'd got a chance at a stage production in Dublin. Why they'd picked on us, I don't know. They knew we'd hated him, we told 'em that, but so did half the town. He could laugh anything off, most of the time, but there were other things . . . it's down here.'

She did an abrupt right turn. Now we seemed to be on the far edge of the town. The street-lights were more economically spread. A hundred yards away, light spilled out on the pavement. Groups cluttered the gutters, scattering paper and chips.

She pushed through them, throwing out the odd, 'Hi!' As though she'd seen them the evening before. It wasn't Fletcher's any more, it was Soo Long's. But the expertise had been preserved; the atmosphere, hot and oily, was solidly there. We pushed past the take-away into the rear, the restaurant. Formica-topped tables, tubular steel chairs, ketchup and HP Sauce bottles with messy tops. It was crowded. We had to share a table with two sex-starved kids, who couldn't wait to get out into the night.

She was known, remembered. She was our Bella. The older people leaned over and chatted with greasy lips. Our Bella. I didn't think they knew her as Roma Felucci. After all, she now looked ten years younger than Roma, and the star of *Colossus* would be seen as 'just like our Bella'. But it was all too close, too difficult to make the mental adjustment that it was a local girl who had become a famous American actress, who could not possibly be sitting now in a fish and chip restaurant down the dingy side street, splashing vinegar on her chips.

When the young couple left we had the table to ourselves for a few minutes. Bella had cod and chips and mushy peas, me the plaice. The batter was crisp, the fish melted in the mouth. I asked casually, 'And where is she now?'

'What? Who?' She was handling a huge mug of tea like an expert, her eyes huge over the rim.

'Your sister. Tonia.'

'God knows. She got tired of waiting for the coppers to let us go. She just went. Like my father.'

'Went? In the same way, you mean? No luggage or anything.'

'How far would she've got, carrying a case? They were watching the house. She just said to me, "I can't stick this any more, Bell." One night, this was. In the morning she'd gone.'

Then she deliberately turned her mental back on the subject.

This evening was her nostalgia trip. The good old days – which sounded lousy to me. We called into a pub on the way back. Even more, she was recognized there. There were her contemporaries. There was not one mention of *Colossus*. She was the teenager they'd known. Certainly, now with a few drinks inside her and her hair flying loose, her mouth a bit loose too, she was three thousand miles from Roma Felucci.

I had difficulty getting her back to the hotel, difficulty getting her up the stairs. She was giggling, maudlin – alternating.

I tucked her up in bed. *Her* bed. Half asleep, she muttered, 'G'night, Tonia.' I thought she was weeping.

In the morning she was terrible. I had difficulty forcing her back into reality, but over breakfast she recovered a little. 'I'll take you out in the car,' I offered. 'A look at the countryside.'

'Ugh!' she replied, and, 'Why go out?' she grumbled, in the lobby.

'We'll go mad, sitting around in here.'

'The police . . .'

'I know. They'll be watching you. Let's give 'em a run for their money.'

She brightened. It appealed. 'Yes. Let's do that.'

The drizzle outside was so fine it felt like a damp cloth on my face. The mist was constantly changing, plunging us into heavy gloom, then lightening. Easing the car out of the yard behind the hotel, I asked, 'Which way?'

'I'll show you the house.'

'Oh . . . goodee.' I didn't want to see the blighted place.

'Left, then right when we get to the crossroads.'

I wished I hadn't suggested it. The visibility was tricky, the wipers seeming to do nothing. It was as though the glass was permanently misted.

'I only stayed another fortnight,' she said.

'What?'

'After Tonia left. There was this offer in Dublin, see.'

'You mentioned it.'

'I sneaked off and caught a train. Easy.'

I'd had the impression that Jay had come for her. Or was that to Dublin? Perhaps she'd so slanted the truth for the police that it was no longer real and solid. It was no wonder they'd been waiting for her.

28

'And you've heard from her since?'

'Who? Oh . . . Tonia. No. How could I? I didn't know where she'd gone and she didn't know where I had.'

'She'd have recognized you in *Colossus*, though.'

'I suppose. Turn right here, and then left, under the trees.'

Under the trees it was worse. I put on the lights, but they weren't much help.

'Hold on,' she said suddenly. Her hand clamped on my arm. 'There was a row of cottages . . .'

I stopped. She wound down her window. 'They've gone.' The loss seemed to choke her.

I drove on, slower now because she seemed disorientated. 'The chapel!' she cried out. 'Where's the old chapel?' It was as though it'd been taken away to annoy her.

There was a throbbing in the air that I couldn't identify. Theoretically, we were in a quiet residential area, running into country. But there was an undeterminable noise. The right-hand side of the road was piled high with earth, bricks, chunks of wood.

'Where *is* it?' she moaned as we drifted along.

'There!' I said, leaning forward. 'Isn't that a house? Up on the left. Short drive. Is that it?'

'Yes, yes. But there were trees,' she whispered. 'What've they done with our trees?'

I left the Rover nose-in to the drive, as I didn't think I could drive up it. There was nothing but mud, where the trees each side had been torn up by the roots, leaving earth and stray rootlets now under our feet. Bella clambered out of the car in a panic, trying to run but slipping, falling to her knees and struggling up again. The roaring, snarling noise was louder now, just beyond our vision to the right. She was whimpering and moaning, heading towards the heavy dark shadow that was the house, tripping on the first step because she was looking up, looking round, everywhere but at her feet.

The front steps were crumbling. There was no front door. The bay window to the right, which was about as far as I could see, was glassless, the frame smashed. I followed her into the hall, but slower. The wood block floor was slimy and damp, the blocks lifting. Bella ran for the stairs, but I managed to reach her and hang on to her arm. The banisters were sagging, the treads broken in places.

29

She turned on me, her eyes wild. 'The house!' Her voice was hoarse, as though she'd been screaming silently.

But they'd all abandoned it, ten years before. It'd since been stripped of everything, desecrated. The throbbing noise was now very close. I knew we should not be there. Nobody should. But she slipped from my grasp and ran into a side room. There was no window at all in there, and the mist invaded it.

We rushed to the gap. She grasped at the remains of the sill, leaning forward so that I thought she might fall out. 'It's gone!' she moaned. 'Next door. Another house. It's gone.'

All her youth had been spent in this house, but she surely could not mourn it, from what she'd told me. She'd hated it, and had deserted it. But nevertheless, it was something of her life that had been snatched from her.

I saw it then, an indistinct and formless shape, hard and angular. But it was the shape belonging to the noise, and my brain put the two together. It emerged from the mist as I identified it, coming in from the left, heading for this house, for us. It was a huge, tractored digger with a shovel a mile wide, thrusting, lifting, turning and dumping.

Bella made a choked, screaming sound. With one quick thrust she threw herself from the window, landing on her knees. 'Bella!' I shouted, but my voice was a tiny sound, which was lost. I had to follow, jagging my slacks. She was stumbling through mud ahead of me, pushing forward towards the tractor. 'No! No!' she screamed. The driver couldn't have heard her. She was waving her arms, but I doubted he would see her.

I caught her just before she went too far. The digger would have grabbed her with its next mouthful. Then at last he must have seen us. The tractor stopped, throbbing, the shovel high with its last grab, tilting, tilting its load towards our feet.

I dragged Bella backwards. The load tumbled and trundled in front of us, speading so that our feet were covered in the wet earth as it flowed. And as I watched the flow settle, a human skull rolled to the surface, grinning as it turned to face us.

Bella clamped her hands to her face and screamed and screamed. Slowly, I fell to my knees, nothing left in my legs at all.

3

She lay on her bed, face down but rolling her body from side to side, whimpering and swearing and crying, beating the pillow with her fists.

For a while I stood and watched, then I became a little tired of it. What could she have expected, after ten years? That it'd all be there, pristine and fresh, awaiting her key in the lock? And she'd hated the place. For her, it had been a house of doom. There was the skull, of course, but I began to wonder whether she might have expected that, too.

So why all the fuss? It was overdone – hammed.

'All right,' I said eventually, forcing in the words between two bouts of sobs. 'That's enough, Bella. Enough.'

Her feet pounded on the bedcover in comment. No words.

I'd managed to get her back inside the Rover, after the first of the police had arrived. There'd been time for me to discover that the house next door had been the twin of Bella's home, but had been empty even longer. It didn't take a great stream of mental effort to understand what had happened. So we had to talk, Bella and I, serious and fast talk, before the police turned up. There was no time for hysteria.

It was the skull that'd sent her over the edge.

I sat on the side of her bed, talking quietly and seriously in a matter-of-fact voice, trying to strip it of drama.

'You've got to realize you're in difficulties, Bella. Listen! Stop moaning. It's ridiculous. You're in trouble, and all you can do is moan! There was suspicion of an illegal killing from the moment your father disappeared. Now they've unearthed a skull. Oh, for pity's sake, it's only a skull. Not a body. An inanimate object.'

31

'Go to hell!' But she was listening.

'Where it was dug up, as far as they can tell, was where the foundations of the next-door house would've been. It looks as though it was a body buried in the ground beneath the floor-boards. Bella, the police are going to face you with this, and soon. Think. Listen, and stop moaning. Don't you see, the fact that you and your sister disappeared two or three weeks after your father did is a suspicious circumstance. Now they've got evidence of a death. Positive evidence.'

She lifted her head and stared at me. She'd aged ten years in half an hour, but I knew it would all come back. But now her eyes were wild, and flickered from me, then back again. 'Oh-oh!' she moaned.

'I expect you girls used to play in that empty house,' I suggested. She put the corner of the sheet in her teeth and tugged at it. She'd abruptly shed twenty years. Remembering the playing, no doubt.

'So the police', I went on, 'are going to suggest that you and your sister killed your father, knew you could lift a section of floor-boards in the empty house next door, so you buried him in the earth beneath.'

'It's a lie!' she yelled, flinging the damp bit of sheet aside. 'A friggin' lie! We never. We never.'

'And there's also the coincidence, you see,' I went on, ignoring her irrelevancies.

'What soddin' coincidence?' She was still in her swearing mood.

'That you should come here, after ten years of absence, just at the time the houses were due for demolition. You must have known, Bella. You must have heard . . . been tipped off perhaps.'

'No!' she cried, jerking her head in dismissal. 'No!'

'Everything's pointing straight at you, you foolish creature.'

'No-o-o-o!' she screamed, flinging her arms around and plunging about, nearly hitting me in the face.

I caught her wrists. She was still half-sprawled on the bed and I was now on my feet, so I had the stability advantage and could control her, sit her up, shake her, then lean closer for emphasis. Her teeth snapped at me.

32

'Yes!' I said into her face. 'They've got a very good case against you.'

Her eyes held mine for a few moments and her lower lip quivered, then she clamped her hands over her face and was away again, weeping and whimpering like a child.

I stood back, my patience close to slipping its lead. 'Now – there's a grand sight for you! Where's the hell's Roma Felucci, our fiery and gutsy heroine? Don't tell me you're prostrated, and licked already. You've got to have an answer for them, Bella. Not a load of tears that wouldn't help you one bit. Do you hear me? Get on your feet and fight back, or act it if you've got to. Get a hold on yourself and face the thing. You're supposed to be an actress, I believe. Or is that all a fake? Is it all for real, and what you see is Bella Fields? If so, let's have a look at her. Stop snivelling like a child and fight back, for Chrissake!' I was shouting when I got to the end of it, and not acting one word of it.

But it seemed I'd got through to her. She came at me from the bed in one smooth and fast movement, hands flying, nails flashing. I'd been waiting for something like that, and caught her wrists in my hands again, and held her. I was the fitter, it seemed. Her red, swollen face was inches from mine. I laughed at her.

'And if this performance is real,' I said, allowing contempt to enter my voice, 'and if you're genuinely upset and near hysterical, then for heaven's sake stop overdoing it. So far, I've never seen such a lousy performance. And you look terrible.'

Then she stared at me while her face crumpled, and I felt the tension go from her arms and the strength ease from her fingers, and we were in each other's arms, both of us weeping, because, frankly, I was not a little shocked myself, not having had previous experience of rolling skulls.

Then she was calmer, and we sat facing each other on our respective beds. Shaking my head, I repeated, 'It's really the coincidence that's the big snag, you know.'

'They happen,' she said miserably.

'Certainly they do. But sometimes they're prodded a little in this direction or that. Look at it – even if the houses were going to be demolished, there'd be nothing in that to bring you all the

33

way from New York. It's as though you *expected* them to uncover a body. That's what the police are going to say.'

'Let 'em say what they like.' But there was no force in it.

'They'd be saying it in an interrogation room. They could confiscate your passport. You—'

'I've got to get back!'

'In that case, the police'll have to hear something convincing. Let's have it now. Let's hear how it sounds to me.'

Her eyes scanned my face wildly. Then they were still, with reason and understanding in them. She protruded her lower lip, swept a hand over her hair. 'Why?' she demanded.

I didn't know what she meant. 'You hair's a mess.'

'Why should I talk to you? You're nothing in this. Why're you sticking your nose in?'

I shrugged. 'I'm interested. Involved, if you like.'

'And if I don't like?'

'Then I'll pack my things and leave,' I assured her, rather too emphatically because it would be agony now to leave it behind me. 'If the police would let me,' I added, giving myself room to manoeuvre.

'Why shouldn't they?' Her eyes weren't leaving my face for a second, now.

'Because I *am* involved, like it or not.' I leaned forward, trying honesty, which is sometimes convincing. 'I can't say I think of you as a friend, Bella, because I don't know you. It's almost impossible to see the real you, behind all the pretence and deceit.'

Her eyes darkened. She looked away from me and plunged a hand for the bedside table and her cigarettes. 'What the hell d'you mean – deceit?'

'What else can it be, if you can't stop acting when the cameras are switched off? I can't see the genuine Bella. Heaven knows, I don't seem to have come across her.' In the fish and chip restaurant perhaps, in the pub, but that had been a former Bella, a younger one, before Roma Felucci.

She blew smoke at me, adopting the best form of defence and going on to the attack. 'And what about you? Who are you? You walked into my life. Not my idea, that wasn't. Yours. Pushing yourself on me. Who *are* you? A woman copper? Yeah, that'd fit. You act just like one, always asking questions. I've had

34

enough of you, Philipa Lowe. What's your interest? Go on, convince me. Isn't that what you're always saying?'

Because I didn't understand my own interest, and because I felt I had to, when it was something subliminal and elusive, I got to my feet and walked around. I couldn't concentrate when I was staring into her eyes. They troubled me.

'Frankly, I don't know,' I admitted. 'Sometimes something human shows through, and I could find myself liking you. Then it all gets lost, and I can't feel anything but dislike. There's a hardness. Oh yes, I told you to fight. But it's not that sort of hardness. A callousness, say, or a complete selfishness. Yes, that could be it. As you say – I can't see why I'm troubling with you.'

'Now just you stop right there.' There was an ominous note in her voice, a bite.

I turned on her angrily. 'I'm a trained psychologist, Bella. I've spent my life probing people, to discover whether they fit the top executive positions they're applying for. I had to try to ferret out their failings and weaknesses. I'm an expert, Bella. Don't tell me to stop, just because you don't want to face yourself.'

'I've had enough of this. Get out of my room.'

'It's mine.' I laughed at her expression. 'I booked it, and I'm paying for it. Shall I help you to pack?'

She pouted, too lazy or too tired to make a greater effort. 'I'm not having you saying . . . those things you said about me.'

'Callous? Selfish? Damn it all . . . your father! You hated him. All right, so you did. But when he just disappeared, you didn't *care*. As long as he'd gone. And your sister! You were close, devoted to each other, but when *she* went – did you care? Not one tittle, you didn't. You didn't even keep in touch . . . and yes, of course, she would know you're Roma Felucci. But you didn't keep in touch! If she ever tried, did you brush her off? Did you tell her to keep out of your life, as you've just told me? Have you got *any* genuine friends? Tell me that.'

She bounced to her feet and pounded the cigarette to extinction in the glass ash-tray. I thought she was going to throw it at me.

'We kept in touch, damn you!' she shouted.

'Ah!' I said, grinning at her. She had previously lied with casual expertise, so I didn't trust her now.

'She went to Ireland, when she left here. We arranged it. She went, with nothing but a shoulder bag. She phoned me from there, so I sent some of her stuff on. She said there'd been no trouble, so I followed. It was easy. We were together, me acting, she helping around. Later on, she was a continuity girl in the film. Jay got her that job, but I don't think he realized she was my sister. She came to the States after I'd settled in, but she drifted away. West. Did some modelling. We kept in touch. Sort of.'

'So it was she who tipped you off about the demolition?'

'No . . . o . . . o.' She said it on a rising inflexion, genuinely surprised that I should think that.

'Then who?'

She hesitated, having previously denied it so firmly. 'It was a man.'

'A name?'

'No. Just said, "They're going to knock down the two houses." And hung up.'

'No clue? Local or distant? The voice?'

'You can't tell local calls from international ones, now. It could even have been from here. The call came to the studio.'

'But you felt you had to come, because you knew there was something to find? To be uncovered, say.'

'No.' She turned away.

'It's so obvious, Bella. Don't back out now. You *must* have known.'

Now it was I who was standing still, she pacing. Something of the genuine person was appearing. Her guard was down. 'I guessed,' she said at last. '*We* guessed. Use your imagination, Phil, if you've got any. My father was in a right tangle at that time . . . thirty or forty people after his guts—'

'Oh . . . come *on*.'

'It's true. Quite apart from the husbands of women he'd been fooling around with . . . there was the football pool swindle, you see.'

'I've never done the pools. You'll have to explain.'

'He ran a syndicate. Thirty of his mates. They each gave him a pound a week, and he sent in a perm. You know, permutation. Any eight from fourteen, it was. I remember that. The same fourteen numbered on the coupon every week, so they all knew

36

what their money was on. Here – do you know this? Dad told me.' It was the first time I'd heard her use the affectionate 'Dad'. Her eyes and her hair were now dancing with fun. 'The chance of picking eight score draws, as they called them, if that was all there were that week, out of fifty-something matches, is twenty seven million to one. It can be worked out mathematically. Don't ask me how. But you can see, with his perm giving them three thousand chances on the one coupon, it was still nine thousand to one against winning the big one.'

'And so?'

'He played the chances. He was always doing that. All his damned life he was playing chances.' Again a flash of affection crept in. 'So he played that one, and didn't ever send in the coupons. Pocketed the money instead. Any small divvies that came up, he paid out of his pocket, but he was always well in hand. Then, one week, the Saturday before he disappeared, it came up. They got the only eight score draws that week. First dividend, and it was nearly one and a quarter million pounds! So there were thirty of his mates expecting about forty thousand when the cheque came – and he hadn't sent in the coupon! Can you *imagine* what they'd do to him!'

I shuddered. 'He'd certainly have to get out of town.'

'Yes . . . but with nothing? You're stupid, Philipa. D'you know that? We *knew* something nasty must have happened to him.'

Stupid? Perhaps, but not completely. 'But – why the house next door?'

'Me and Tonia, we'd been keeping out of the way. Hell – we weren't going to be caught up in it! We'd both got work waiting for us. Bits, here and there. So we left his friends to do . . . to do what they liked with him, what they'd got to do, and the obvious place . . . the house next door . . . under the floor.'

'They wouldn't have to take him far,' I agreed, somewhat distastefully. 'And I can see why you girls wanted to get away. But Bella – why come back now?'

'I had to *know!*' she said curtly, dismissively.

'All right. But why – if you found you couldn't keep away – why didn't you fly? Why the QE2?'

'I hate flying.'

37

'You hated coming here. The flying would take a back seat – wouldn't be so scary,' I amended, as it had sounded strange.

Then she gave a small, childish grin, almost of embarrassment. 'If I *had* to come, I wanted to be not too early. Oh, Philipa, surely you can see that!'

Oh yes, I could understand that. I looked at her calculatingly. She *was* an actress, after all, and she'd succeeded in capturing my pity, if not my sympathy. And she could have been very much more clever than I'd thought.

'But will the police believe you, Bella? That's the point.'

'Piff!' she said, elegantly flipping a hand. 'They can believe what they like.'

'Now,' I told her, 'it's you being silly. You can parade all your cuckolded husbands – lovely word, that – and your cheated pools syndicate, but the police are going to aim straight at you. Make no mistake. So don't dismiss them—'

'I haven't done anything!'

'And how long d'you think it'll take you to convince them?' Before she could answer, I glanced at my watch. 'We can get some lunch in about an hour . . .'

'If you think I could swallow a mouthful!'

'. . . so I think I'll pop along to the house and see how they're getting on. Coming?'

'What! Back there? Wild horses—'

'Right. Then I'll be back for lunch. Probably with Inspector Connaught tagging along.'

'The one that's grown the 'tache? Hey! He's real scrumptious. Drag him back with you, Phil.' It was a flash of sheer bravado. Her eyes shone. She tossed her head, swinging her hair back, glanced at the mirror in the wardrobe door. Stupid creature! Or perhaps not. It depended on how susceptible he was.

To tell the truth, I was glad to get out of that room. Bella could pack so small a space with the crowding aura of her personality. She was a vital and vibrant creature, setting the air tingling with her unique electricity. I had to get out into the open air, to breathe it in and shake her weight from me. I wasn't sure how she'd managed to fool me, but she had. I felt it. Call it an instinct. Somewhere along the line she had deliberately misled me.

The fine rain had now ceased, the drops being sufficiently

separated to allow me a fair range of visibility. The mist had lifted and withdrawn. Nevertheless, the journey was not simple, as I'd previously had Bella to guide me, and it was now difficult to recall which twists and turns we'd taken. My impression was that we'd headed in the direction of the factory chimney, and certainly we had left behind the main bulk of the town. She had spoken of a row of cottages that should have been there. Of trees. Yes, we'd driven along a dark and obscure road beneath an arch of overhanging trees. I thought I had it right, and pressed on.

And there was the stretch of naked foundations where a row of cottages might have been. I could see no reason for their removal, but perhaps a more modern development of houses was due. The road swung round a bend, and plunged towards the outbuildings and yard of a farmhouse. I couldn't recall it. There were no dogs, no farm animals, empty and desolate barns, and no curtains at the windows of the farmhouse itself. Although the farm still stood, its very emptiness emphasized the deserted impression of this portion of the landscape. It was October. The wheat, or whatever, would be safely gathered in, though the fields gave no indication of stubble. And there . . . there ahead, but forking away to the left, was what must have been my tunnel of trees.

I drove into it. Now it was really gloomy, the fallen leaves mushy beneath the tyres, the nearly naked branches tangling above. Then at the top of a rise, as the trees fell back, there was further evidence of recent occupation. Gardens. What had been gardens, anyway, but now with no delineation between what had been lawn and what flower beds. Houses had lived along here, sprinkled in the countryside like cast seed, but now sagging and lost, some half destroyed already, the others shells, almost flinching from the distant sound of the tractor diggers, though this was no more than a distant mutter now. Subdued.

None of this had I noticed on the drive back to the Crown. I'd simply driven in the general direction, my attention more on Bella, whimpering and gasping in the other seat. Now I was more alert, eyes everywhere, absorbing impressions. The two houses had been isolated. Desirable residences in their own grounds. That's how they would have been described. And there they were, on a rise of ground to the left. What was left.

I'd parked inside the entrance of the drive that previous time. This visit, I parked out on the road. Lane? Was that a fairer description? It was narrow, its surface entirely covered in a mushy sludge. A pity I didn't have my wellies, but I'd been unable to imagine in what circumstances I'd need them on the QE2. In my low-heeled walking shoes, I picked my way up to the house, past police vans and cars, past a wagon with an open back, past the remains of Bella's previous home. Ivy House, I saw on a plaque, twisted against the porch entrance. And eventually I faced the neighbouring house, now barely recognizable as such. This was where the skull had been unearthed.

Then it all became clear to me. There was no mistaking that swathe of battered and naked earth that swept towards me from around the factory, away out there, a two hundred yards width of rutted and pounded mud before me, the detritus piled, almost with contempt, on each side. They were putting in a motorway, or a spur. The houses had stood in the way. A push and a shove and a snarl of engines, and they'd be gone, a few tossed bricks in the heaped piles of ruination.

Yet a single skull, so small in that extensive construction, had brought it all to a halt. Any clearing activity was way over the other side of that sweeping sprawl of flattened ground, seeming paltry, the tractors now like beetles, crawling slowly over a dung heap.

He was there, Detective Inspector Connaught, in a short waterproof coat and a tweed hat on the back of his head, feet apart, hands clasped behind him and flaring the skirt of the coat. Beyond and below him his men were working, about twenty of them, up to the tops of their wellies in mud, fumbling and slipping, using spades and sieves. On the only stretch of flat and as yet untrammelled ground, there was spread a brown tarpaulin. On it they were placing bones, as they were recovered. A sergeant (I guessed his rank, he being almost completely enveloped in a police-issue waterproof cape) held a clipboard. He was recording each discovery as they washed it clean with a hosepipe and numbered it with an indelible pencil. Care – oh, such tender care! They were reassembling Rowland Fields.

Connaught turned as I took my place beside him. He nodded, but said nothing. His eyes lingered for a moment on my face.

'The weather's not ideal,' I commented.

He shrugged. 'You take what you get. Where is she?'

'Back at the hotel. She's not going anywhere, you know.'

'Yes. I know that.'

'She's recovering.'

'I'm sure she is.' He swayed, his coat swinging. 'And you?'

'And me – what?' I glanced sideways. His eyes seemed to be mocking me. 'Oh, I see. No, I wasn't too upset. If that's what you meant.'

'It wouldn't be so personal?'

'Of course not.' Yet it hadn't been a casual enquiry.

One of the searchers raised his head. 'That's three of these, sarge.'

'So what? Mark it, Tyler, mark it, and get on with the job.'

'Three legs, sarge?'

'What d'you know about it?' the sergeant demanded. 'You're always falling over yours.'

It would be necessary to treat the operation with impersonal levity, I supposed.

'I'll have to see her,' said Connaught thoughtfully.

'She seemed to want to see you,' I told him, not exactly truthfully.

'Really? In the mood for confession, is she?'

I shook my head, and grinned at his expression. 'Something more personal, I gathered.'

It worked. He betrayed himself. A hand appeared from the folds of his coat, a finger swept over his moustache. Another egotist! Their meeting would be packed with interest; I hoped I could be there. His eyes were bright, one eyebrow lifted. I had the impression he'd dismissed me from conscious thought. But no. Breathing out heavily and producing a cloud of steam, he went on: 'You came over together on the QE2?'

'I wouldn't put it quite like that. We were on it. We met there. I found her interesting.'

'Of course,' he commented, assuming I would. 'Very interesting, it seems.'

'Meaning what?'

He turned to face me, smiling his damp smile, switching on all his practised charm. 'Three or four days of acquaintanceship, and you chased her all the way from Southampton to here. You

41

booked a double room at the Crown, you took her along there, and you were at her side when the skull turned up. Now . . .*that* I consider to be something rather special in the way of interest.'

I didn't like his eyes. Too close together, I suppose, beneath eyebrows too bushy. I shrugged. 'We'd become kind of friends. I'd got the idea she was heading into trouble.'

'The idea? From what?'

'Impressions.'

'How easy you make it all sound. I wish I could go on impressions. They can trip you up, Miss Lowe. It is Miss, I suppose?'

'Miss will do. And it seems my impressions were correct. You'll hear, when you speak to her. It took a fair bit of extracting, but I think she'll admit it now. She was tipped off that this demolition was under way. So she was concerned.'

I wasn't giving away anything critical. She would tell him, and she could explain her feelings better than I could.

'Yet all the same, at that time you had no more than an impression. And on that you've involved yourself . . .'

'I suppose I'm just plain nosy.'

Then he unveiled the full perfection of his smile. It was a singularly unpleasant experience; a touch more and it would have been terrifying.

'I don't believe you, Miss Lowe,' he said softly, and the light died from his eyes.

I tried to shrug, tried to find the correct voice with which to tell him I didn't care one little jot what he believed, but suddenly I knew I did care. I'd involved myself, so I'd been able to decide when to walk away from it. Now he'd involved me, and I wasn't going to escape anywhere.

The same constable rescued me, raising his voice. 'And another of these, sarge!' he shouted, just a little personal triumph in it.

I turned. There'd been urgency too in his voice.

He was holding aloft a second skull.

4

I drove Inspector Connaught back into town in the Rover. He sat moodily beside me, plucking at his moustache, but when he was satisfied I knew the way he suddenly broke the silence.

'Not one word about this second skull, d'you hear! Not a gesture, not a sign to her.'

'Of course not.' I glanced at him. His eyebrows were lowered. 'You'll allow me to be there, then?'

I got a sharp glance. 'Daren't let you out of my sight.'

'Should I be flattered?' No reaction, so I went on, 'Of course, we'll discuss it together after you've left.'

'That might not be possible,' he said placidly.

'Why not?'

'Separate cells.' He was morose, his thoughts assembling themselves elsewhere. I was unable to tell whether he was serious.

We were leaving the factory behind on our left, the view of it gradually decreasing to no more than the top of the chimney. He suddenly said, 'Turn right here. We'll come into town from the other direction.'

I obeyed, though not seeing his point. The road began to climb as we rose out of the valley. Along here were neat rows of newer houses, mostly detached, tidy and evenly spaced. Further up, the houses became larger, more carefully and expensively laid out, use having been made of the great old oaks and beeches for landscaping purposes. There were a large number of For Sale signs.

'Anticipating the motorway spur,' he said suddenly, reading my mind. 'This development's been completed two or three years. The motorway plans got bogged down. When it's completed, these properties will become choice, and therefore very expensive. Very.'

We rose above them, leaving the last behind as the road swept round to the left. It was open countryside here. I'd probably driven into the town this way, though unable to recall it. He said, 'Pull in here.'

It was a lay-by. An old farm gate still stood to one side, strong enough for us to lean on. Companionably. I couldn't understand his purpose, and simply waited for him to say something. The town now lay below us, and there was a clear view of half a mile of the curving swathe of motorway footings as it swung round behind the factory, now fully visible again.

'They make plastic mouldings,' he said eventually, apparently guessing my thoughts. 'The slip road will give the factory a good feed-in for its wagons. Tudor Kemp owns that. And owns a fair number of those houses you saw for sale, and the land the motorway's gobbling up. Rowland Fields owned both of those houses – he of the first skull, we'll assume for now. You can see what trouble Rowley could cause by opposing the land purchase. Two houses, rotten old things, and he was putting every possible objection to the motorway coming through there. You understand what I'm getting at? He wouldn't be able to hold out for ever, but he could cause a deal of delay.'

He was silent. The breeze ruffled his hair. He was waiting for me to say something, but I was busy wondering why he was telling me this. Making an effort, I murmured, 'They could declare him legally dead after he'd been missing seven years.'

He cast me a sharp glance, something of approval in it, as though I might be his favourite confidante. 'Which is what happened. By that time, of course, the Fields's own house had been plundered. So all was ready for the motorway to go through. And . . . think about it . . . a man had disappeared, and there'd have been seven years of uncertainty for all except the one person who knew Rowley Fields was dead, and wouldn't be coming back. Seven years in which one man could quietly buy up land and property, *knowing* Rowley Fields wasn't coming back. You see my point?'

What I discerned was the fact that he had a personal dislike for this man, Tudor Kemp. But I spoke brightly. 'With piercing

44

clarity. But there wasn't just your friend, Tudor Kemp. Lots of other people wished Rowley Fields dead.'

'Oh yes,' he agreed, smiling at me in approval. 'The football pool winners, or rather non-winners – yes. Half a dozen husbands and boy-friends whose women Rowley had charmed, though I don't think he ever went further than that. Charmed. A lovely delicate word, that is, but he *was* a charmer. Some men have got it,' he said, a hint of complacency in his voice.

'I never seem to meet them,' I admitted.

'The point I wished to make, is that there are forty or more possible suspects for the killing of Rowley Fields. I know them all. I was a sergeant at the time he disappeared. It's a large and complex investigation now, Philipa Lowe. Not for one individual, but for a large team.'

'You want to get rid of me,' I decided.

'How did you guess! Shall we say for my own peace of mind.'

'Very considerate of you. Is that why you've been telling me all this background stuff?'

He didn't answer that, but turned from his contemplation of the horizon. His hand rested on my arm. Sincerity was heading my way. 'I don't know you, Philipa Lowe. You could be a news person, out for a scoop. Or involved in some other way. For all I know.'

'I can prove . . . my passport . . .'

'Never mind your damned passport. Philipa Lowe! There's a false name if I ever heard one.'

'It's real.'

'It smacks of Raymond Chandler.'

'My father was a Chandler fan. He wrote a book about him. Chief Superintendent Lowe. Look him up, Inspector. He told me he was glad I was a girl, so that he would name me Philipa. It's Philip Marlowe, but without the M and the R.'

'Without the mister.' He gave me a twisted grin, not certain I wasn't kidding him. 'Clever.' He shrugged then, accepting it, sighed. 'Then you'll be in a position, my dear Miss Lowe, to understand what you've involved yourself in. A big and time-wasting investigation.'

'You'd advise me to pack and depart?'

'Exactly.'

'But, my dear Inspector, what you've been saying related to

45

only one death – Rowland Fields. Now you've got two skulls. It's an entirely different ball game.'

The smile expanded on his face slowly, as though it took a vast effort. He'd urged me round to his real point. 'Which . . .' He touched my arm again, '. . . is going to make things very unpleasant. Narrows it down from forty-odd possibles to one specific person, who's been lying her head off like the excellent actress she is. But I intend to get to the bottom of it. Do you believe in intuitions, Miss Lowe?'

'When they've got some backing, yes.'

'Then my feeling is that this business is going to cease to be unpleasant and become rapidly very nasty indeed.'

'You're not scaring me.'

'No? Then consider again this relationship you've developed. Consider it beside the fact . . .'

He stopped, as though realizing he'd gone too far. He took a breath. It was almost a sigh. Then he decided to carry it on.

'You saw the sergeant, recording exactly where each bone was recovered. Yes. It's routine. Forensic will have to do a lot of reassembling. They'll be able to tell us heights, sexes, possibly even ages. But there's one thing you must bear in mind. We'd already noted that those two bodies were buried side by side. Lying together. Think about that.'

He didn't mean at that moment, he meant over a protracted period of contemplation. It took me five seconds. 'You mean, at the same—'

'Yes. Now let's get on. We're wasting time,' he said severely, as though I'd been the one doing it.

We got back into the car and I drove on, not needing much in the way of directions now. He left me to it, brooding darkly. I had time to think. Side by side. That had to mean they'd been buried together, at the same time. Surely? Probably. I couldn't think of any other explanation. Two people buried by one person. Oh God! And I'd felt it – felt that Bella had been lying to me in some respect.

I missed a turning. He muttered, 'First right, and right again.'

This I did, and there was the Crown. I drove round into their tight and cobbled car park, so that we entered the lobby by the back door. No one was around. We climbed the stairs silently and I used my key in the door. Put my head in.

'You decent?'

Decent! She'd had time to give herself the grand treatment, wearing casual slacks and a short jacket over an embroidered white silk blouse. Nothing showy, but by heaven they all fused together into a single impression of majestic confidence, with no hint that she'd anticipated this encounter and was anything but completely relaxed, even appearing surprised to see us, but pleased.

'Philipa! You've been ages. And the inspector! How pleasant to meet you again, Mr Connaught.'

'It's Arnold,' he said, smiling, disarmed by her magnificence.

'I know.' She smiled at me.

I would have expected him to have arranged for a woman officer to be waiting downstairs, but there hadn't been one. Now I knew why he needed me. It was all to be informal, no notes taken, no warning given. I was there merely to testify, if necessary, that there'd been no pressure, no coercion.

Bella tossed me one quick glance, then her attention was fully on Connaught. She was pleased to see him – as a man. She chose not to be aware of the police inspector behind his bland and switched-on charm.

'I've been so worried,' she admitted. 'Can't sit still . . . but I was sure you wouldn't want me to go out. And I just knew you'd bring me news. It's so good of you, Inspector.'

'All in the day's work, Miss . . . do I call you Fields or Felucci?'

'My married name's Messenger. Mrs Messenger. But I'll soon be getting rid of *him*. Call me Bella, please, like you used to.'

'Very well. Getting rid of him?' A smile, confiding. 'I hope you don't mean that as it sounds.'

She gave a token, breathy laugh, wiggled a hand. 'Divorce, actually. But stick a gun in my hand . . . and who know!'

'Hand-guns are a bit thin on the ground in this country, as you very well know, Bella. In America . . .' He wasn't smiling now. 'In America they're relatively common, I understand. But I was forgetting – you're English, so you'll know. This was your home town, after all.'

'I have an American passport.'

'American by marriage, of course. But why're we talking about hand-guns? Already we know – I'm sorry to put it so bluntly – but we know that the skull bears a cleft. A blow from a heavy and sharp instrument. No guns involved.'

She stared at him, then turned away. One hand cupped her other elbow, fingers twiddling with her lips. She turned back. 'Do we have to have these disgusting details?'

'I didn't intend to upset you. It's been a long absence, though, and you've also had quite a while to get used to the idea.'

'This morning—'

'I meant on the trip over on the QE2.'

'I was not . . . I came over to . . .' She stopped, collecting her thoughts, seeming momentarily lost, and turned away for her cigarettes. Connaught watched her. I saw his lips twitch.

I moved quietly round the room and slid into the one easy chair they allowed us. She lit the cigarette, her eyes following the billow of smoke. She'd played this scene before in the TV series. It was superbly done, a woman gathering her defences.

'It's the coincidence, you see,' he explained.

'I've heard all about the coincidence.' She dismissed what I'd told her with a shake of her head, a swirl of the hair, not glancing in my direction. To her they were alone, testing each other's nerves, alone with three cameras and a battery of lights, a floor manager, a producer and a director. But she'd trained herself to be unaware of them, always. Everything she could call on went into each performance, as now, pure concentration isolating her.

'If you've heard about it,' Connaught said flatly, 'you'll surely have realized it's too wild to be accepted *as* a coincidence. You came because you knew the two houses were due for destruction. You came *expecting* something.'

'Such as a blasted skull?' she demanded in disgust, now quite callously accepting it as no more than a stage prop. 'Alas, poor Yorick!' she added, confirming it.

I realized, at that moment, that her approach was the only way in which she could carry this through. It had to be unreal for her, something in the script, from which she could isolate her real self.

Connaught wasn't slow to realize this. His voice took on an edge, trying to cut through from Roma to Bella. 'Not a blasted skull. Cleft. By a savage blow from a sharp and heavy instrument. Possibly the edge of a spade.'

Her face froze as though he'd had the effrontery to slap her. 'You're trying to over-dramatize this. Admit it, Inspector.' A tiny smile lightened her face. 'I expected something, yes. I'd been informed that the work was going on. Tipped off, if you like. Can't you see? Why is it that you official people haven't got the slightest imagination? It baffles me. In *your* job, I'd expect it to be critically important. But there's not a touch of it. Not a hint.'

'I do assure you . . .' He extended a hand. She was getting to him. Past him.

'Oh, don't apologize. Please!' She was now moving around, showing him her profile of disgust. Giving camera 3 a bit of work.

'I can imagine,' he said, plodding on, 'that you anticipated something. Because you came. Slowly, on the QE2, but came. Not simply in order to watch your old home being destroyed, I'm sure. But you came. Slowly. In time.'

'Hurrying like a snail unwillingly to school,' she said distantly.

'A pity you didn't take a plane, then,' he said, somewhat acidly. 'You'd have been here for the act one curtain, and been prepared for act two.'

So he was fully aware of what she was trying to do. I saw her blink, then she was her old self. 'Unless I decided not to stay for the last act.'

'Oh . . . I think you'd have had to,' he told her, displaying his imagination. 'Knowing what to expect, you'd have had to wait for it.'

'I did . . . not . . . know.'

'You must have done. You used your imagination, Bella. Admit it.'

She raised her chin. She'd been trying to keep him at a distance, but he was edging in close. 'We had a feeling, Tonia and I. I'll admit that. Intuition. Putting one or two things together. If you knew anything about the situation at that time, Mr Connaught . . .'

'I did. I was involved as a police officer. As you very well know.'

'Good. Then you'll remember his life was hanging on a thread. We expected something.'

'We being your sister and yourself?'

49

'I've said that. Yes, we expected trouble. And then when he disappeared . . . I ask you, with nothing, not even his clothes! Of *course* something nasty had happened. We felt it. I remember . . . we got to watching from the bedroom window, that last week or two. Not watch exactly, but stare at that empty house next door. It was the ideal place. For a body, you see. We'd played in it as kids. You know, you know. Any empty house, kids play in it. We knew the floor-boards were loose. I'm telling you this . . . for you to understand. Or at least try.'

'I understand.'

'Good.' She nodded her appreciation. 'So you'll see that after a while we convinced ourselves he was there. His body was. You know. Then, of course, we couldn't stay.'

Her eyes were now huge, slightly moist. In some way – I hadn't seen her reach to it – her hair had become slightly disarrayed. This was the genuine Bella, she was informing him, the slightly agitated Bella, but sincere. Oh, completely sincere. The teenager he remembered.

'I seem to recall that it was she who left first,' he commented.

'Well yes. She was younger.'

'That matters?'

'Of course. Tonia was always the frightened little mouse.'

'But not you?'

'Frightened – yes. Oh, I can remember being frightened. But I had to hang on and give her a chance to get clear.'

'Very commendable.'

'Then I went, myself. Left. Packed and left.'

'To meet up with her?'

'By accident really. I'd got this offer in Dublin. It led to a part in a film. Tonia got a job on set. Continuity. We went on from there to America. The States,' she added, in case he wasn't sure.

'You're telling me you kept in touch?'

'Vaguely. You know . . . birthday cards. Phone calls.' She kept varying this.

I could see it coming. He'd been very clever, allowing her to do most of the work, leading herself into it. He found something to interest him, down in the street. Glanced out, then back over his shoulder.

'You can contact her now, perhaps?'

'I expect.'

'Only expect? Your own sister!'

'Yes. I've got a good idea where she is.'

'In that case – if you could contact her – I'd have expected her to come with you.'

'She'd have been too scared, I can assure you.'

'Too scared, I'd have thought, to allow you to come alone.'

She couldn't understand that. His approach was unnerving. Her temper flowed to the surface. 'What the hell does that mean?'

He smiled, recognizing the break. 'I think you've been lying to me, Bella. I think you haven't contacted her, spoken to her, even set eyes on her, since you left that house ten years ago.'

She stared fixedly at him. 'Believe what you damn well wish.'

'You'll note,' he said placidly, 'that I've come here without a colleague. You've had no official warning. I can't use one word of what you tell me. So we can both say what we like, and certainly believe what we wish.'

'Warning?' she snapped, seizing on the essential word. 'What about?'

'The warning we give that anything you say may be taken down . . . etc. It usually helps to prevent too much lying. But . . .' He shrugged. 'No warning, so we get plenty of lies. I believe you're lying about your sister. I believe she is dead. I believe she died when your father did, or shortly afterwards.' He paused. 'In any event, before you left.'

'Believe! Believe!' She sounded disgusted but uneasy, and shot a glance at me, almost the first since I'd entered the room. 'She's alive.' As though it was I who had to be convinced.

'And you could produce her if necessary?'

'Yes.' She breathed the word in desperation.

He seemed to relax. 'Hamlet was joking, you know. Pretending he could recognize Yorick from a skull. It's not possible, I assure you. Not even male from female. You've assumed that the skull you saw was your father's. If that's so, then the second one we've found must be your sister's. Or vice versa, of course. If you want to be fussy on details.'

'Two!' she whispered. 'You've found *two*?' If *that* was acting, it was superb. No hysterics, no screams, just blank disbelief.

'Two skulls, yes. Two bodies, then. That follows.'

'Somebody,' she said, her voice now husky with passion, 'is

51

playing funny buggers. It can't be so. That's why you didn't bring anybody, because it's you who's bloody well lying, Inspector Arnold Connaught.'

He turned to me, gesturing. I was being invited to put in a word. 'There are two skulls, Bella. I saw them.'

Then she laughed, and hysteria at last peeped through. '*You* can say that! There's irony for you!'

'What does that mean?' Connaught demanded.

'Two, you say. Two, you both say. But one of them can't be Tonia's. Just can't be.'

'Then produce her,' he offered practically. 'If that isn't your sister, then where is she?'

The look she gave me was one of mute appeal, as though I might help her. Then it all dissolved and she spluttered, hand to her mouth. It might have been all a huge joke. She gestured to me, a tiny flip of the fingers.

'Ask her. She's the best to know.'

Connaught turned to stare at me, eyebrows raised, moustache twitching, but with something special in his expression. More than expectation. Hope, perhaps?

'Oh my God,' he said. 'And didn't I say it sounded like a false name, Miss Philipa Lowe!'

It was like a blow between the eyes. For a few moments I couldn't breathe, couldn't see clearly. The two others seemed fixed, like a black-and-white still; time was fixed as I fought to retrieve my mind. I knew I was holding out a hand, fending it off, fending off something, fighting for time. Then there was nothing but a sharp and cold clarity, bright and highly coloured. I could see every detail, the tiny design in her blouse, the fact that his tie was silk, that his eyes were not quite the same brown, that her hair was brighter than I recalled, closer to my own colour.

As Tonia's might have been! I heard myself saying, 'Hey!' It felt harsh, a nothing sound. I licked my lips, my brain clicked in, and I shouted, 'What the bloody hell's all this about?'

They were staring at me, Connaught with a stiff expression, almost of shock. It was new to him, too, but Bella was viewing me with a sad-eyed look of hurt, that she'd needed to say it, that she'd absolutely *had* to say it – and betray her sister. If I'd had something heavy in my hand I'd have thrown it at that expression.

Then Connaught laughed lightly, shattering the tableau. 'Fancy that,' he said. 'I've seen some things . . .'

He moved to the door, had his hand on the knob. 'Wait!' I shouted.

He turned his head. 'What for?'

Bella now had her back to us. I threw her one quick glance, but she was standing at the window, indifference in her stance.

I said to Connaught, 'I can prove I'm Philipa Lowe.'

'Can you?' His lips were dry and seemed to stick together. 'Then I suggest that you start assembling your proof.' And he walked out.

5

I waited, silent, until my restraint forced her to turn, her nerves tight. Just the sight of me seemed to provoke a flinch. But I was not about to indulge in violence. Oh, the fury was there, make no mistake. I ached to break something. Yet I knew I had to keep control of myself and of the situation, and was rather proud that I could talk below a shout, a little tightly, perhaps, but approaching rational comment.

'Bella,' I said, 'you're going to go after him and retract that statement.'

'I didn't make any statement.'

'Don't play with words, for pity's sake. You as good as claimed I'm your sister.'

'I had to do something,' she said simply.

Then I lost it. 'Do you realize what you've done, you stupid bitch?' I shouted.

'I know exactly what I've done.' Now she was icily cool, the real and practical Bella who had complete control of herself and her actions. 'It's known as self-defence.'

'It's known as blind idiocy from my point of view.'

'It seems to me . . .' She smiled pityingly, '. . . that it's you who doesn't understand. He was one snap of the fingers from arresting me. *That* close.' She snapped them. 'If it isn't a trick of some sort – two skulls! He could've made that up.'

'I *saw* them. With my own eyes. Two skulls.'

'There you are, then. It's as good as saying I killed my own father, and then my sister, to keep her quiet. A touch away from saying that. It's what he was working round to. And I had to do something. Surely you see that, Phil. Come on, it does you no harm. But it's my whole life at stake. And don't smile like that.

54

It is. If I'm arrested, then where'll I be? I'd never be able to get back to the States in time, and Roma Felucci'll be dropped, written out. Discarded like an old glove. It's my life, Phil. Can't you appreciate that! I've fought for it, clawed my way up to it, acted my head off for it. If I'm written out, that'll be the end – and I might as well be dead.'

'Surely not so serious . . .'

'I *am* the boss of *Colossus*. It's the way the viewer gets to think, and that's how they see me. It's happened before to lots of people. A hit series and you're on top. Then, if you're dropped, nobody can touch you again. In anything else I'd still be the boss of *Colossus*, and it'd all be unreal. Phil, you must try to understand.'

I knew she was correct. Lord, it had to be sheer murder, being so prominent in the entertainment scene – and then becoming nothing. As good as dying, it would be. As bad as dying.

'So you had to land me right in trouble? Oh, fine! Great for you.'

'I can stall them off. Long enough for them to catch the real killer. It's all I want.' The appeal in her voice was genuine, the eyes not meeting mine, which was what you'd expect with the embarrassment of having to appeal, she normally so confident and majestic. I felt it to be real.

'And if it comes to it you can trace your genuine sister,' I suggested.

'You can surely prove your own identity,' she said shortly, not in any way answering my question.

But could I? So few people really knew me in England since my husband's death. Inspector Oliver Simpson. My solicitor, Harvey Remington, his secretary . . . and . . . and . . . well, nobody really.

'I'd prefer you to trace your sister,' I said, no warmth in it. There was no response. I had to use a sharper tone. 'Pick that phone up and start things moving. *Do* something, Bella, blast you. Don't let it all roll over you.' Over me, I meant.

She was hunting for her cigarettes. They had been in her hand only moments before. It was a ruse to avoid my eyes.

'Bella!' I said sharply. 'Are you listening?'

She turned back to me. I have to credit her with a shaded look of sympathy and distress in her eyes, an unwelcome line of worry appearing between them. 'I told him a lie, Phil. Sorry.

From the moment she left that house, left this district I assume, I haven't heard a thing from Tonia. Not a word, not a sign. And that's the truth.' It was said as though the handing to me of *that* particular item of truth was a gift!

I stared at her for so long, so fixedly, that in the end she turned away and went to sit on her bed. In fact, I was trying to make sense of it, or rather, trying to see some alternative to the very obvious truth. Finding none, I went and plonked myself on the edge of my own bed, facing her. I felt I was now talking to the real Bella, with all the attitudes and stances of her acting hammered out of her. She was clearly terrified. Her fingers shook as she tried to extricate a cigarette from its pack.

'Do you really understand what you've done, Bella?' I asked softly.

'Playing . . . for time,' she whispered.

'Think. Look at it. You could well have persuaded that very nice inspector that I'm really your sister. Just might have. I don't know. But there's one thing you don't know. Are you listening?'

Eyes huge, she nodded.

'Those two bodies, Bella, were buried side by side. That has to mean by the same person, and at the same time. Now . . . are you listening?' Her eyes were moist with shock, but she was listening. 'To Inspector Connaught, if you've persuaded him I'm your sister, that would have to mean that one of those bodies is not Tonia's. Which is what you intended.'

'Well, then . . .' she muttered. 'Of course.'

'But I *know* I'm not your sister. I know your father and your sister disappeared at about the same time. I know you haven't heard from her since – you've just told me that. So – as far as I'm concerned – that second body could well be Tonia's. So I *know* the odds are that you killed them both. Me. This is me . . .' Tapping my chest. 'Philipa Lowe, who can prove who I am. And this Philipa Lowe knows you killed them. That's what your trickery has done for you. Look at me, damn you, Bella. Let me see your eyes. I want to see whether there's guilt in them.'

She raised her face again. The eyes were limpid, with defeat in them. 'I never harmed anybody in my life. It's not fair!' she wailed.

'It's not fair to be killed and buried under a house.'

'You're hard. D'you know that?'

'You killed them. I can be as hard as I like, and still not match you.'

She looked at her fingers. The nail polish was cracked. She frowned. 'You said . . .' she whispered. 'Told me you didn't know what you would do when you got home. Well, you're here. So that's what you can do.'

'What?'

'Prove I didn't do it. Them. Whatever.'

'You must be—'

'Joking!' she cut in bitterly. 'Oh, I feel just like a bloody good laugh. I didn't do it. So you can help me out.'

'You've dropped me in it – now you expect help!'

Her face was like a child's, mischievous and tentative. 'If you can prove that, then it wouldn't matter whether or not you're my sister.'

She was magnificent in her complete absorption. It was a flatly stated proposition; it would surely be done.

I slapped my thighs. 'D'you realize we've missed lunch downstairs? And if you mention fish and chips I'll crown you.'

'Give me time to change . . .' She'd come alive, not realizing I was merely wearied of the fight, not complying with her request.

'Change be damned. Repair your face, and you can take me somewhere very expensive and buy me a huge and satisfying meal. Wine, brandy, the lot.'

'You're on.'

Like a chameleon, she was, except that I believe they change their colours slower.

She was all eagerness now, so bright and optimistic that I ought to have felt flattered, her faith in my ability being so pathetically naïve. It took her longer to repair her face than for me to do mine, and really I needed to change, felt like a bath actually, but even the most expensive establishments are not going to serve lunch too late in the afternoon.

'The Rendezvous,' she said. 'I used to know the head waiter. Wonder if he's still there. I wish I had your hair, really I do. You shake your head, and it's back in place. No, not that shirt, dear. Too mannish. We're women, you know. Let's look wildly feminine. And not *that* blouse. The collar ruins the line of your chin. You really ought to learn how to make the best of yourself.'

I could've killed her for that alone, and chose the shirt

anyway, with a straight, dark skirt, which slims my thighs a little. She tutted, and waited in the foyer until I'd brought the car round, as though I was her chauffeur.

'You're pointing the wrong way,' she said.

'If you'd come with me into the yard . . . oh, never mind. And fasten your seat-belt. It's legal here.'

The Rendezvous was a low, squat building along the Shrewsbury road, with an entrance drive long enough to hide it behind trees. Very dignified. They knew her, sure enough. The head waiter hadn't changed, and might have been her uncle, the way he fussed. He called her Miss Felucci, was probably Italian himself.

We were definitely late for lunch, as most of the diners were leaving, but nothing was too much trouble for the famous Roma Felucci. The chef came to the table and listened gravely to her instructions, the wine waiter polished his corkscrew. She laughed and preened, and charmed the eyeballs nearly out of them, but the result was a splendid and protracted meal. I had no intention of paying for it, and she clearly didn't expect to. But no bill was presented, and we were shown out like royalty. Roma Felucci Ate Here. I could imagine the notice they'd already be preparing, and the odd pound or two being added to the items on the menus.

'Aren't they splendid!' she cried. 'Nobody ever lets me pay.'

It didn't happen to me. Never.

As I turned on to the drive, I noticed a Ford Fiesta, dark and anonymous, pull out after us. Not a member of the staff, not a late customer; we were the last. Connaught had us under observation, I reckoned. I caught just a glimpse of a man's profile. And what report would Connaught receive? That we'd dined, laughing and arguing together, just like two sisters.

Had it been intentional on Bella's part, adding verisimilitude to the fiction? Come to think of it, it was she who had contacted me on the QE2. Not quite contacted, perhaps, but had stumbled and cursed in a way to attract my attention and interest. She might well have picked me out, being the right size and having the correct colouring to be her sister, with the possibility of a deception looming ahead of her. But surely that would've been too complex to be planned.

Yet she'd adopted an austere and distant aura, keeping

58

everyone else clear, and ensuring that our relationship had been enviously observed. In case anybody official enquired at a later date? And hadn't I followed her here! Surely she could not have motivated that – yet she'd managed an eloquent appeal with no more than her eyes. Those eyes! From which she had, possibly on purpose, swept her dark glasses to be left at my feet? How effectively she could use those eyes! Then on arrival I'd booked a double room. Playing straight into her hands. How useful this background would now prove to be, especially as I'd confided to her the details of my long stay at New York and my scarcity of contacts in England.

I glanced sideways at her. She'd put on the car radio and was tapping her knee in rhythm to whatever it was. No care in the world, you would have thought. But why should she have? Hadn't she now got Philip Marlowe trying to establish her innocence? Admittedly without the mister, but you can't have everything.

I dropped her outside the hotel. 'I'm getting fed up with this dump,' she said. 'We'll go out later.' It was an order. She marched majestically up the steps and into the lobby.

But now it was becoming dark, darker still in that cramped and over-shadowed car park. As I opened the car door and put a leg out, a shadow moved to my side. By that time my nerves were becoming tense, and I couldn't suppress a sharp little, 'Eek!'

'It's only me,' said Connaught.

Only? Had she punctured his ego? 'Did you think we'd flown the coop?' I slammed the car door behind me.

'Years since I've heard that,' he said appreciatively. 'No coops now, it's battery farming.'

'Why do you have to be so literal?'

'It's police training. Have you given it a thought?' he asked, assuming I had, expecting a report on the result, and meaning the two skulls.

'Yes.'

'And?'

'It appears that if they were buried together and at the same time, the apparent choice is Bella.'

'Apparent?'

'I'm becoming convinced she didn't do it – them.'

He seemed to find that amusing. 'Charmed you, has she?'

'I'm not a man. Have you got any more information, yet?'

'In what way?'

'The skeletons. From Forensic. Have you had any sort of report?'

'It's a long job.'

'Surely . . . sex. They'd have decided sexes. There're bones that're different. Have they said?'

'Who's asking the questions around here?' He was being gentle but cool.

'You've just asked one. It was me. Have they?'

I caught the gleam of his teeth. 'One female, one male.'

'Ah. As you thought.'

'The female was about your height.'

I thought about that. If Bella had picked me out . . . 'It's to be expected.'

He was silent for a few moments. Then, 'So you haven't given it serious thought.'

'I told you. The apparent—'

His voice was suddenly rough, angry. 'You disappoint me.'

'Is there more?' I asked meekly, mocking his anger.

'Of course there is, you ridiculous woman. Don't you ever think of yourself and your own welfare?'

'Of virtually nothing else, with you on one side, and Bella on—'

'Never mind sides. Hasn't it occurred to you . . .? Look at it. Think. Here you are, suspected of being her sister. If the dead female is her sister, then she can't produce *her*. So there's you. You say you're not. You say you can prove it. But you've been in the States. Your contacts are very few. All the same – one creditable witness that you *are* Philipa Lowe, and she'll be proved a liar and therefore most likely a murderess. Ruthless with it, too.'

'I'm beginning to see . . .'

'What do you see?'

'If I should die . . .'

'Unpleasantly, say . . .'

'In a way making identification difficult.'

'Then there'd be no way . . .'

'Of proving I'm not her sister,' I completed it breathlessly. It *did* take my breath away.

60

'Mind you,' he added, his voice now more cheerful, 'I'd then be absolutely certain she was the guilty party.'

'But you'd be further away than ever from proving it?'

'That is my fear,' he admitted.

'Thank you, Inspector. I appreciate your concern.'

'Think nothing of it,' he offered grandly.

'Fear not, I don't.'

He touched me on the arm with one finger. 'Look after yourself.'

'Your man,' I asked. 'Is he to watch I don't make a run for it? Or is he there as my protector?'

He paused, half turned away. 'Man? I haven't got a man watching you. Nor a woman, if we want to be pedantic.' He hesitated, seemed about to say something else, then he moved round and past me. I saw that he'd been hiding a sign with his broad back. GENTLEMEN. It was hanging against a wall, vertically by one nail. A man cleared his throat, and I was through that rear door and into the lobby in three seconds.

Bella was just hanging up the phone, looking annoyed, when I entered the room. 'Well?' I asked.

'Well what?'

'Been on to New York – I assume.' I was watching her eyebrows climbing towards the fringe. 'No? I thought you'd been getting things moving. A private eye on the job over there.'

She was frowning and distant. 'Job?'

'Tracing your sister,' I suggested. 'Or at least, making the motions.'

Her gesture silenced me. So much anger in a mere gesture! She was superb. But the anger was not levelled at me. 'It was New York – yes,' she snapped. 'Our flat. I was trying to contact Jay.'

'You feel we need some male muscle on the job?'

'The only muscle *he* uses isn't going to help. But I want him here. Where I can watch him.'

I thought about that, and realized what she meant. 'You spoke to him?'

'A woman answered,' she spat out.

'Oh. You knew the voice?'

'No, I didn't. How the hell could I ever keep up with them! He snaps his fingers and there they are, panting. I'll kill him! I swear I'll kill the pig.'

61

'Hmm! Never the same one?'

She paced a little, trying to work off the anger. Then she spoke quietly, subdued now, with her fury in a tight, compressed mass. 'We've got a holiday place in New Haven. I don't get time . . . God, I'll make time, if I ever get out of this mess. But I'm sure he's got some female or other settled in there. The nerve of it! Can you just imagine! I could slip up there, and if I caught them at it . . . oh hell, what's the use of talking! What *would* I do? Stand in the doorway, blasting away with a bloody gun?' She gave a short and bitter laugh of self-disgust. 'I'm . . . I'm actually scared of facing the truth. That's what it is. Scared that I wouldn't be able to do anything. Doesn't that sound marvellous! The tough and ruthless Roma Felucci – and I know I'd turn and run away from it. And do nothing. What *could* I do? Run to a lawyer? Then what? Divorce? Yeah, I've sworn I'll divorce him, but Phil . . . Jesus, I couldn't live without him, and that's that.'

She turned away from me. I wasn't sure whether her shoulders were shaking.

Did she realize she'd stepped into the jaws of her own trap? The current performance could be intended to persuade me that she was quite incapable of murder. To reach out for my sympathy at this stage of our relationship I found vaguely insulting.

'If you've finished with the phone . . .' I said.

She gestured, not turning. 'Help yourself.'

I looked up the dialling code for Penley, my home town. I owned a cottage there, though I had no intention of going back to it, after the tragedy it had witnessed. My solicitor was at Penley, the family lawyer. I had a friend in the police force. It wasn't much to form the basis of claiming it to be my home town, but it was all I had. I checked with my notebook and dialled my solicitor's office, glanced at my watch to verify he ought still to be there – it was nearly five – and heard it ringing out.

'This is a recorded message,' I got back. 'Please wait for the pips before stating your name and business. Mr Remington will be away until the seventeenth of November.' Then I got the pips, said, 'Go to hell,' and slammed the phone down.

The voice had been that of his secretary, Florence. What a time to go away, and on holiday, I assumed. But I knew Harvey.

He'd be off for a month in Tenerife, or somewhere else distant, with, if my guess was correct, Florence.

I asked Directory Enquiries for the number of Penley Police Station, then dialled again. The desk sergeant.

'Is Inspector Simpson in his office, please?'

'Is this a personal enquiry, madam?' he asked.

'It is personal.'

'Your name, please.'

Feeling uneasy now, I gave him my name.

'Well . . .' he said. 'Miss Lowe . . . I'm afraid he's on sick leave. In hospital, actually. St James's.'

Time ticked on.

'Madam?'

I cleared my throat. 'Can you tell me . . . is it serious?'

'The inspector was involved in a shooting incident. A shotgun. He's out of danger—'

'Where?'

'At Pearson's Farm.'

'I mean . . . the wound.'

'Ah yes. The shoulder, madam. Right shoulder and upper chest. Painful but not lethal, if you get what I mean.'

'Clearly, Sergeant. Thank you.'

I hung up. The room seemed dark, then Bella had her hand on my arm. 'Bad news? Here, come and sit down.'

'I don't want to sit down,' I whispered.

'Is it . . . your friend? You mentioned him. Oliver Simpson, wasn't it?'

'Oliver. I've got to go to him, Bella.'

'But if he's in hospital, how can he help you?'

I stared at her. 'Help me?'

'You wouldn't be able to bring him here, to identify you.'

I shook her off. 'If you don't know what friends are for, Bella, perhaps you've never had any. Sometimes I can feel very sorry for you.'

'You're going out?'

'What d'you think? Yes, I'm going out. It's only five. I'm getting away from this town, and away from you. I may be back. Perhaps not.'

Of course I'd have to be back, but all I wanted at that moment was to be on my way to Penley.

63

She watched me quietly, sadly, as I snatched a few things together. 'There could be somebody else,' she suggested, worried for me, for somebody.

'Somebody else . . . what?'

'For you to bring back. To identify you.' She nodded.

I stared at her for a moment, then laughed. It sounded flat to me. 'Oh, you're marvellous, Bella. Unbelievable.'

I slammed the door after me and ran down the stairs, in a sudden panic because I hadn't been able to put my hand on the car keys, which had to mean I'd left them in the car. What a stupid thing to do. I almost snatched at the car door, and I'd been correct. There they were, now illuminated by the interior light, the keys still in the ignition lock. I breathed out. What a problem it would have been if the car had been stolen!

I sat in the driver's seat and took a good look at my map. To Bella I'd tossed the remark that my home town was only forty miles away. On the map it looked more, but it was mainly major roads, and the evening, dark now, was clear. I reckoned on an hour and a quarter, but wanted to keep south of Shrewsbury if I could. At this time of the evening the Shrewsbury bypass would be packed, nose-to-nose, shuffling along at walking pace. The snag with my proposed procedure was that I really needed a passenger to read the map. It's so easy to be lured into taking a wrong turning when you're on your own.

This was what I seemed to have done, because I found myself on a winding B road, though proceeding roughly in the correct direction, as the moon was bright and I had to do no more than keep it ahead and slightly to the right. There was little traffic, so I was able to ease the speed higher as I became more used to the Rover's handling. It was a neat car to drive. I'd discovered that on the drive from Southampton. But this was the first opportunity I'd had to push it into fast corners. It liked to be powered out, the tail never once wagging.

It was quite abruptly that I felt an uncertainty in the steering. Not much; a judder on coming out of a corner, which could well have been due to an unevenness in the road surface. But when it did it again, with quite a frantic scrabble of tyres this time, I knew something was wrong. I slowed. Lay-bys on this class of road were rare, but I found one in the next half mile, pulled in, and got out to have a good cuss.

I reckoned it had to be wheels. The tyres were nearly new, so it couldn't relate to treads. I went round, grabbing opposite sides of the wheels and wiggling them. It took all my strength, but in two of them, the front ones, I thought there was a slight play.

There was no torch in the car, so I had to manage with the moon and with the doors open for whatever light might filter out from the interior. The boot had its own lighting, so I had no difficulty in finding the jack and the levers and nut-wrench. I hesitated. There was a quicker way, without jacking it up. I levered off the front near-side wheel disc, and a nut fell out.

The other three were loose.

Before allowing myself to give it any deep thought I banged on all four nuts solidly, then I went round the other three wheels. Only the two front ones were affected. The offside front was the worst, all four nuts about to fall off. As I was tightening these a small car whipped past, its headlights flooding me. It swerved as though about to stop, but didn't. It went within a foot of my back, in fact. I stood up and stared after it. It had the general shape of a Ford Fiesta.

There are several ways of rendering a motor vehicle lethal. They usually involve the braking or steering, but these are not really satisfactory methods, as either can fail at a non-dangerous time, braking or turning for corners, when you're moving slower. Loosening the wheel nuts can cause you to lose a wheel, most likely at a high speed, and can be very lethal indeed. The assumption has to be, though, that the driver is so stupid as not to notice anything going wrong, such as a female person, who is not supposed, by the bulk of motoring males, to know a steering wheel from a speedometer.

Yet I'd been warned, well and truly, though the only person who would want me dead before I could prove my real identity seemed to be Bella. I could think of no one else. And Bella could not possibly have got near the Rover, even if she could have forced herself to put her delicate and beautifully manicured hands anywhere near a tool of any description.

So I had to assume that someone else wanted me dead. The only question outstanding was whether I was wanted dead as Philipa Lowe, or as Tonia Fields.

6

It was visiting hours at St James's. I'd dropped lucky for a change. Yes, they had an Oliver Simpson in Cassandra Ward, on the fourth floor. Easy, apart from the fact that this was an old building with no lifts available, except to patients on trolleys, so I had to walk up, the snag being that my legs were still foolishly shaking unless I could keep moving.

He was in a four-bed ward, two of them empty. His sole companion was asleep, Oliver reading a collection of Sherlock Holmes, which was supported on his raised knees. His right shoulder and chest were swathed in bandages, his face seeming drawn and grey.

'Phil!' He tried to lift himself higher. 'Is it really you?'

I walked round the bed, trying to smile as though I wasn't devastated by his general appearance. He seemed shrunken, his body drained by pain. I kissed him on the lips. They were dry.

'Oliver! What *have* you been doing?'

He moved uneasily at the memory. 'He'd gone crazy. Old Pearson. His wife was hiding in a barn, and I tried to take his shotgun from him. The old confidence trick, you know. "Now hand it over, Charlie. You know very well you're not going to fire it." But he didn't know, and he did fire it. Lucky, I suppose, that he didn't blow my head off.'

I studied him with my head on one side, knowing the approach that would appeal to him. 'No harm to your face, though. Still the same old good-looking bastard.'

'Sarcasm, Phil? What about you? Have you come home to stay? Well, that's cheered me up no end, I must say. I'll be out of here—'

'Don't cheer yet, Oliver, please,' I said, looking round for a chair and dragging it across so that I could sit beside him, perhaps hold his hand.

'Don't tell me you're going back! New York calls, does it?'

'I don't hear it. No, no.' I secured the hand. 'But I'm a little caught up in something at the moment . . .' I allowed it to tail away.

'How did you know I'm in here?'

'Easy. I rang the station.'

He tilted his head. Even that drew a tiny wince. 'Rang it? Does that mean you're not staying here, Phil?'

'I'm at a place called Horseley Green. Heard of it?'

'I know it. Go on, tell me what you're caught up in. Lousy sentence, sorry. Tell me what it's all about.'

But now I didn't want to. My own troubles seemed so paltry compared with his present condition. I felt guilty that my visit might present itself as being less than a hundred per cent on his behalf. The last time I had seen him, he'd been so full of energy, a burly man, brushing six feet, though with touches of grey above his ears. It hadn't, then, shown much, his hair being very light, like bleached straw. Now it did show, because his hair seemed darker, probably with sweat. He'd aged, looked fifty, though I knew he was no more than in his mid forties. But I couldn't continue to stare at him. He was waiting, attentive.

I told him all about it, every detail that I could squeeze from my memory, from the moment I'd met Bella on the QE2. He watched me closely, his eyes roving over my face. Those grey eyes seemed to darken with his concern. There was not a word from him; he was always a good listener.

'But Phil,' he protested, when I'd worked up to the present, 'this is ridiculous. How can she claim you're her sister? All you've got to do is deny it, and leave her to offer some sort of proof. Tell her to go and jump in the lake.'

'She hasn't claimed anything,' I said. I couldn't get much emphasis into it.

'And that inspector . . . hasn't she?'

'No. It was all implication. The nod and the wink – and a lot of background confirmation she could produce if she had to.'

He was clearly in pain, moving uneasily in the bed. He wasn't going to waste much time with paltry claims.

'Then you simply tell her to go to hell.'

67

'If she prefers that to the lake?' I pouted at him. 'It's easy for you to say it. But don't worry about that, Oliver. I'll—'

He wasn't to be diverted. 'And that Inspector . . . Connaught, was it? He couldn't go along with something like that.' He shook his head stiffly and reached for a glass of fruit juice he had on the bedside table.

'He *is* going along with it,' I admitted reluctantly.

'Then it's a trick he's playing. He's probably leading her on. He knows she must be guilty—'

'I don't know what his thinking is, Oliver. But I'm not so sure she's guilty. Of anything.'

'Ah! Got you interested, has she?'

I didn't reply. Damn the man, he always managed to lead me into saying more than I'd intended.

'He's playing it canny, you can bet your life,' Oliver went on with confidence, because that was what he'd have done. 'He's waiting for her to trap herself.'

'I'll bear that in mind. It's comforting.'

But now his grey eyes were watching me keenly. Oliver never missed anything, and he could build mountains out of impressions. He'd detected the worry in my voice. 'Does it concern you so much, Phil?'

I shook my head.

'No lying, now. Don't ever keep anything from me – d'you hear?'

I pouted, smiled at the 'ever', and admitted that there'd already been an attempt on my life.

'You didn't mention this,' he accused.

'If I were to die now, in such a way that I could be buried as Tonia Fields, then I wouldn't be in any position to deny it.'

Behind his eyes I saw the anger grow. The fingers of his left hand clenched; I removed mine just in time. 'That blasted Connaught! Irresponsible, that's the word for him. Right . . . we've only got to identify you formally, and that'll be that. I can be out of here—'

'Oh, no, you won't!'

'A day or so . . .'

'*No*, Oliver. Don't be stupid. Somebody else, perhaps.'

'Superintendent Grossman? *He* knows you.' He tried a twisted grin. I shook my head. He nodded. 'Right. There's another way. She'd know her sister's abnormalities.'

'Abnormal?' I hadn't heard of anything like that.

'Have you got any birthmarks – which she wouldn't have?'

'A raspberry mark on my left cheek. I wouldn't call it an abnormality.'

He squinted at me. 'I see nothing.'

'On my bottom.'

'There! You see. Ask her about her sister's birthmarks, not mentioning her bottom. If sister Tonia didn't have one, and you've got a witness present, then you can prove—'

'To Connaught?'

'I didn't quite mean—'

I laughed. 'But it wouldn't work, anyway. Bella's seen me stripped.'

'Pity. I haven't been so privileged.' He pouted.

'Now don't start that.'

We grinned at each other, almost as freely as we used to before. I felt we'd steered clear of the seriousness of it. Really, look at it from the correct angle and the whole thing was positively ridiculous. I shrugged. Perhaps the loose nuts had been pure chance.

'I'll manage,' I assured him.

'There ought to be somebody who could help you, though.'

Behind me the door opened. I heard it sigh. He looked past me, his face lightening. 'But of course, there's always Jennie!'

I turned, rising to my feet. Yes, there was always Jennie, and there she was. Trim and bright, a busty redhead, that was Woman Detective Constable Jennie Lyons, who had been far too intimate with her inspector for my liking, and, judging by her grin and Oliver's suddenly uplifted response, still was. But she had one very large plus mark. She knew me.

'Just the person we need!' he cried.

We smiled at each other in cool formality and bumped cheeks in an empty kiss at the air.

'How splendid to be wanted.' She looked from one face to the other. 'What is it?'

Oliver told her briskly and precisely, she nodding. Very quick and smart, was Jennie. She watched his face as he spoke, not once glancing at me. They shared a tight intimacy in those few moments. But I saw that her lips twitched. She found the situation amusing, and when she'd heard the last of it she turned to me with her eyes dancing.

'Of course I'll come,' she said without hesitation.

But I didn't want Jennie. She would be doing it for him, not for me. Yet her smile was for me, and her enthusiasm was for the adventure of it. There was nothing but friendliness in her expression. But we had always been friends, in the brief time I'd known her, which had been during the trouble arising from my husband's death. She'd never been anything but uncritically sympathetic. I felt mean that I should have considered rejecting her offer, and tried to match her warmth.

'But it's so much trouble for you!' I protested. 'And all over a silly misunderstanding. I can't ask—'

'Nonsense. It'll be fun. I'm off duty at ten.'

'At nine,' put in Oliver helpfully. 'My orders.'

I doubted he could give orders, being off on sick leave, but I didn't say anything.

'I'll be there just after ten,' Jennie told me, placing a hand on my arm, squeezing. 'We'll sort this crazy woman out, you'll see.'

I knew that there was no doubt that Jennie, when she got going, would be able to overwhelm Bella completely with her fiery personality, which didn't need any acting to boost it.

So there I was, feeling caught again, when in fact I'd got what I'd come for, if not in the way I'd expected. I gave her directions, but she knew Horseley Green. I told her it was the Crown. She said she knew it. I told her she could park round the back. She seemed to know that, too. She was one of those people who infuriatingly know everything.

'We're in room seven,' I murmured, trying to find something she didn't.

'I'll come straight up to the room,' she said. 'Walk in on her. Say ten to ten-thirty. If you could get this Connaught character there, it could all be cleared up in a few minutes.'

'And there'd be time for a drink before the bar closes?'

'Precisely.'

I was, of course, reluctant to leave before she did, but I'd had my share of visiting and she'd really had none. So I kissed

Oliver chastely on the chin, nodded and smiled at Jennie, and left.

I sat in my car and tried to work out how I was going to tackle it. A phone call ahead would best guarantee the presence of Inspector Connaught, on duty or off, because he'd clearly considered the question of my identity to be of importance. I therefore went back inside the hospital to where I'd noted a coin phone, discovered I was short of change, but was lucky to get straight through to him at once. In a few brisk sentences I told him where I was, and that there'd already been one attempt on my life. The idea was to shake him a little, but it didn't work.

'Really? I didn't expect—'

'Never mind what you expected,' I cut in briskly. 'If you can be at the Crown at about ten-fifteen, room seven, I'll be in a position to put an end to it. WDC Jennie Lyons is her name, of Penley Police. She'll no doubt have her warrant card with her. All right?'

'Yes. This attempt on your life—'

'I'll tell you later.' I hung up. I'd heard the pips and my time was running out. Not, perhaps, an auspicious thought to present to myself at that time.

I left the Rover in the hospital car park and walked the short distance to the nearest café, got a couple of cups of tea and an over-poached egg on hard toast, went back to the car . . . and remembered to check those wheel nuts once again. You never know. They were firm. I climbed in and got going.

There was, I discovered, a certain satisfaction in pushing the car way beyond a safe speed on those roads. It was a gesture. If the car was going to kill me, I dared it to get on with it, throwing challenges at it on every scrabbled corner. There comes a time when you realize your concentration is at its peak, and that you are anticipating and calculating to perfection. And in so doing, you thrust behind you all background concerns and the intricacies of your problems. When I turned into the yard behind the Crown I was in a state of complete and relaxed readiness. That drive had done me the world of good. It seemed, now, that I was on top of my difficulties and in charge of my destiny.

At night, that yard was a dingy place, with no more than a single pearl globe on a bracket from one wall. I wasted no time getting away from there and hurried into the lobby, pattering

71

up the stairs, anxious to acquaint Bella with the fact that her stupid plotting was about to come to nothing.

But of course – and this was something that had slipped my mind – it would then leave the double-skeleton problem wide open. Or firmly closed, I suppose. With me out of the reckoning as a possible sister, there could no longer be much doubt that the female corpse had to be that of the real and genuine Tonia Fields. Bella would be in trouble, and I cannot deny a little eagerness to get to her and tell her so, face to face.

My hand was on the doorknob before I heard the raised voices within, one of them a man's. For a moment I assumed Connaught had arrived early. I opened the door and walked in.

Bella was standing with her back to the window, her long and flowing skirt still settling, as though she had just completed a whirl. Her face was flushed with anger and I thought perhaps she had been weeping. The man had his back to me. She was shouting, 'And you can just bloody well get back . . .' She stopped as she saw me.

The man turned. Not Connaught. This one was taller and more craggily built. He was wearing casual slacks and a chunky, hand-knitted sweater, which must have cost a mint. There was a motif of J's worked into it. So I didn't need any introduction. This was Bella's Jay, a very masculine man indeed, over six feet and balanced with it, heavy shoulders and deep chest tapering down to a narrow waist. She had said he was in his fifties, but by heaven he was fit. To maintain this pitch he would have had to spend a good part of every day working out, a process that either builds you up or strikes you down. At the moment he was very much alive, with a tensed eagerness about him and suppressed triumph that blazed from his eyes. Blue-grey eyes, they were, under craggy brows, set in a sunburnt knobbly face that somehow contrived to look like an experienced thirty instead of a jaded fifty. Bella had at one time implied a series of face-lifts, and any number of tucks and pleats could have gone into forming his half-handsome and half-distorted face. But his mouth was soft, wide, expressive. At the moment, as he turned, fury and scorn still controlled it, and then it melted into a wide smile of sheer pleasure, unadulterated joy at the sight of me, whilst his eyes, in one quick and experienced glance, took in every aspect of my figure from top to toe, stripping me of all dignity.

'Well, well,' he cried. 'At last, the little sister.'

I knew he had to be mocking somebody, me or himself or Bella. He'd made the instant connection with what she must have told him about me, my name and its derivation. Otherwise, he'd not have used the Raymond Chandler title: The Little Sister. But he had the required appearance of tough resilience to have enabled him to play Philip Marlowe in a film. I would have thought, though, that he could not have conveyed Marlowe's deep understanding and muted passion. Nothing deep about this man, nothing muted. But passion, certainly. It shouted out at me.

'Well, well, well,' he repeated, using up his reserves. He raised his arm as though to slap me on the back, but instead it fell along my shoulders as though it lived there, and perhaps I was expected to bask in it. Smiling, I slipped free.

'What was the shouting about?' I asked Bella.

It was he who answered. 'Shouting? We were discussing—'

She didn't allow him to finish. 'Shouting – yes! That was me. I was telling this idiot . . . oh, this is Jay, my husband . . . telling the stupid fool to sod off back to where he came from.'

I glanced at him. He raised his shoulders heavily, grimacing. 'What've I done?' he asked me ruefully, in an intimate way not justified by our short acquaintanceship.

'You've come here, that's what,' Bella snapped.

'All I did . . . plane to Heathrow . . . hired an auto . . . came to you, sweetheart. I've brought you news. Special news. Have I got news!'

'I don't want to hear your news.' She turned a shoulder to him, and he raised his eyebrows at me.

'They picked it up in the States,' he explained. 'It's in all the papers. Star Of Colossus Seized By Brit Police.'

'I haven't been seized!' she protested angrily.

'No? That's what they said. I bought every paper I could get.'

I thought it time I put in a word. 'She was wanted for questioning.'

'And that's been done, has it, this questioning?'

'You could say,' I informed him cautiously, 'that some questioning has taken place.'

He slapped his palms together, then spread his arms. 'That's just great. So you can get packed, Bella my love, and I'll book a return flight for two—'

'Don't be more ridiculous than you can help, Jay,' she said coldly. 'You're acting like a demented clown.'

Indeed, he seemed to be riding a high on something, tension, triumph, excitement, but certainly not drugs. He wouldn't allow such contamination to get anywhere near that perfect body. And he had not asked the vital question: on what had his wife been wanted for questioning? Perhaps she had already told him. Now, he seemed to realize the impression he was making, because he was abruptly serious, glancing at me as though for encouragement, then at Bella with his brows lowered.

'It'd look better,' he suggested, 'for you to come back voluntarily. Better than holding out until they apply for extradition.'

'Extradition!' They could have heard her in the street.

'Though I suppose . . .' He looked doubtful. 'With a good brief—'

'What the hell d'you mean by extradition?' But now her lips were thin, and there were red patches high on her cheeks.

I looked from one to the other. This was not, apparently, an unusual scene for these two. I had gathered that they must be used to snapping and snarling at each other, pecking away at tender spots and trying to establish a position of ascendancy. In an attempt to dash cool water on their emotions, I intervened.

'You don't have to worry about that, Bella,' I told her. 'Even if they try to extradite you, you'll be safe. They couldn't get you, because the British police will have a prior claim.'

It had the required effect. Perhaps because they were not used to their squabbles being interrupted, they were now both standing very still, and staring at me intently. I glanced at my watch. It was a few minutes to ten.

'In half an hour or so there'll be a woman arriving here. A policewoman, who knows me under my real identity, which is Philipa Lowe and not Tonia Fields. She'll be able to testify as to my name and the rest. Inspector Connaught will also be here, so in half an hour's time I'll be able to walk out of your life, Bella. Won't you be pleased! Do you understand what I'm saying, Jay? Has she explained what's been going on?'

He nodded, jaw firm, eyes bleak. 'Get on with it.'

'What else is there? Oh yes, of course. It'll mean, you see, Bella, that from that moment on the police will have a reasonably solid case against you for the killing and burial of both your father and your sister. So you don't need to worry. The New York police won't be able to have you back.'

'Is this supposed to be a joke?' she asked huskily.

'A joke!' I was angry with her. No – furious. Suddenly I felt hot with fury. 'And who's been playing jokes?' I demanded forcefully. 'Who's landed me in no end of trouble with stupid claims that I'm your sister?'

'I claimed nothing.'

'And denied nothing!' I shouted.

There was silence. Then she shrugged, possibly because there was nothing worth saying. The anger drained from me, leaving me cold.

'So you're safe here, Bella,' I said emptily. 'Unless the police in New York can produce a charge better than two murders, then you're safe.'

She made a movement with her lips, very like spitting. It didn't become a word.

But it seemed that Jay had himself completely in hand. He was composed. Composed but puzzled. Perhaps the visible exterior of such a superior being hid the possession of an inferior brain. Certainly he didn't seem to have a full grasp of the situation.

'It's New Haven, actually,' he observed. 'Not New York. And it *is* murder over there, too. But only one.'

Bella made a choking sound and sat down on the edge of her bed. 'What? Who?' she whispered.

Jay was pleased to offer an answer. The big, complacent bastard was enjoying himself. 'A woman. Dead on the floor in the living room of our holiday place. You know that little pistol you keep, locked in the bedside table? It was lying there beside her on the rug. That Bokhara of ours . . .'

'What does it matter which rug?' Bella demanded, searching for anything that would break down his story.

'Three little holes in her,' said Jay. 'Bang, bang, bang.'

I remembered clearly what Bella had said about walking in on them with a pistol in her hand.

'One of your whores!' she snapped, nodding, nodding. Too much nodding for the remark.

'No, no.' He shook his head with confidence. 'Not one of mine. I wouldn't dare. What would Odile say? And Dawn would cripple me, and as for Felicia—'

'You filthy rotten bastard!' she shouted, and he laughed, throwing his head back.

'By God, you're a gullible fool, Bella. No, this wasn't one of mine. Nobody I could recognize. The police seem to think she came to see you. She'd flown in from the west coast. They reckon you took one look at her, and you assumed she was one of mine. Bella – admit it – you do have these strange ideas.'

'This is some sort of trick!' she cried wildly, thumping the bed with her fist. 'You're a liar, Jay. You always were a damned liar. Besides . . .' A thought twisted her lips into the best she could manage of a sour smile. 'Besides, I've been here, and my passport will confirm it.'

'Me too,' I murmured.

'They've set the time of death at two days before you boarded the QE2, as a matter of fact.' Jay was calmly practical.

He'd come armed, his speech rehearsed, probably in front of a mirror so that he could perfect that near-casual smile with a hint of pity in it, that Bella should be in trouble, but I didn't think he'd been able to master the light in his eyes. He was enjoying every minute.

'Name?' I put in, as Bella seemed unable to bring herself to ask.

'No name.' He shook his head. 'Nothing on her but the return half of her air ticket from Los Angeles. Nobody I'd know, nobody you would, Bella. They fetched me – drove me there. Not that I wanted to see, but somebody had got to. About thirty, they said, but she looked a damned sight older. Really old and worn out. They told me she'd been on drugs, cocaine and heroin – probably both. You wouldn't have liked to see her, Bella. You know what I thought at the time? D'you want to hear?'

She mumbled something and shook her head, premonition tightening the lines round her mouth. He smiled wickedly, though there was pain in his eyes.

'I thought, seeing as she'd possibly come to see you – not me, not a woman like that . . . I thought – maybe it was sister Tonia.

You know, come to see whether she could get money to keep her going on her habits. I didn't say anything. It was just a thought,' he said soothingly. 'And how could she be?' He nodded to me, smiling, as though we were in conspiracy.

Bella gave a small moan, her eyes rolled and her head slumped. I went to her quickly, but Jay thrust me away and lifted her chin with his left forefinger. Then he slapped her face, rather harder than necessary, I thought. She came out of it spitting in his face, her nails going for his eyes, but he'd had practice and was anticipating it. He caught her wrists, laughed in her face, and flung her away from him, sprawling across the bed.

'How many sisters have you got, Bella?' he demanded. But he was still smiling.

He glanced over his shoulder at me and winked. I looked away quickly before I did something stupidly violent, and grabbed one of my cases, flung it on my bed, then began to stuff clothes into it. No time for delicate folding. They were silent. When I risked a glance I saw he was standing, those huge and powerful hands on his hips, gazing out of the window. Bella had found her way to the dressing-table and was examining her face. Then she seemed to notice my activities.

'What the hell're you doing, Phil?'

'Packing.'

'Where're you—'

'With your husband here, I'll book another room.'

'Don't you dare!'

Jay laughed.

'Don't you laugh at me!' she shouted. 'Do you think I'd have you in here? Not while I can stand. Get out of this room, Jay. Get out! Before I kill you.'

'Kill, kill. It's all you think about.'

'Out!'

He held up his palms, backing towards the door. 'Don't worry, I've already booked another room—'

'Not even in the same hotel!'

'A room at the Clarendon, lover. Somehow, I guessed you wouldn't be pleased.'

She threw the ashtray. He closed the door behind him. She didn't even hit the door. I sat on my bed and waited.

77

I had to wait a long while, through all her fury and passion, her hatred and her tears. I had to endure the listing of his monstrous parading of a dozen or more females. Privately, I thought he'd invented them, partly for use as a torture instrument, partly to boost his own ego. There are men, vast macho objects, who openly parade their wares, and yet are not greatly sexed. A wife would probably be all that Jay could manage, but he wouldn't care to have it known. Was it possible that he was a one-woman man? If so, he was caught in the trap of his own public image. He would certainly have to hide it, especially from Bella, and how better to do that than to torment her with a promiscuity he didn't in fact practise? In any event, I'd caught no messages from him, no hints, no special glances. I admit to receiving such messages from time to time.

It was then, at the moment that I rounded off this pleasant theory in my mind, when she was weak and lost and in need of a confidante, that she completely destroyed my reasoning.

'We haven't', she whispered, 'slept in the same bed for five years.'

'Oh,' I said.

I glanced at my watch. Nearly ten minutes past ten! What the devil was happening? Where was Jennie Lyons? And just when I needed a diversion.

The tap on the door jerked up my head. It was unlike Jennie to knock, especially in these circumstances. Walk right in – 'Here I am!' That sort of thing.

I went to open the door. Inspector Connaught said, 'Here I am. Where is she, this witness of yours?' His practised sweep of the room with his eyes told more than just the absence of Jennie. 'What's been going on? You two been fighting?'

'It's just Bella's husband. He's turned up.'

'No cause for distress, surely.' So casually that was said, even dismissively, but it was clear he felt it to be of importance. 'What time is she due?'

'Who? Jennie? We reckoned ten to ten-thirty.'

'Late, then.'

'Not really – the road can be tricky.'

'Hmm!'

He went to stand at the window. Bella had a handmirror perched in front of her face and was frowning at something.

She'd be itching to repair the damage. Connaught's stance was casual, hands in his trouser pockets. But his shoulders were tensed. Without turning, he said, 'What car does she use?'

'I don't know.' He was making me nervous.

He leaned closer to the glass. The white-painted window frame was flushed orange from the street lights. He leaned forward, the glow tinging his shoulders. As I watched it, the colour shaded to grey, wavering and waning, orange, grey, orange, grey. Not grey though now, more blue as the predominant colour took over, until it was blue, blue, blue.

Connaught stiffened. He flattened his face against the glass, peering downwards. There had been no siren. The blue shading ceased and the frame was restored to orange.

He snapped, 'Stay here,' and was across the room in three strides.

The door slammed behind him. I heard myself whispering, 'Jennie! Jennie?'

Bella demanded from behind her mirror, 'What is it?'

I didn't answer, but backed away, turned on my heel. 'I'll be back.' I didn't know whether I said it. I crashed through the door and ran, stumbling, to the head of the stairs, my heart pounding, fumbling my way down the staircase, trying for two steps at a time but my feet missing the treads. Then through the lobby into the yard, which was packed with people and cars. There was no room for more than half a dozen, but those had their lights on, with the beams concentrated on one patch beside the gaunt outline of a Citroën 2CV.

I thrust through, panting. Connaught was crouching there. I fell heavily to my knees beside him. Jennie's red hair was redder still, the lights blazing on to the colour, the blood soaking it. Beside her lay the GENTLEMEN sign. There was blood on that too.

'Jennie,' I whispered. 'Oh, Jennie, Jennie . . .'

And Connaught put his arm round my shoulders and said softly, 'I'm sorry. Sorry. She's dead, Phil.'

Before I passed out, I registered the fact that he'd called me Phil.

7

I was sitting alone in the little Green on one of the two benches, having discovered a tiny gate in the low, spiked fence. The seat was damp, and maybe I would develop rheumatism in my behind, but I had to have solitude, air around me and nothing near. My skin felt tender, the nerves close to the surface. I would scream if anyone touched me. The huge chestnut to my right was trying to throw a shadow, as the sun was doing its best to push its way through the morning mist. Perhaps I was cold. I could feel nothing.

The street seemed very busy, with traffic edging along nose to tail and pedestrians flooding the pavements. Maybe it was Saturday.

I was procrastinating, no other way to look at it. Sometime I was going to have to drive over to Penley and tell Oliver what had happened. And yet I knew, miserably, that I wouldn't need to. They would know at Penley. Oliver would know, and I was close to tears at the thought that the news hadn't come from me first. I'd been afraid. No arguing about that. Couldn't face it. A coward. I ought to have been able at least to dial the hospital's number before the sedative grabbed hold of me.

Miserably I sat, knowing that each second's delay made it worse.

A man's voice said, 'What're you doing here?' There was concern in his tone.

I turned. I hadn't seen him arrive, hadn't noticed he had sat beside me.

It was Detective Inspector Connaught, fumbling in the pocket of his anorak and producing a tin of tobacco and a bent pipe. A

Sherlock Holmes pipe. It would be part of his image, I supposed – the quiet smoke and the contemplation.

'Sitting,' I answered shortly, not wanting company, certainly not his. He was a complacent and egotistical ass, I thought. Why wasn't he on the job? Go, go, go. 'What about you?' I demanded.

'Aren't you cold?' He was avoiding having to look me in the eye.

'I don't feel it. Aren't you on duty?'

'That sedative didn't take, did it?' he asked mildly, untouched by what I'd tried to be, which was unencouraging.

'I'm all right.'

'Good.' He was rubbing flake between his palms, then he began to pack it into the huge bowl of his pipe. 'Meerschaum,' he explained, as though I might be interested. 'It's a kind of clay.'

I didn't reply. On the pavement the far side of the street Bella was parading, the mirror glasses there again – a new pair, they would have to be – and in all her exotic finery, now deliberately exhibiting her other self as Roma Felucci, welcoming it and encouraging it. She might have been 'our Bella', but she was set to dispel the past. Head high, swinging her hips and her long skirt, she paraded her beauty and authority, and very soon she'd have the traffic stopped.

'Have you done *anything*?' I demanded abruptly and angrily, though the anger was aimed at Bella.

'We've been at it all night,' he said flatly. 'The team, the lot. And . . . nothing. That metal sign had been torn off the wall by somebody wearing gloves. Your friend must have parked her Citroën, shut the door, and he struck. One blow. It's all it took.'

'He?' My voice shuddered.

'We believe it was beyond a woman's strength.'

'Depends which woman.'

Scented smoke was drifting around my head. He gestured with the pipe. 'Not *that* one, certainly.'

No, not Bella. She had been with me in the room. Not Bella with the wheel nuts, either. I'd already decided that. And yet, she was the only one . . .

'But she's the only one who had *any* reason to keep my real identity secret!' I burst out.

There was no reply. I turned and looked at him, for the first time really examining him. He'd been on duty all night, but he was cleanly shaven, his moustache carefully arranged, hair by hair, and he was wearing a tweedy suit I hadn't seen on him before. There had been time to restore the external part of his personality, but it had done nothing for the internal. This was an Inspector Connaught I'd not previously encountered. Gone was the self-confidence, gone was the man who had to impress. His ego had taken a hammering. The bath, the shave, the change of clothes were no more than a gloss. He was repressed and hurt, as though he'd been slapped across the face.

But of course, he'd probably encountered few murders in this small and tight community. If any at all, they would have been domestic, with no mystery involved other than the question of what had driven the perpetrator over the edge. Connaught was lost in this.

Then at last, as though he'd had to force his mind to the task, he answered my question. If it had been a question.

'You've got to admit that Bella Fields – as I'll call her – had good reason to be worried. One skeleton popping up, and it would've been a good guess it was her father's. There was half the town who would have been honoured to kill Rowley Fields at that time, so that she'd have been a very minor suspect. But two skeletons, buried side by side . . . then the assumption has to be that the second was her sister's. Then our Bella would have to start worrying. She wouldn't have known that there's a possibility we'll be able to put a name to both of them in due course. All she would see was that everybody would say, "That's her pa and her sister, you can bet your life". So it would suit Bella to be able to produce a live sister.'

'You don't have to explain to *me*!' I stared at him. He stared at the bowl of his pipe. 'It suited her, you said. You mean – you knew it was false?'

'I believed it to be,' he admitted cautiously. Then he turned and surveyed me with consideration. 'There *is* a resemblance, you know. But Tonia was only seventeen when I last saw her.'

'Believed!' I was furious. He had seemed convinced. 'But you allowed it to—'

'To go on . . . yes. It suited me, too. I wanted to see how far she would take it.'

82

'You mean, how far before you had another death on your hands? All right. Sorry. But you distinctly told me . . .'

'Perhaps I was leading you on, as well.' He was placid about it, even smiled. 'It's the truth I'm after.'

'What a dirty rotten trick!'

'I couldn't take it seriously. It *wasn't* serious, just a slippy bit of confusion thrown in my path.'

'Jennie was killed, damn you. Is *that* serious to you? Or are you going to trip over it? If you hadn't been so amused by it all—'

'That's rather unfair,' he protested.

With stronger words poised on my tongue, I stopped, and bit my lip to keep it still. He was correct. It was unfair. He'd had no chance to intervene.

'My apologies,' I murmured. 'It was all my fault in the first place.' I didn't really feel I owed him an apology, I was simply clearing the air. 'Jennie came to help me – I *feel* responsible.'

'You found it necessary to prove who you are,' he said, a little pompously. 'It's a natural reaction, but you ought to be careful with it. Push it far enough, and discover that you still can't establish it, and before you know where you are you'll be wondering, yourself. It's a kind of self-induced schizophrenia.'

'Well, thank you, Mr Freud,' I said bitterly. 'Are you *laughing* at me?' I demanded, not fully in control of my voice.

He grimaced, holding up his palm. 'Trying to help, really. Trying to get you to see it's not a serious problem. Bella Fields has been trying something on, but she couldn't have expected to keep it going much longer. No. What we've got now is the vicious killing of Jennie Lyons. I can't see the connection. Perhaps there isn't one.'

'You think not?' I ventured gently, when what I really wanted was to scream. 'You don't think it's somebody who prefers me to be Tonia Fields?'

He grinned at me. I had to assume he was sincerely trying to be helpful, to reassure me. 'No, I don't. Different style – different person. Somebody who's . . . well, desperate, shall we say.'

'Nothing,' I whispered, 'for *me* to worry about?'

'Nothing. Leave me to do the worrying.'

Was he insane? Or was he treating me as a delicate and

inexperienced female who would sigh with relief at his specious encouragement, coming as it did from a mature male police officer? If so, he had failed miserably. Any desperation hanging around was mine, while I fought grimly to cling to the basic fact that I was Philipa Lowe, who wasn't going to be frightened by bogies and whispers in the dark, not even by somebody who was desperate! Yet creeping into my bones was the chill awareness that perhaps Bella had done too good a job, and that for somebody I was really Tonia Fields, who'd been a frightened little mouse, and who seemed now to be wriggling on that damp bench with her briefs sticking to her behind.

'What are you intending to do about it?' I asked coldly.

'Do?' He seemed surprised. 'Why . . . wait, of course. Until the forensic people give me something to work on. Here!' He flicked a smile in my direction. 'I didn't tell you . . . we already have a good guess as to the age of the female skeleton. When she died, that is.'

'Tell me.' I tried to sound uninterested.

'Late teens to middle twenties.'

'It fits,' I said quietly. 'Tonia!'

'Doesn't it!'

It seemed that my nerves were being teased from all directions. The fact that he'd deliberately approached me, not to interrogate but to inform, and that in the most formal and prepared way, indicated that he was applying a test. Did he intend that I should make a run for it? Or hang on like a worm on a fish-hook?

'Am I allowed to leave the district?' I asked meekly.

'You're under no restraint.'

'You don't want me for statements and the like?'

'I'll know where to find you. In fact, I'd prefer you to be somewhere else.'

I nodded. 'So that in the event of another violent death, with me in the lead part, it won't be on your patch? You're as transparent as a sheet of ice.' And as warm, but I managed not to say that.

'I'd still be interested.'

'Thank you. Then I'll tell you that I'm going to my home town, Penley. Amongst friends.'

'And a very good idea, too.'

I didn't reply, having suddenly become fascinated by the drama I could see about to unfold on the far side of the street. From the left Bella was approaching, doing a return run. From the right Jay was approaching, he in his full persona as a co-star of *Colossus*, and basking in the instant recognition. Traffic slowed, groups paused, hesitated, then stopped. They sailed magnificently towards each other, like fighting ships under full sail on the Spanish Main, the encounter inevitable. People stood aside in respect. The imminent clash was recognized by the sun, which made a vast effort, flung aside the residue of the mist, and burst through. Colours were at once more brilliant, and none shone with more piercing clarity than Bella and Jay, who had now seen each other, who flung their arms wide and rushed into each other's embrace as though separation had robbed them of a vital element, which now acted as a catalyst to their emotions. How many times they'd done it for the cameras! They kissed hungrily, passion at last released, the mirror glasses dangling in Bella's fingers behind his head, and dancing to the rhythm of her ecstasy. The traffic stopped, the pedestrians stopped. Many hearts hesitated, then beat faster.

'Very touching,' said Connaught. He blew something unpleasant from his pipe stem.

I stood. My briefs stuck to my bottom. Indecorously, I detached them. 'I'll no doubt see you again, Inspector,' I said.

'They'll start a riot,' he muttered uneasily.

I walked away in the opposite direction. It was possible that Bella and Jay, their attention most certainly not being on each other, might spot me and include me in the touching scene. The idea made my toe-nails curl. I sneaked off round the back and hurried away, dreading the calling of my name. But I'd be able to ignore it if they called me Tonia.

Head down, I trotted up the steps and into the Crown, my intention being to sign out immediately, throw my stuff together before Bella returned – inevitably in a flaming temper – and get moving fast away from Horseley Green.

But intentions are not necessarily fulfilled. Oliver Simpson was standing at the desk, luggage all round him, and with his old tweed hat cocked at an angle that ridiculously caught at my throat. They'd managed to reduce the bandaging, and had the arm now in a sling, his jacket and coat hanging free on that side.

How do you approach a person so severely handicapped when your body cries out to be thrown into his arms – arm? He solved it.

'Phil!' And his good arm was pulling me tightly to his chest, where it didn't hurt, and his tired kind eyes were looking down into mine. We didn't need to say anything more. Nothing demonstrative; he kissed me on the forehead. 'I'm so very sorry,' he whispered, when it was I who should have been apologizing and comforting.

I had to look away from his face. The journey, however it had been accomplished, had strained him. It was there in the wounded line of his mouth.

'I'll book you in,' I said, my own plans way up in the sky now.

'It's done. A double room.'

'Good. I'll move my stuff in there, then.'

'I've made arrangements, Phil.' Grimacing, half in amusement, he gestured. 'Constable Terry Alwright.'

I hadn't noticed him there, he'd been so self-effacing, a large and doughy-faced young man in his mid-twenties with wide shoulders and a firm stance. There was pink in his cheeks, his mild blue eyes dancing, his blond hair slipping over his eyes.

'Hello, Terry.' With friendliness, I hoped.

He nodded, smiling.

'I'm on sick leave,' said Oliver, 'so this is unofficial. Jennie was on my team, but it's still unofficial.' A little terse anger touched his voice. 'Terry's on loan, also unofficially. Therefore, it's Terry and not Constable. So . . . This is Philipa, Terry. This is Terry, Philipa.'

'Philipa,' he murmured, even more embarrassed now.

'I need help, you see, Phil,' Oliver explained, but not looking me in the eyes. 'Dressing, undressing, washing, shaving. I'm like a great big awkward baby. Isn't that right, Terry?'

'Right . . . sir.'

'Terry's the strongest they could find for me. He's been instructed to take me to the hospital here, once a day, for dressings. I think we'll manage.'

But *we* could've managed, Oliver, I wanted to shout at him. I said, 'Right. Got your key, have you?' He dangled it. 'Terry, if you'll grab hold of the boss-man – there's no lift, I'm afraid – I'll bring up what bags I can. Then we'll settle you in, Oliver, and Terry can . . . can . . .'

I'd wanted to say evaporate for a while, because Jennie was still there between us, and we had to be alone. But I couldn't order Terry around. He delicately lifted an eyebrow because I was doing exactly that.

'Yes, ma'am,' he said quietly, which I suppose I deserved.

We managed it to their room, which was on the same floor as Bella's and mine – probably this was the only floor catering for guests – but at the far end of the corridor. Terry handled his inspector like candyfloss, equally crushable and just as light. The muscles of the man! Oliver was no light weight, even taking most of it himself. He lowered him gently to sit on one of the beds. Oliver groaned. I stared silently and miserably at his harrowed face.

'I'll get the rest of the cases, sir,' said Terry.

'For heaven's sake!' There was no snap in Oliver's voice, just weariness. 'We can't operate together if you're going to be so damned formal. On this operation it's Terry and Oliver. It's informal, lad, this trip. All right?'

'Yes . . . Oliver.' He had a pleasant smile.

I was left alone with my poor distressed and pain-racked Oliver.

'Why did you come?' I asked softly, tentatively.

'To see you, Phil.'

'I would've come to you. I was going to do that. Oh Oliver, Jennie! I couldn't . . . poor Jennie!'

And I could hardly collapse on the bed in tears, on his operative side, because Terry would be back any second. And because Oliver was watching me sternly. No time for tears.

'We'll get him, Phil.'

'Or her.'

'Or her, if necessary.'

'We could've done that together, Oliver, you and I. You know we could. I could've managed.'

'I need Terry. His strength.'

But not his comfort. 'We could've . . .'

'No, Phil. Listen. I admit it. I'm not strong, something I never expected to say. Besides, I couldn't have left him behind. He threatened to resign if I insisted, and come anyway.'

'I don't understand. You could have had your choice. Dozens of big coppers.'

'Phil – Jennie was his woman friend. They were living together. You can see—'

'Oh heavens, yes. Of course.' Poor Terry, too! I tried to grin at him, just to lighten the mood, but my lips felt stiff. We'd always managed to grin at each other. 'By God, Oliver, we'll make such a team.'

Terry's hip hodged the door open. He was festooned with cases.

'One more trip, Chief,' he said. He'd had time to work out a compromise. Then he was gone again. I wondered what he would think up for me. Chiefess?

As the door closed behind him, we grinned at each other. Finally.

'Does it hurt much?' I asked.

'I've got tablets.'

'That's no answer and you know it.'

He nodded. 'It hurts. But I'm mobile. I can still use one fist if necessary, and Terry's got two.'

'And me, Oliver?'

'I know you. Grab anything that's available.'

'So we're really working on this together? What about Connaught?'

'He'll have been told I'm here. He won't like it, but he'll have no grumble so long as we keep him in touch.'

'And fully informed?'

He rubbed the stubble on his chin. He had obviously departed from the hospital in a hurry. 'That depends – doesn't it?'

'It depends,' I agreed, longing to lather his face and shave him clean. Somehow, I knew he was a lather and blade man. 'So where do we start?'

'We start right here, and when Terry's back.'

Which he was, that moment, so that I was spared a comment.

'That's the lot,' he said. 'Coming up to lunch-time, Chief.'

'Lunch? You'll have to learn, laddie, that in the CID eating comes when you can find time. And sleeping. Everything.'

'Oh,' said Terry, dropping himself on the bed beside me, 'I thought this was informal. Not official,' he amplified. 'Chief.'

There was a wicked little gleam in his eyes. This young man was a droll one, addicted to dry humour. He'd need watching.

'All right,' said Oliver. 'So unofficially we sit here until we've decided on a line of approach, and then we eat. Let's have it, Phil, from the beginning.'

'You already know—'

'For Terry's benefit, and for me to hear again.'

So, slowly and carefully, trying not to miss any detail, and stopped from time to time for clarification by both of them and with Terry all the while growing in confidence, I told them the lot. Apart from the bit where Jennie entered into it, where I faltered and Terry grunted as though I'd punched him and Oliver looked down at his hand, I managed to work through to the end without, I felt, missing anything.

'And now,' I finished with relief, only at that point realizing how this affected my personal situation, 'you're here, on the spot, to identify me. Positively. Finally.'

'Umm!' said Oliver.

'What the devil d'you mean by umming me?' I demanded.

'Logic indicates that it might no longer be necessary,' he said formally.

'But Chief—'

I cut in quickly. 'Logic tells me I'm scared, Oliver.'

'You!' Oliver laughed wickedly.

Terry darted his head back and forth. 'I can see what the chief's getting at, Phillie . . .' He stopped when we both stared at him. He shrugged. 'The difference now is that I'll be around.'

So I was to be the informal Phillie! Fair enough, particularly as he seemed to be on my side.

'All right,' said Oliver. 'So Terry can read my mind. OK then, laddie, let's hear what logic dictates.'

Was Oliver being cruel? Surely not. But there was a wicked gleam in his eyes.

Startled to have it thrown at him so abruptly, Terry glanced at me, then at Oliver. 'I don't think . . .'

'Nonsense. You'll have to learn, Terry, that when a senior officer asks for an opinion it's when he's stuck. Then he can claim any bright ideas as his own. Let's have it, while you've got a witness to swear the ideas are yours.'

'I haven't got any ideas.'

'Thoughts, then. Don't think you're going to get away with offering your muscles and nothing else. Thoughts, Terry.'

'I don't know about thoughts,' he replied doubtfully. 'I can't even understand what that Bella Fields has been playing at. I mean . . .' He looked anxiously from one face to the other, and we nodded. 'Even assuming she knew something nasty might be dug out of the ground . . . one or two skulls, depending on how much she knows . . . what's she gained by involving Phillie? Time, that's all. Sooner or later Forensic will tie things down, and they'll put names to them. Sure to.'

'But she wouldn't know that,' I explained. 'She was terrified of being taken into custody, and not being able to get back to her TV studio in three weeks' time.'

'And the second skull meant something special to her?' Oliver thought about that with his lips pursed. 'Tonia?'

'Something like that.' But I wasn't happy with it.

'Anyway . . .' His eyes were on mine, detecting my concern, but not quite understanding the full extent of it. 'Anyway, that's all over now. We're here. We can prove you're the one and only Philipa Lowe.'

The tone of levity irritated me. 'And how does that leave me?'

'You, Phil?' Oliver cocked his head.

I breathed in heavily. 'Say it gets to the point where I've proved my identity—'

'Which will be very soon,' Oliver promised soothingly.

'When I'm able to stick it under Bella's nose?' I demanded. 'You think it'll all be over when she turns to me and says, "Sorry, Phil, but I had to do something, just in case"? And I'd call her a cold and cynical bitch . . . and a few other things—'

'You'd do that, I'm sure,' Oliver agreed.

'But I'd be alive, Oliver! Don't you see? It's not Bella who's got to be persuaded – she *knows*. Jennie's death, the attempt to crash my car – neither of those fits with Bella. And Bella wouldn't want me dead, anyway. She wouldn't *need* me to be dead.'

'Ah, yes,' he said. 'I get your point.'

'Somebody,' I told them heavily, because I could detect no undue concern, 'wants me dead. No, I'll rephrase that. Somebody wants Tonia dead, and I'm the surrogate Tonia, so I'll do. Have you two bright characters thought of that?'

They were smiling at me. Damn them – smiling. Both nodding.

'Isn't it lucky we're here,' said Oliver placidly.

'To do what?' I demanded.

'Well . . . Phil, you've not been attending. To prove you're not Tonia Fields.'

'To whom?' I shot at him. 'Who is this person you're going to convince?'

Oliver frowned, concerned not for me but for my attitude. 'Connaught, of course.'

'But it *isn't* Connaught who's got to be persuaded.' I ruffled my hair with both hands, absolutely exasperated with them. 'It's somebody who unscrews wheel nuts, somebody who killed Jennie—'

'Somebody, then,' cut in Oliver, 'who doesn't want you proved as not Tonia, somebody who therefore *knows* you're not.'

'You're just trying to complicate things!' I cried. 'There's somebody anonymous. Out there! And how does *he* get to know I'm the genuine Philipa Lowe, and, whatever he's got in mind, it's too late to do it now? Does Connaught send a street-crier with a bell through the town, shouting, "Oyez! Oyez!" and spreading the word? Do we put an advert in the evening paper? Philipa Lowe is not Tonia Fields! Ha! If he heard, he'd assume it was a trick, and not believe a word of it. And there I'll be, all relaxed, thinking I'm in the clear – and with the bastard still on my tail. Oh . . . great! That's just fine! Where can I run to?'

I was aware that I was going over the top on this, could hear the hint of hysteria in my voice, but really I felt that I was still a potential target. There's a cold feeling you get in the back of your neck, and it creeps down until you can feel the flesh . . . flinching. That's the word. My whole body was flinching. And here they were, lowering their guards already, certain of my future safety.

Oliver said, 'Easy now, Phil.' I could have hit him for that alone. 'You simply go away. Disappear.'

'And leave it to you two great lummocks! One of you a nursemaid and the other barely able to stand!'

Then I felt my face crumpling at the enormity of what I'd said, and I was in a storm of tears, with my hands clamped over my eyes.

Oliver would have known what to do, but he was in no condition to do it. Terry was rigid with embarrassment. They simply waited me out, until I could lift my face and let Oliver thrust a clean handkerchief into my useless fingers so that I could dab away, and whisper round it, 'Sorry. I'm sorry.'

I sniffed. Found my voice somewhere down there and dragged it to the surface.

'I want to find out who killed Jennie,' I said, no tone in my voice. 'And I don't care whether I do it as Philipa Lowe or Tonia Fields. As long as it's done. But I am not going to go away anywhere, not for you, not for anybody, Oliver. Is that clear?'

They looked at each other, searching each other's opinion without having to do it aloud. I saw Terry nod slightly. He'd look after me. Oliver was worried.

'I'd like to know more. I'm not sure I could give my permission, Phil, for you . . .'

I opened my mouth to tell him what he could do with his permission, but was interrupted by a tap on the door. Before anybody could say another word the door opened, and Inspector Connaught put in his head.

'Can anybody join in?' he asked happily.

8

I got to my feet in order to make the introduction. Connaught was clearly unsure of his approach, and was poised to pounce in any direction, according to the temperature of his reception. He was alone. His gaze flicked to my swollen eyes, and away again.

'This is Inspector Connaught,' I said. 'My friends, Inspector Oliver Simpson and Constable Terry Alwright.'

Connaught stepped forward, on his toes and alert, and thrust out his left hand. 'Pleased to meet you, Mr Simpson.' Then he remembered to nod towards Terry. 'Constable.'

'And this', said Oliver, half rising to his feet, 'is Miss Philipa Lowe. We can identify her officially.'

I knew that smile of Oliver's. Connaught should have read the message; he was not making a good impression. But it seemed to pass him by. He was bubbling with news, and so proud you'd have thought he had created it himself.

'It's a pity you've put yourself out,' he said, looking round to locate a chair. 'A bit less panic and you'd have saved yourself a journey.' Collecting the easy chair in one hand, he swung it across the room as though it weighed nothing. He sat, his legs spread and elbows on his knees, his hands spread like semaphore signals. He waggled them. 'Don't you think our forensic people are wonderful?' he asked.

'We probably share the same team,' said Oliver coolly. 'I always found them efficient, if a little slow.'

'Ah!' One hand came down in order to waggle a finger. 'You have to push 'em a bit, then they scuttle around.'

I saw now, with the two inspectors close together, that Connaught was several years Oliver's senior. It didn't, though, justify his condescension. Their ranks were the same. Connaught couldn't have been outstanding in his grade, or he'd have climbed higher, though he'd seemed quite clever to me.

But he was clearly insensitive in this situation, or he'd have adopted a different approach.

'I take it,' said Oliver, dangerously mild, 'that you've been doing your bit of pushing, and that you've got a report from them.'

Connaught leaned back, beaming. 'I'm not going to give them all the credit. Some of it goes to my team. They dug out facts. Ask around, and ye shall find. What we found was that Tonia had an accident when she was about fourteen. Bicycle and a car. The usual thing. But the relevant information is that she had a fracture of her right leg. Not serious – it knitted well and she didn't limp. And she broke some of her teeth. Upper jaw. These were capped, and we've got the dental records.'

'Good work,' said Oliver. 'Don't you think so, Terry?'

'Yes, Chief. Smart. We'd never have thought of that.' He turned to me and whispered in a penetrating hiss, 'We'd have asked Bella Fields.'

I coughed into my hand, and after a bleak smile Connaught continued.

'So they checked the female skeleton. And guess what!'

'No knitted leg fracture, no capped teeth,' suggested Oliver.

'How can you know that?'

'If it had definitely been Tonia, you'd have said so straightaway. To Philipa. To relieve her anxiety,' he explained blandly, 'you appreciating how worried she's been about being mistaken for Tonia herself.'

So Oliver did understand, but certainly must have realized that this news did not completely relieve my anxiety.

Connaught stared blankly around the array of our unenthusiastic faces. 'Well – doesn't it *do* that? We know now. Positively. The corpse isn't Tonia's. No more doubt clouding the issue.'

He'd been over-explaining, trying to force his way through a tight and concerted lack of enthusiasm.

'Doesn't it?' he repeated.

'Not really,' said Oliver. 'What d'you propose to do with this information?'

'What?' Connaught seemed not to understand. 'File it, of

course. Discuss it with the Super. Set up enquiries to find somebody else, some other young woman, who disappeared at the same time. If she was around twenty . . . well, it might not have been reported to us at the time. But we'll cover the area. You can be sure of that.'

Oliver didn't take his eyes from Connaught's. 'And you'll let the media know? That it's not Tonia Fields,' he amplified.

'It could help. Somebody might come in . . . their wife or daughter disappeared . . . you know.'

'It wouldn't be a good idea,' Oliver went on steadily, boring in. Connaught was clearly uneasy. Oliver's grey eyes were becoming very cold indeed. 'It doesn't assist Phil in any way. On the contrary. Can you include in your interview with the press and the TV people and what-not a mention that Philipa Lowe has now been able to prove her real identity?'

'As long as *I* know, I can't see it matters.'

'No!' said Oliver sharply. 'As long as *everybody* knows.'

Connaught still seemed doubtful and stubborn. 'Can't pile it on too much,' he said, moving uncomfortably in his seat, sitting back in order to get as far as possible from those cold grey eyes. 'The skeleton isn't Tonia. Philipa Lowe isn't Tonia. Christ, everybody isn't Tonia!'

'Except Tonia herself.'

'All the same—'

'But you don't want to have to face that, do you?'

'I don't know what you're talking about.' Each word was painfully separated from its neighbours.

'Somebody's going to ask, "Then where the devil *is* Tonia Fields?" And you'll have to find out. Oh, don't try to pretend it's not there. You've got to locate Tonia.'

'After ten bleedin' years!'

'Yes. Somehow. And if it all gets too big for you – more than you can handle – an international job with Interpol co-operating and a chief super taking over . . . well, that's what you've got to put up with. Because, make no mistake, Mr Connaught, that is the centre point of all this. Where Is Tonia?' His tone gave it the capitals.

'You're making a mountain out of this,' Connaught accused him belligerently.

'No, my friend, it's you who's made the mountain, by letting

95

it get out of hand. You should've put your foot down on any suggestion that Phil could be Tonia, from the very first moment. Squashed it. Somebody, Connaught,' said Oliver coldly and decisively, 'somebody out there is trying to kill Tonia Fields. That's what it comes down to. Don't you see, man, that you've got to find her now! Somehow. And for God's sake clear Phil out of the reckoning right now.'

'It might not be possible.'

'Then make it so.'

Connaught got to his feet, the chair twisting under the tight grip of his hand. His finger pointed, and was jabbed in emphasis.

'You come here, to my patch, and think you can dictate! Let me tell you, friend – you sign out of this hotel and you sod off back home, taking your Philipa Lowe with you. This is *my* case, *my* patch. Bugger off out of it.'

Terry was rising from the bed in slow motion, like a spring lazily unwinding. 'No,' he said. 'We're going to stick around.'

'Don't argue with me, Constable! I'll have you out—'

'No,' Terry repeated. 'Jennie was my woman. Does that make it clear?'

'I shall report the whole meeting . . .' He made for the door.

'Oh,' put in Oliver. 'One other thing. If I were you, I'd spread my enquiries around, if you'll accept a bit of advice. You might not be hunting simply for somebody who disappeared ten years ago.'

'I don't know what the hell you mean.'

'Don't assume they were buried together and at the same time.'

'Well of course . . .' Connaught allowed himself a small sneer. 'How else could they have been buried side by side?'

'Different times, but buried by the same person.'

Connaught stared at him for a protracted few seconds, then he slammed out of the door.

Still on his feet, Terry stared at the door. His colour was high. 'I'll kill him,' he muttered. 'So help me!'

'Sit down, laddie,' said Oliver. He seemed more pleased than upset. 'We've got some planning to do.'

Terry sat, again beside me. He pouted at my smile. 'Temper!' I said quietly.

'What do we know about him?' Oliver asked, mainly to me. 'This Inspector Connaught is interesting.'

I too thought him to be interesting, but in a way I couldn't analyse, and found disturbing. 'What's there to know? I don't get your point.'

'A bit unconventional, isn't he? I mean, you'd expect him to travel around with a sergeant or constable at his shoulder, to take notes and record circumstances. That sort of thing. But Phil, he's interviewed you and Bella, and both together – and he's always been alone. Have you been asked to make a statement? Has he done anything in an official way?'

'From you,' I said, 'that sounds marvellous! You've always worked like that . . . off the record. With me—'

'That was different.'

'It's your own style, Oliver. Admit it.'

'Hmm!' he said, frowning. 'All the same . . . he plays cat and mouse. Who knows what's true and what isn't? He's a local man. He was probably born here, and knows everything.'

'You're making too much of it,' I said quietly. I didn't want him stressed, and wasn't sure that already the strain under which he was operating wasn't affecting his concentration, blunting his perspective.

'All the same, we'll keep it in mind. Now . . .' He slapped his left knee. 'There's planning to do. Where to start. Terry?'

'What? Sir?' Terry had been immersed in his own thoughts. 'I'd suggest food, Chief. As a priority.'

'It'll have to be a sandwich, then.'

'I can do better than that,' I told them. 'A fish and chip restaurant. How's that sound? A Chinese fish and chip restaurant. I bet they never close. Fish and chips and Cantonese takeaway. What d'you say?'

They smiled and they nodded. It would do famously.

So, the three of us together, with me in the middle feeling minuscule between two such large men, we walked through the town in a glorious and pure sunlight, the air clear and crisp, and all the world flooding the streets. Saturday afternoon. They'd have driven in from miles around.

It's the way to get the feel of a town, on foot in the streets. You could sense the throb and progress of a thousand years through the soles of your shoes, or cast wary eyes up the narrow alley-ways, still cobbled and with drainage channels, all bearing ancient and honourable names. Sheepfold. Luke's Acre. Tuesday Pasture. History thrust out all around. Shops actually thrust out, willy-nilly, constricting the pavements for a few yards, narrowing the already tight roadway. And there *was* a car-park after all, behind the modern flare of Sainsbury's, its surface old and pitted, and obviously the now abandoned livestock market. But no more the chattered mumbo-jumbo of the auctioneer and the stench of meat-on-the-hoof. Now the spinning of engines, the blast of horns, and the stench of pollution.

It was a nervous, tight little town, with tension in the air and crackling with static. Struggling to accommodate new ideas and the already visible spread of its boundaries, it had not yet decided whether the future was to be better or worse. Certainly it would not be the same. Perhaps only the venerable Green would survive, isolated in a new and thrusting metropolis. At one time everybody had known everybody, a time not much more than forty years in the past, one could guess. Already, they were strangers in their own streets, we three no more strangers than the rest. Anonymous – one woman and two men, jostled and stepped round by people who knew nothing of a ten-year-old tragedy, and to whom the discovery of two skeletons was a one-day wonder.

'It's along here,' I said. 'I think.'

'There'll be money flooding into this town,' observed Oliver, apparently not listening. 'Money to be made when that motorway goes through.'

'I'll drive you up there later,' I told him. 'You'll need to see the location of the two houses and the general set-up.'

'Yes. We'd better have a look at it. Terry?'

'I smell fish and chips,' said Terry, his thoughts elsewhere.

Now I recognized the side street, looking so different, and in some ways more squalid in daylight. There would be a couple of hours before the light began to disappear, perhaps more with the sun in a clear sky, but that side of the street was shaded, and the lights were on in Soo Long's, strangely making it seem darker than its surroundings. But to me, fish and chips were associated with newspaper wrappings, walking dark streets companionably with greasy fingers.

It appeared that, although we were in a hinterland between

lunch and evening dinner, the restaurant was nevertheless busy. I led the way through to the seating area at the rear. There was one empty table with four chairs, near the door. We took it. 'Lord, I'm starving,' said Terry, and he ordered cod with two servings of chips. Oliver likewise, but I stuck with plaice, one serving of chips, and mushy peas.

Oliver, staring at a chip on his fork, said, 'He's put a follower on us.'

Terry didn't look up. 'I thought so, too, Chief. Chap in jeans and an old tweed jacket.'

'That's him.'

'What do we do – drop him?' Terry asked.

'We do not . . . we ignore him – as we have been doing.'

'Unless . . .'

'Unless we wish to be unaccompanied. Then we drop him – or his relief – but gently, Terry, gently.'

It was then that I realized we had company. A hand wearing a white cotton glove was placed on the table surface. I looked upwards and sideways. A woman, in her late seventies I'd have guessed, a tiny creature with a crumpled face and small, dark, glittering eyes, was standing with her other hand on the back of the spare chair.

'Wasn't you here last night, luv?' she asked.

I nodded. 'I was.'

'With . . . *her*?'

'I was with a friend,' I agreed, stretching our relationship a little. I was trying to be non-committal, wondering whether or not to encourage the approach. In the corner of my eye I saw Oliver's head nod gently. 'Bella Fields,' I amplified.

'Here . . .' She swung round, and was seated in a second. 'You can settle it for me. My friend . . . Gladys, that is . . . she said it was that – you know – that Roma creature in what's its name . . . that American thing. Couldn't be, though. I said to Glad, couldn't be. Not here! You'd expect it in Hollywood. Not here, eatin' chips . . .' She darted a hand sideways and filched one of Terry's chips, chomped it in half, her teeth clicking.

I smiled. 'But it was, you know. Roma Felucci is her screen name.'

'Well . . . what d'you know! Our Bella! From here!'

'She'd have to be from somewhere, wouldn't she?'

'She don't even speak our language.'

'Here, she does.'

'Fancy that.' She looked round at Oliver and Terry, then tried one of Oliver's chips. 'Mind you,' she explained to them, 'you can see it there. That Roma! Jus' like our Bella. A right little hell-cat, she was. Her an' her sister, Tonia.'

'You knew them, then?' asked Oliver, keeping it going, shoving another chip in her direction.

'Knew them! Everybody knew them. Listen. Here.' She thrust her head forward and we obediently joined her. 'Hot little bitches they were. After all the lads. You'd never guess. Not like in my time . . .' She pursed her lips, poised the chip, then it was gone.

'Oh, I'm sure it wasn't so different,' I said, smiling at her. 'I bet you were a right little raver yourself.'

'I never . . .'

'It's still there,' I assured her, and by heaven it was, when I looked carefully. The bone structure was there, and the features, if now somewhat decrepit individually, were neatly placed. 'I reckon they all came running.'

She simpered horribly. 'I had me a time, I've got to admit. But them two . . . you'd never believe . . .'

But I would.

'Took after their mother,' she told me, nodding. 'I knew her. Dulcie. That was their mother. Was at school with my girl Gwen. Drove poor Rowley wild, she did.' She blinked at me. 'Now *there* was a beauty. Queen of the May, she was.' She giggled. 'Lordy-me, but my Gwen *was* jealous of Dulcie. Lovely, she was, give her that.' She blinked at me again. 'Here . . .' Her hand flew to her mouth as she tilted her head, her eyes unwinkingly on me now. 'Oh, I *have* been makin' a ruddy fool of meself! You're not Dulcie's second, are you? You're not Tonia! Lemme have a good look at you. Yes – the eyes, it's her eyes to a tee. An' that hair. Had it curled, have you? Oh heavens – I *am* sorry. An' the things I said!'

I put my hand over hers on the table. 'I'm not Tonia,' I said gently. 'It's all right. I've been mistaken for her by other people.'

She whipped the hand away and clamped it to her chest. 'Oh, I *am* glad. Gave me a turn, that did.' She glanced at Terry, who was grinning, and I thought for a moment she was going to slap

100

him on the back, to express the extent of her gladness. Instantly she was laughing, at herself and at her social blunder, a choked clatter of a laugh.

'And how,' asked Oliver, when she subsided, 'did Rowley's wife, Dulcie, drive him crazy? Here, have a bit of fish.'

I was still struggling to reconcile the image I'd gathered from Bella, that Tonia had been a frightened little mouse of a creature, with this old lady's description of one of two hot little bitches. I was inclined to accept the latter description, though not keen to be accepted as Tonia if that was how she'd been. There was a distinct twinkle in Oliver's eye. I knew he was pursuing the same thought, and perhaps fitting me in exactly with the image, blast him. But perhaps the two pictures were not completely irreconcilable. A frightened little mouse could well play the game of demure and virginal availability.

'Y'want to ask Flora Porter about that,' she said. 'About Dulcie.'

'But *you* know, and you're here,' I pointed out.

'So I am. Here! You three havin' another mug of tea, are you?'

Terry got the hint and went to get them, he being the only one capable of carrying four mugs at the same time. We kept the old dear happy while he was away, going back in time to when *she* had been in the running for Queen of the May, and to me it sounded more like guerrilla warfare than a beauty queen contest, all roses and laughter you'd expect. All brickbats and tears, it had been.

'Dulcie,' Oliver reminded her, when we were all supping very hot, strong and satisfying tea. The old dear sucked it from the edge of her mug. 'Drove poor Rowley crazy, she did.'

'You mentioned that,' I told her quietly. 'In what way?'

'You know. Before'n after.'

'Before and after what?'

'Before and after she married him, that's what. P'raps he wasn't very good at it. Him and his laugh and his slap on the back, and his leer and his suggestive wink! So p'r'aps there wasn't anythin' behind it. You know. An' p'r'aps she played her game with him as well. They ain't gonna take that, are they. The men. Not when it gets legal. Not anytime, these days, so I hear. It's there in the marriage service, it is. Love, honour and cherish – an' that bit about begettin'.' She nodded suggestively.

'But he did his bit of begetting,' I told her. 'Bella and Tonia.'

'Ha!' The salacious leer was ugly on her face. She wiped it away with back of her gloved hand. 'There's some as says he might not've had much of a hand in that. Or . . .' She spluttered hideously. 'Much of anythin' else!'

'But surely . . .' I was only prodding her on, trying not to laugh, desperately trying not to catch Oliver's eye.

'Reckon she went on as she'd always bin. There was a word for it then. They called Dulcie a cock-teaser. Never hear that these days, somehow.'

'It's sort of gone out of fashion,' I informed her solemnly.

'Well, that's what she was.'

'So you're saying—'

'Don't ask *me*.' She drew herself together in majestic dignity. 'I'm not one for gossip. You'd better ask Mrs Porter.'

'And who's she?'

'Don't you know? Then I'll leave you to find out.'

'But how can I do that?' I asked. 'I don't know where to find her.'

'Waterford Farm,' she said, nodding. 'The cottage. It's about all that's left now, an' I reckon when they've got that new road done the traffic's goin' to shake it down. Waterford Farm. Tell her you met Edith Payne. We're friends.' She began to lever herself awkwardly to her feet. 'Here. You'll get me chatterin' all day. You hadn' oughta encourage me.' She stood as she'd arrived, one gloved hand on the chair back, one greasily on the table. 'I'll say goodbye to you good people. You're sure you're not Tonia?'

'Quite certain.'

'Hmm!' She crimped her lips, still not convinced. Then she turned away and headed for the door.

We said nothing until she was well clear, as though her essence still sat at the table and eavesdropped. Then Oliver slapped his knee. 'Well, what did you get out of that, Phil?'

I shrugged. What I'd really got was a sense of uneasiness, that I'd been introduced to people who were becoming important in my life, and that I suddenly saw them whole and real – and didn't much care for what I was seeing. Bella! Well, Roma *was* Bella, and that was that. A hell-cat the old dear had called her. And so she was. As was Tonia. No – perhaps not. She was

102

welcome to her demure sexuality. It had perhaps been an act for her, too. A dangerous one, I'd have thought.

But these people I'd never met were taking on substance, had become clothed in personality – or unclothed. They now seemed rounded to me, living their exciting little lives in this confined valley town. Dulcie! Ah yes, Dulcie, who to me had been no more than their mother, who had gone away, Bella had told me, though later Rowley had changed it to died. I'd thought it strange for a mother to leave two little girls, and simply go away. But she'd been a teaser, and there are dangers to that, too. There can come a time when you're teasing yourself, especially if your husband (if Edith Payne was to be believed) wasn't very good at it. Then, with the right partner, something special could spark, and her life would abruptly flame with passion, so new to her perhaps, so wonderful, that nothing would matter but to perpetuate it. And if going away with this man, who'd need raise but one finger and the teasing stopped, ah, then there'd be no thought left for two children and a husband. Only for self, the only difference now being that she'd no longer found herself able to control it.

And yes, that would explain Rowley's story to the children. She had gone away, certainly. But later, when she'd failed to return, even knowing he wouldn't hesitate to welcome her, he'd told them she had died – as she had in his heart. Bella had said he was a man who took chances. The big one he had taken was in marrying Dulcie.

Now I understood his laugh and his shoulder slap, his bounce and his *bonhomie*. It had been an affectation of continual joy in living, to cover a blank despair that shadowed his life. Perhaps Dulcie had always teased him. Rowley sounded too soft, too understanding, too tender to strike sparks. Dulcie had been primed and charged, but Rowley had been like putty when she'd been yearning for a flint. I could have cried out in pity for his frustration. I could even, now, excuse his attitude to the girls. They were reproductions of Dulcie, and he could afford to shower on them a playful patter of sensuous slaps, because he could hide safely behind the knowledge that they would neither of them reciprocate, would repulse him. Safely. Nothing to fear. It was all a bit of fun, and life was like that. A bit of a lark, really. Wasn't it?

103

'Phil!' I heard Oliver saying. 'You still with us?'

'What? Oh yes.'

'I asked you what you made of it.'

'What I think, Oliver, is that we've got to go back a long way on this one. Back to Rowley and to Dulcie.'

'I thought that, too,' said Terry.

We both stared at him.

9

We walked, in a leisurely manner, back to the hotel. Oliver decided it was a good time to have a look at the two houses, while there was still enough of them left to make possible an assessment of the general situation. So we decided to do that.

The two men headed straight for the bar, while I went up to change into something practical, such as slacks and low-heeled shoes. I'd need to freshen up a little, too. It was something of a surprise to find Bella in the room, my mind being so preoccupied that I'd assumed I'd be walking into my room rather than ours.

She was smoking nervously by the window, and turned quickly, her eyes suddenly wild before she had herself in hand.

'Oh – there you are!' As though I'd kept her waiting. Then the mood fled away, and she was all welcome, all excitement. 'Have you heard the news? Have you, Phil?'

I'd forgotten that I hadn't met Bella since Connaught had told us the female skeleton definitely wasn't Tonia's. For a moment I hesitated, forcing my mind to it, trying to remember whether I was supposed to be pleased or disappointed. 'About the skeleton . . .' I suggested tentatively.

'Yes, yes. Isn't it a *relief*, darlin'?'

'Relief?'

'That it's definitely not Tonia. Go on. You can smile. You're relieved too. Admit it, Phil.'

'Am I supposed to be relieved?' I demanded, annoyed at her stupidity. '*You* can be, for all I care. Go on, enjoy your bit of relief. But where does it leave me? Where I was. That's where.'

Dismissively, I went across the room to sort out some slacks and the little jacket I rather liked, knitted but half-lined. The air had been feeling cooler. While my back was to her she said

105

nothing. People were supposed to be looking at her while she was speaking, so that they wouldn't miss one nuance of her expression or fail to admire her sincerity. As I turned . . .

'Now . . . Phil . . .' she said, all contrition. 'Don't be angry—'

'Angry! Who's angry? I could scratch your eyes out, but I'm not angry. You had to foist me off as your sister. A pretty game, that was.'

'But Phil! I had to do something. I had a feeling . . . I *felt* there was going to be something turn up. Kind of. And if it did, there could be two . . . well . . . bodies. And Phil, I was so worried they'd assume one of them had to be Tonia.'

I flung my skirt at her, but it fell short and on my bed. Not wishing to watch her face, not welcoming the raw triumph in her expression, I sat down on the edge with my back to her, sliding into the slacks. 'What you mean,' I said, slowly and intensely, 'is that you damn well *knew* there'd be two skeletons, and it was going to be bad for you if they assumed one was your father's and one your sister's.' I stood up, yanked the slacks to my waist, and whirled round, catching her with one finger to her lips, and went on, 'So you had to have a sister Tonia on hand, and I was a good substitute. No!' I snapped, as she opened her mouth. 'Let me say this. *Now* I'm expected to open my arms wide and clasp you to my bosom and tell you you're forgiven! Christ, Bella, you must be stupid if you think—'

'But Phil,' she cried, 'I'll tell everybody it was a mistake. *Everybody*. Then they'll know you're not—'

'Never mind me!' I shouted. 'Don't you understand what you've done to yourself? And don't stand there gawping. Try to use what bit of brain you've got. By using me as a substitute Tonia, you've made it too clear you had prepared for it. Planned. As though you knew there'd be two corpses, and one of them female. Knew!'

'Oh Phil . . . come on now . . .'

'Bella,' I pleaded. 'Try to concentrate. There's only one way you could've known there would be two skeletons, and one of them female. Only one way. You can work out the rest for yourself.'

She was shaking her head, her lower lip poised in quiver

position, like a child being shouted at for a tiny indiscretion. Don't scold me, mamma, please!

I ignored her, pretending she wasn't there, walked into the bathroom and wasn't pleased with what I saw in the mirror and tried to wash it away. My face doesn't wear anger very daintily. Repaired, more resigned than relaxed, I walked back across the room, changed my blouse, and slipped into my little jacket.

'You're going out,' she said dully. Not asked.

'Yes.'

'Why can't you stay? Oh Phil, I'm so bored . . .'

'Work to be done.'

'Work?' There was envy there.

'Trying to discover the truth.'

'Then you don't think—'

'I don't think anything, Bella. I'll see you later.' I turned to the door, but her sulky voice held me.

'Why is it that you've got two men, and me none?'

So she'd watched us from the window. 'You've got Jay.'

'Jay! I'd need to be desperate. He's gone out jogging, anyway.'

Certainly, she sounded desperate. Did she expect me to ask her to join us? I said nothing more, but opened the door.

'Phil!'

'Now what?'

'You can't wear that jacket without something at your throat. It kills your eyes, just kills—'

'Go to hell.' I slammed the door behind me.

Why was it that even when she most exasperated me, she still had the ability to excite my sympathy? She seemed so vulnerable, behind her hell-cat image, so eager to be liked and wanted when she seemed to be exerting herself in her efforts to repulse. Had she, I wondered, always been like that, observing her hair-trigger temper abort any friendly approach before it matured? It seemed to me that after all Jay could be her natural soul-mate, closing his eyes to the flashes of rejection, flouting the fighting stance, riding the aggressive blows. And laughing her out of it – or shouting her down – or slapping her down.

I found them in the bar. Oliver turned and frowned at my expression.

'What is it, Phil?'

'That damned Bella!'

'Forget her. She can't harm you now.'

'No?' Sometimes, Oliver disappointed me. 'Are you two ready? We'll have to get moving or the light'll be gone.'

We went out to pick up the Rover. I was still worried about those wheels, but Terry got out the wheel-nut wrench and managed another half turn on each, so that I had to pray that I'd never need to change a wheel, because I'd be quite unable to undo them again.

'It's becoming an obsession,' said Oliver. 'We could've used my car.'

It was parked right beside mine. I said, 'I'll be doing the driving because I know the way, and I'm used to the Rover now.'

I hoped neither of them had noticed the shake in my voice. It was here that Jennie had died, but I didn't want Terry to realize that.

I took us out of the yard. The traffic seemed to be lighter, but of course the shops would soon be shut. 'I'll take you the back way,' I said.

Oliver was beside me, Terry in the rear. I was keyed up, just waiting for either of them, no doubt both trained at police driving schools, to comment on my technique. But perhaps they sensed my mood. In any event, they said nothing, even when I jumped an amber. But police drivers are probably trained to do that.

'Why the back way?' Oliver asked.

'So that you can get a general impression of the size of the town and the way it lies, and to show you the housing development along the rise at the far side of the valley.'

'We'd be interested in that, d'you think?'

'It's a question of motivation,' I explained.

'For what?' You'd have thought I was a suspect.

'The murder of Rowley Fields.'

'That's assuming the male skeleton is in fact his.'

'You *can* be annoying, Oliver Simpson. Who else could it be?'

'I don't know. And we don't know who could lay claim to the female one.'

I drove a quarter of a mile, placidly, I hoped. You get these times when everybody seems to be setting out to be annoying.

In the end I said, sighing, 'Let's assume it's Rowley Fields. He went missing, and he's not turned up.'

Of course, Terry had to get his word in. 'Tonia also went missing, and *she* hasn't turned up, either. Unless . . .'

'Don't say it!' I warned. 'Don't even hint.'

There was a long silence, into which Oliver eventually inserted a comforting voice.

'No doubt, in due course, they'll find some peculiarity of Rowley Fields and match it to the skeleton. In the meantime, assume it's him, and tell us why you brought us along here – unless it's just for the view.'

It would have been worth it just for that. 'It's not for the view,' I assured him. We were passing the scattering of high quality houses that Connaught had shown me, so many of them still unsold. 'It's this development here. I'm told that they're owned by a man called Tudor Kemp, a local, who also owns the factory with the tall chimney, and a lot of the land the motorway spur's coming through.'

'So?'

Oliver didn't sound interested. I glanced sideways. In profile his face was sharp, with lines bitten deeply into it.

'It's only that Rowley Fields owned both those old houses, and they were in the way of it all.'

'I don't get your point.'

I sighed. 'If Rowley disappeared, then there'd be seven years to wait before he could be presumed dead, and during that time a man might invest his money—'

'A man?'

'A man called Tudor Kemp, then. Do I have to spell it out? The point is that if Kemp killed him, and knew he was dead—'

'Which seems likely, if he killed him.'

'Yes!' I bit it off, then forced myself to relax. 'He'd be the only one who could be certain Rowley wouldn't be coming back to block the planning permission.'

'Who told you this?' Oliver demanded.

'Inspector Connaught.'

'Hmph!' Thus Oliver dismissed him. 'Probably pulling your leg.'

'Or slipping in a distraction,' Terry said lightly.

I let it lie. Connaught being crafty, perhaps. But I had an

inborn suspicion of big business. I'd had close contacts with it in my work in New York, and it hadn't done much to change my opinion. Yet a man might risk his own money on a chance, and stand to gain if it worked out. All to his praise; it was he taking the chances. As Rowley Fields had done with his football pools fiddle. It was all a matter of degree, Rowley with his thirty pounds a week, Kemp with his several millions.

'It's along here, I think,' I said. 'You can just see the motorway work, beyond that dip in the ground.'

In two minutes I was certain I had the correct lane. The mud was there, the tattered hedges, and, when we reached the site, most of the Fields's house still standing. But the wrecker's ball had been busy. I could see the crane, poised beyond the building. I turned to swing into the drive, and a uniformed policeman suddenly stood dangerously almost under my wheels. I ran the side window down.

'You can't go up there, miss.'

'I just wanted to show—'

'There's nothing to see, and what there is isn't pleasant.'

'I know that only too well.'

Why wasn't Oliver saying something? Did a detective inspector become a mister the moment he moved off his own patch? Then he did speak, a gentle murmur.

'It'll do in the lane, Phil.'

So I backed out, and slowly we drove on up the lane, me knowing it was going to come to an abrupt and probably dangerous end. There was a slight curve. Because of this I hadn't seen that there was already a car at the far end. Behind it, we drew to a halt. It was a sleek, black Daimler Sovereign.

We got out, Oliver slowly and awkwardly. Terry caught my eye and shook his head. Oliver looked grey and old when he unwound to full height.

Beyond the Daimler, only feet from the front bumper, there was a line of cones barring the way. Beyond them the lane surface ended abruptly. The digger had run along at a right angle and chopped it off, not cleanly, for the layer of tarmac heaved and writhed as though in its terminal agony. Beyond that there was a fall, not steep, not so steep that your feet might run from under you, but of slashed and impounded clay.

The air was still, the sky a flaring red over to our left, touching the soft wet edges of tumbled soil with lines of blood. Clear in the glowing evening I heard the double bark of a shotgun, so much deeper and carrying more weight than the snap of a pistol or the crack of a rifle. It came from not far away, but its source was difficult to locate amongst the mounds and terraces of upflung earth out there, spread below us and swinging round in an arc into the sun.

But a man stood with his back to us at the very rim of the fractured tarmac, hands above his eyes, and by following the direction of his attention I could locate the gunman, who was moving slowly across from left to right, plodding, head moving as his eyes darted around. As I watched, the gun was raised and two more shots cut the silence. Nothing tumbled down from the sky, nothing was picked up, limp from the ground.

'Rabbits,' said the man at the edge, as though I'd asked. Into that one word he condensed a bitter anger and a deep contempt.

Then I realized it was Jay Messenger. I ought to have recognized those wide, firm shoulders from behind, and the trim hips, but he was out of context here. To me he lived in a world of spurious sets, or surrounded by hysterical fans. But here he was alone, and he must have walked or jogged, as it seemed unlikely he'd have hired a Daimler Sovereign just to travel from Heathrow to Shropshire. I glanced down. He was wearing tattered jeans and running shoes. All right, so he'd jogged, as Bella had suggested. The man had to keep fit. One day of relaxation and he'd sag into decrepitude.

I was aware that Terry and Oliver had now joined us. Jay glanced round, and I made the introduction. 'We haven't met,' said Oliver, but I noticed he'd become enlivened and that his eyes had lost the lack-lustre look.

'Bella's told me all about it,' said Jay. 'I reckoned I ought to come and have a look myself. But it's nearly all gone now.' He meant the house. 'And that officer won't let me near. No way.' His accent was harsh New York, with a bite to it.

We were looking across a shallow valley with the battered swathe running from right to left. On the far reaches of it, now silent for the weekend, the diggers and shovers and dumpers rested in a yellow group. The lowering sun flushed them with orange, transforming them almost into a romantic setting, the ploughed lines, themselves rimmed, leading the eye to that one spot of colour in an empty landscape. Beyond, the valley rose, scattered with small copses of trees and sheep, climbing towards the summit where a large house perched like a magic castle, crouching in trees.

'The diggers,' said Jay suddenly in an empty tone, 'flush out the rabbits. He waits down there, and slaughters them.'

The figure had now turned and was walking towards us, his stride more purposeful as he saw our waiting group. The shotgun was under his right arm, broken open in the approved manner. As he came closer, I saw that he was rather more old than his youthful stride suggested. He was fit, slim, almost gaunt, and must have been in his fifties, but still handsome in a sharp and clean-cut way, with an aquiline nose, a forceful jaw, and bright eyes beneath heavy brows. He was wearing a waxed belted jacket, tweed trousers and rubber boots, fair hair blown over ears and forehead. There was no wind now. Perhaps there had been. From a small and distant figure he grew, when he halted just below us, to about five feet ten.

'You're trespassing,' he said dismissively. 'Do you realize that?'

'This is a public roadway,' said Oliver quietly. 'Where we are standing. Where you have come from, you've been trespassing. Shooting over someone else's land—'

'It's my land.' It was a bark.

Jay gave a snap of harsh laughter. 'And your rabbits. Home is the hunter! Must take a lotta guts, slaughtering rabbits.'

The hunter stood facing us, legs slightly apart. Not angry, not demonstrably so, but his voice was like acid. 'My land. I shoot over it if I wish . . .'

'I think not,' said Oliver, still gently. 'Not now. It's corporation land, I'd guess.'

'Who the hell're you?'

'The name's Simpson. And you – sir?'

Just that single word – sir – lent the question authority.

'Kemp,' he snapped. 'Tudor Kemp.' He turned. 'This . . .' He gestured embracingly, 'as far as you can see, is mine.'

The house? Those extensive acres? And those sheep? He could have walked across from that house, if that was his too. Across and back. Yet he'd used his Daimler. Had it been no more than show? Here I am, Tudor Kemp! As he turned back

112

his right arm jerked the gun, and it snapped shut. It could have been unintentional.

Jay had observed it, though. 'I'd watch what you do with that.' His voice had become more harshly American, the tone deeper, in the growl that the politicians affected. I glanced at him more intently. He was poised on the balls of his feet, but there was the trace of a smile in the corners of his mouth. He'd wanted this. It suited him. I had the impression this antagonism had a deeper base than the wanton killing of rabbits.

'Get out of my way.' Kemp thrust himself forward. The angle of the gun was slightly raised.

Jay did not move. Standing as he was on a firmer surface he had the advantage of height as well as the more positive stance. 'Raise that barrel two more inches,' he said, his voice now carrying an English inflexion mockingly, almost Kemp's own accent, 'and I'll break it over your head.'

Perhaps he'd observed a lack of cartridge cases in the breech. Perhaps not. The air in this valley seemed to instil a taking of chances.

But Kemp smiled, broke the gun again, and walked past, pausing as he came opposite Jay. Then he frowned. 'Do I know you?'

'I'd never admit it.' We were back now with the New York accent.

Kemp went to his car, then noticed the Rover directly behind it. In that second his temper snapped. 'Will somebody move this sodding car!' he shouted.

'Certainly,' I said blandly, and I pushed past him, touched his arm, and smiled up into his face – just to see what might happen. The effect shocked me. One corner of his upper lip began to move into an unpleasant shape, then his eyes held me, and he blinked. His smile was ghastly.

'Please,' he said softly.

I backed into the house drive, and the Daimler swept past, backing at such a speed that I didn't know how he did it. I pulled out again, nose now in the direction of the town.

The three men were still standing there when I joined them, not speaking. Jay was staring out towards the house on the rise.

'Would you care for a lift back into town?' I asked him.

'What? No . . . no, thank you. I'm supposed to be jogging.

113

It's thataway.' He told me, laughing now. He jerked a thumb vaguely towards the right. 'I think.'

Then he jumped down into the ruts and set off at a steady, loping pace, away to our right, heading for civilization.

We got into the Rover. I said, 'Seen what you wanted, Oliver?'

He grunted. 'More than I wanted. They knew each other, Phil. Don't you think?'

'Jay certainly knew who he was talking to,' I agreed. 'But Kemp was uncertain.' I drove along slowly, half expecting, at each bend, to find the Daimler stuck in a hedge. 'Bella told me Jay spotted her on the stage in Dublin, and got her into films, but he'd met her before then, in Birmingham. So Jay's probably been in this area before. They could've met then. But that would've been ten years ago, which would be a few face-lifts back for Jay. Kemp could've half recognized him.'

For a moment I toyed mentally with the possibility that Kemp had known Bella in some way intimately. From their respective bedrooms they might have watched each other's windows alight at night, across the valley. But ten years ago Kemp would have been twice Bella's age. As would Jay, come to think of it.

No . . . Kemp was more the age group of the mother, Dulcie. But I couldn't imagine their hearts calling to each other across the valley. Dulcie would not be able to play her teasing game at a distance. Closer, very much closer, she would have needed to be. And my imagination rejected the mental image of Dulcie flitting away from the big house in the dark, with Kemp crying out in agony from his open window, 'Dulcie! Dulcie!' Unlike Heathcliff, he would more probably have sent a couple of barrels of buckshot after her.

'What's funny?' asked Oliver.

'Nothing,' I said, 'that you would appreciate, Oliver.'

And Terry said, startling me with his perception, 'You're thinking of Dulcie, aren't you?'

'But *she* went away,' I reminded him, 'with another man. And Kemp, you can bet, would never have been persuaded to leave his empire here.'

Oliver was silent. His silence was beginning to worry me. He should not have come. He should not. I glanced at him. He was pensive, but nevertheless sensed my attention. He tried to smile.

'You know what, Phil?' he asked, his voice bitter. 'I felt

helpless back there. I could feel violence on the very edge of breaking free, and I knew there was nothing I could do about it.'

'There was me, Chief,' Terry said abruptly.

'Yes, you, Terry. That made it worse. You see, I'd spotted there were cartridges in that breech. Not fired ones – he'd have ejected those. Live ones. And I knew you were about to jump in. You scared me, Terry. I thought I'd got over it . . . but, a loaded shotgun . . . I don't know.'

'It needs time,' I said quietly. After all, the physical pain was still there, and the mental wound would surely hang on longer.

But oh how I longed to do something about it, to take him in my arms and reassure him with soft and intimate words. To hell with Terry! I could have managed Oliver alone. I could, I could!

Oliver said, as though we'd been discussing it, 'In any event, it's obvious she didn't go away with another man, leaving little Bella and even littler Tonia.'

'What . . .'

'Dulcie,' he said. 'It's obvious she's that female skeleton. Don't you think?'

And Terry, glad to welcome a change of subject, said, 'Hey, Chief! I never thought of that. Of course! Of *course*.'

There was silence in the car as we each turned over in our minds the possibilities this exposed, if it were true. Oliver finally broke it.

'Forensic will come up with something, you'll see. Bones decompose according to the acidity or alkalinity of the soil. Perhaps not much, but enough, with a bit of luck. If there'd been only one skeleton, its burial would be difficult to date. But with two, side by side, buried in the same soil, you can be sure they'll spot the difference.'

'You're willing to put money on it?' I asked.

'If you're willing to bet against it.'

But I wasn't, because something else occurred to me. 'With Dulcie buried twenty-five years ago – if it's her skeleton – and Rowley only ten years . . .'

'Exactly. That was what I meant, there being enough years in between. Forensic will know.' He nodded to himself, satisfied.

'If you'd let me finish . . . I was going to say – how the devil did they come to be buried side by side? Two illegal burials, fifteen years apart!'

'As I think I said before,' Oliver remarked, considerably more alert now, 'it has to mean they were buried by the same person.'

'Who must, therefore, have killed both?'

'So it would seem.'

'But always,' put in Terry, who'd been remarkably silent, 'assuming the male skeleton *is* Rowley Fields.'

'Assuming that.' Oliver was placidly confident.

'And assuming,' Terry persisted, 'that the female one is Dulcie.'

And nobody said another word, there being so much to think about, until we reached the hotel, had entered it, and stood at the foot of the stairs. Then it was Terry.

'I think I'll go up and have a bath,' he declared.

Oliver and I looked at each other. Terry was being delicate. We watched him walk away.

'Want to go and tidy up?' he asked, offering me the option.

'It can wait.'

'A drink in the bar?'

'Why not?'

Which was what we had.

10

Oliver managed a tray very confidently in his left hand, his pint and my short on it. He grinned at me as he slid the tray on to the table.

'I can manage this much, Phil.'

'You ought to be resting, you know. It's quite ridiculous—'

'I'm resting it now,' he said firmly, though he was managing a smile. 'Bound up and immobile.' He could be very intractable at times.

I touched his left hand. 'I bet you haven't been to have the dressing changed.'

'I haven't had the time. Tomorrow will do.' He took a deep draught from the glass, cocking one eye at me over the rim.

'It will *not* do.'

'You're as bad as Terry,' he complained. 'Fussing round me like an old maid.'

'And so he should. Now promise me, Oliver—'

'What d'you intend to do, Phil?'

'Don't change the subject.' I couldn't help being sharp with him. The fact that he was avoiding a direct answer was worrying.

'But *what* do you intend to do?'

I was being introduced to an unexplored facet of his personality. Previously, we'd managed to get along fine, apart from the occasional fight. But those had been physical, and this was the first time I'd found him so difficult, almost dictatorial. He didn't want to talk about it, and he wasn't far from forbidding its mention. I sighed, looked away from him, and tried to answer his question.

'I thought I'd try to find this Waterford Farm that Edith Payne mentioned in the fish and chip shop, and have a word with Mrs Porter.' I could see no interest blooming in his eyes. He seemed not even to know what I meant. I prompted, 'Who ought to be able to tell us more about Dulcie.'

He looked down at his glass and rotated it between finger and thumb. 'That wasn't what I was talking about.'

'Oh?'

'Do . . . with your life. Now that you're back in England.'

I shrugged, trying to appear indifferent, but I had an unpleasant idea about the direction of his interest. 'I hadn't given it much thought. Then this business cropped up.'

'Will you think about it now.' He looked me suddenly in the eyes, and his cocked eyebrows turned it into a request.

'Need I?'

'It might be a good idea.'

'Later, Oliver. Let's get this thing over first.'

'Yes,' he said moodily. 'Let's get it over.' Then he brightened. I thought the effort cost him a lot. 'You'll be a rich woman, Phil. You could do . . . well, practically anything. See the world . . .' He allowed it to tail away.

'Richer than you think,' I told him. I was now certain as to his interest, and what was worrying him, and felt a prickle of anger I had to try not to show. The best thing now was to present him with the lot. Throw it at him. A worst case scenario, it would be, as far as he was concerned, if my guess was correct. 'I was surprised, Oliver. When I came to sell up the goodwill of the business in New York . . . the files, the background information we'd built up . . . heavens, they clambered over each other to make offers. I'm now very rich indeed, Oliver – by my standards, anyway. I don't know what I'll do. Harvey will advise me. It's what a solicitor's for. I thought maybe I'd buy a yacht. You know, an ocean-going thing. Complete with crew. And go cruising. Drift round the Med and meet people. You never know . . .' That's right, Phil, I told myself disparagingly, pile it on.

'Get married again,' he muttered, not looking at me. 'Somebody with an even bigger yacht.'

'Who's talking about marriage?' I asked negligently. 'I want a bit of freedom – look around. Decide later.'

'Of course you do. You've earned it.'

Not all of it, I hadn't. 'No encumbrances,' I agreed. 'Nothing to hold me back.' I stared into a space just above his head.

'I can understand your reasoning. You've been tied down and restricted by your work.' His left hand fiddled with a loose end of bandage.

'Do you realize, Oliver, what my life's been? But of course you do. Dealing with all those up-moving executives without ruffling their self-esteem, praising them, boosting them. It's as though I've been shepherding one lame duck after the other – if you can shepherd ducks. Holding their hands and leading them where they ought to go.' You're pushing it too far, Phil. Too far.

'I can see your point. I thought you loved it, though. That's the impression . . .' He let it lie, raising his eyes to mine, glancing away. Again he was disappointing me. He'd under-estimated my lying ability.

But he had been correct. It had been my life. 'And d'you know what they all had in common, Oliver? They each thought they were God's gift to big business and high finance. Not a modest claim from any of them.'

'Is that so?' He moved his shoulder furtively.

I allowed a little pause to build up, then I said gently, 'You haven't told me the truth, have you? About your shoulder.'

He shook his head, fumbling for his glass although it was empty. I said, 'I'll get you another pint.'

He said flatly, 'No!' Then he looked up, directly at me at last. His smile was a poor thing, but he seemed to have relaxed.

'Not the whole truth, Phil,' he admitted. 'It's rather worse than I said. Tendons and muscles and things . . . hell, it's all so technical. The fact is, I'm never going to regain the full use of my right arm. They'll pension me off, Phil. No use for a one-armed copper.'

'You won't *lose* it!'

'No! No, no. But I'll have to learn to write left-handed.'

'It'll make you stutter, I've heard.'

'I'll be able to write to you, wherever you are. I'll put the stutters in.' It was a flicker of his old self.

'Thank you. And where shall you be writing from? A bit of a cottage with a bit of a garden? Which, I suppose, you'll dig one-handed. And with an old lady to clean for you and cook one meal a day. You make me mad, Oliver. Furious!'

'It wasn't my fault.' He seemed puzzled and lost. 'Old Pearson—'

'Your attitude,' I explained, clipping my words now. 'The wounded warrior, pensioned off for life. I'll tell you what I want to do with mine, shall I! I just want to do one more job. Devote myself to it. Don't stare at me as though I've gone mad. I'm going to find you something. A future. That's right in my line.'

'Well . . . fine . . .'

'Devote, I said. Oliver Simpson, do you want to live with me? Married or not.'

'Come on, Phil! I can't lumber you—'

'Yes or no.'

His mouth was set in a grim line, but his eyes danced with amusement. 'It's maybe a good idea.'

'Maybe!'

'Maybe a good idea to go and see Mrs Porter, as you suggested. But not this evening—'

'Yes?' I demanded distinctly. 'Or no?'

'Yes, of course.'

'That's that then.'

Thus it was settled. He grinned. 'If this cottage of Mrs Porter's is at all isolated, she won't welcome visitors. I'd have to go with you for protection, but as it is . . .'

'I could hit you. You're as bad as the rest, big-headed and complacent.'

'I'll be guided by you, Phil,' he promised solemnly.

'Or I by you,' I agreed. 'If not Mrs Porter this evening, what d'you suggest?'

'We'll need to know about this football fiddle that Rowley Fields was operating. A trip round the pubs is the best way of doing that.'

'If you think it would help, and if it's what you want to do.'

'I've made no useful contribution so far.'

'You'll injure your left arm, too,' I warned him, 'lifting all those pint glasses. And you won't be able to get back here if you stick to shorts.'

'Now you're being sarcastic. We can all three go.'

'I'd prefer to see Mrs Porter.'

'Then do so. You can take Terry.'

'You'll need Terry yourself.'

'I'm not letting you go without protection.'

'You're not letting—'

'And I'm not good at that . . .'

'Oh, for Chrissake!'

'. . . Any more,' he added, determined to get in the last word. 'He's here now. Let Terry decide.'

Terry slid into the chair beside me, looking all pink and fresh. 'What's this? What's this?' He looked from face to face, smiling, then it faded when he saw our expressions. 'What's going on?'

We spoke together, then Oliver waved his hand, giving me the floor. I explained the disagreement. Terry frowned. He searched our faces again, then he slapped the table surface.

'It's easy. The chief goes round the pubs alone. The two of us together would obviously look like cops. So Phillie and I'll go to see the old lady, then drive back here, and if you haven't come back, Chief, we go round the pubs with the car and shovel you in, if you're in that state, and bring you back here. OK? Isn't that logical?'

'Completely,' I agreed.

'And it's got the advantage that I'll get you on my own, Phillie. Won't that be great?'

'For both of us,' I said emptily. It seemed he was managing to forget Jennie already.

'Then that's settled.'

'Satisfactorily,' said Oliver, 'all round.' But he twisted his lips lugubriously.

'So let's go and eat,' Terry suggested. 'I noticed they're serving in the dining room.'

'Heavens!' I glanced at my watch. 'I'd better just pop up . . .'

I left them talking to each other, heads close. No doubt Oliver was issuing strict instructions as to the guardianship of my person. My impression was that Terry would be sticking fairly close, anyway.

My idea was a quick swill, a change into a skirt, and a dash down again. I burst into the room, and found Bella sitting on the edge of her bed and watching herself on the telly. She looked up.

'Phil, Phil!' She patted the bed beside her. 'Come 'n' look at this. You'll enjoy it. One of our shows.'

'I haven't got—'

'You'll miss the best bit. Come on.'

Reluctantly, I sat. I could spare it perhaps five minutes. The setting was some sort of an impressive office. Jay and Bella were standing facing each other, he with his feet well apart, a sneer on his face, and she raging in fury in front of him, and the more the rage, the worse the sneer. Jay looked magnificently poised, in complete control of himself and the scene. Bella was overacting like mad, but there was something of fear behind it. Perhaps she was a better actress than I'd realized.

'He's just come back from one of his trips,' she told me, for some reason whispering as though we were in a cinema. 'He's heard I've been seen around with that character I told you about, who drives over the cliff. He's jealous, and he's been having me watched. Now concentrate on this. This bit coming up. See the expression on his face? It was suddenly personal, you see. Not in the script. Him and me. Because the bastard *had* been having me watched, and there *was* this really fantastic feller. Oh Phil . . . he was divine.'

'You mean – '

'I'm a grown-up healthy girl, Phil. What d'you expect? Look. Listen. This is where he says his insulting line, and I'm supposed to slap his face – palm, right hand. We'd rehearsed it. He rides it and I pull it. But . . . listen . . . this is his line.'

'. . . not even claim to be a low-class whore,' Jay was saying with passionate disgust. 'You didn't even get paid. I bet you had to pay *him* . . .'

She half turned away from him, to her left. I couldn't see how a right-hand slap could come from there. As I'd been primed, and as Bella's fingers were digging into my arm, I was prepared for it. There was a split-second of blank incomprehension on Jay's face, then she whipped back, bringing her right hand up and across, her knuckles lashing his mouth. His head went back, his eyes were for a second blank, then blood trickled from the corner of his mouth.

Bella laughed weirdly, and clapped, turning towards me. 'Did you see! I caught him unprepared. It made a lovely shot! They kept it in. But Jay was wild, mad. They had to hold him, or he'd have killed me. It was his face, you see. His precious face. It's not all face-lift, you know. In his early days he did his own stunts, before he became valuable, and he crashed a motor bike.

Or so he told me. Mashed his face up good and proper, it did, but when they'd put it all together again, it was better than the original. Came out all craggy, you know, and kind of twisted. Sexy. So he looked after his face, and I'd dented it. His precious face.'

And her own face was aglow with the recalled pleasure of it.

'Bella!' I whispered, because I could think of nothing more to say.

She showed me the back of her right hand. 'My mother's ring,' she told me. It was multi-stoned, like diamond chips. 'Father gave it to me when I was sixteen.'

'Oh,' I said. 'How nice. I've got to rush.' To be away from her.

Rapidly I sorted through what I had. Not too formal, not too plain. I was going to visit an old lady, who would want to be reassured by the presence of another woman, and not have to guess as to sex. There was a two-piece I had hardly worn, a double-breasted blouson top with a hip-snatching basque and a nicely co-ordinated pleated skirt. I clambered into it, stood in front of the wardrobe mirror, and wasn't displeased. Ear-rings? No. Make-up? It would do. Mrs Porter wouldn't go for elaborate make-up.

'You're surely not going down to dinner like that,' cried Bella.

'I shall be wearing shoes,' I said with dignity, meaning my low-heeled wedges.

'Your neck, darlin'!'

'Oh for heaven's sake, Bella, stop worrying about my neck.'

'Borrow my rhinestone necklace, Phil. What it'd do for your eyes!'

'And forget my eyes.'

'You're just hopeless.'

I laughed. She really was the limit. 'Oh,' I said, my hand easing open the door, 'you can probably help me, Bella. Waterford Farm. You'll surely know where it is.'

She looked away. 'Why d'you want to go there?'

'To see an old lady. Mrs—'

'Porter,' she cut in, and there was a snap in her voice.

Gently I reclosed the door, moved towards her, and tried to sound casual. 'You know her?'

'Of course I do. She's my grandmother.' Then her eyes were

123

coldly on mine. She fingered her mother's ring. 'What d'you want from her?'

I realized I had to be careful here. I ought to have guessed who Mrs Porter had to be, if she was in a position to supply information about Dulcie, Bella's mother. Stupid of me! I'd slipped up.

'Just something another old lady said in the fish and chip restaurant.'

She nodded. 'You can bet! They all know everybody and all their business, the old uns. What d'you expect dear granny to tell you, anyway?'

'I don't know. It's just a matter of groping in the dark.'

'Then I'll warn you, Phil.' There was bitterness in her voice. 'Don't believe a word the old bag tells you. Oh, she'll fill your ears right enough, with dirty rotten rubbish. Don't believe one soddin' word, that's all. Me . . . I've had some. She's got a nasty vicious mind, believe me. All smiles and soft words, and every one of them dipped in poison. She was one of the reasons I had to get away from this blasted town, the rotten-minded old cow . . .' She jerked her head up and away. There had been a catch in her voice.

I sat down quietly on my own bed. 'Did she drive you away, Bella?' She was grabbing for her cigarettes, her usual refuge when emotion intruded. 'I had a bad time like that with my husband,' I confided. 'A complete misunderstanding, it was.'

'This was no misunderstanding, believe me. She sat me down, and I felt as though I was tied there. She pinned me to the chair with every word, all dripping with hatred and acid. She was set to turn me against Dad. Oh, her poor Dulcie! My ma, that was. She'd had to put up with his brutish behaviour. Brutish! The very word she used. And his mockery. She said he'd mocked her, jeered at her, wept at her! Oh Christ, the bastard!'

'Your father?' This wasn't sounding like Rowley.

'No. That rotten old bitch. Didn't she see! Didn't she see that all she was doing was turning me against her instead of against my dad, her and that nasty vicious tongue of hers. I hated her then. Hated her. And just . . . Lord, this was just the time I'd worked myself up to going away . . . and she had to hand me *that*.'

Once again, this didn't quite line up with what she'd already

124

said about Rowley, he of the jovially loose and grasping hands. 'When was this?' I asked quietly.

'Just before he . . . my dad . . . disappeared himself. Oh, don't you see, Phil. If *that* was the mother-in-law he'd had to contend with, and if my mother was . . . blast it, Phil, use your imagination for once, will you! I'd heard about my mother. Dulcie. The wonderful Dulcie. D'you know what they used to call her? Duck-out Dulcie. Now ain't that bleedin' lovely! My mother, and they sneered at her, and poor old Dad . . . I was . . . It was that last week or two and I was desperate to go. Jay had turned up – come back into my life.'

'You'd met him in Birmingham,' I reminded her, reminded myself.

She wagged the hand holding the cigarette. 'That's right. I'd met him at a party in Birmingham. I'd had a bit part at the Alex, and gave him my address. You know how it is. You meet dozens. Hell, I don't have to keep records.'

'Of course not.'

'So he came. I wanted to go. Then Tonia'd got something lined up. It was *all* laid on, and that rotten bag . . . oh, Phil, Phil, how could I leave Dad after that? I felt *sorry* for him, blast it. D'you know, I took a good look at him, for the very first time, and you'll never guess what I saw behind all that happy slap-on-the-back bouncy jokey stupid face of his.'

'I couldn't guess. Tell me.' I barely breathed it.

'He was unhappy and he was alone, and he was afraid, Phil. Afraid. And suddenly I didn't want to go. Jay had come and everything seemed to be opening up, and all I wanted to do was stay with that poor lost old bleeder – and that was what dear Granny Porter had done for me. Ruined everything. And I didn't know what to *do*.'

I stared at the top of her head. She had been flinging it about, and her hair fell like a curtain between us.

'Then it's convenient your father went away himself, and made the decision for you,' I murmured.

'Went away!' The head came up. 'He was killed, you fool.'

'We don't know that.'

'Of course we do. That was *him*. That skeleton. You daft or something?'

'Nobody can be certain of that, yet.'

125

She snorted. 'Want a bet?'

I said, 'Not on that subject, Bella. You know too much.'

She was watching me as I got to my feet, and again she managed to halt me at the door. Her voice was dull and uninflected. 'D'you want me to come with you, Phil?'

There was perhaps a hidden yearning to repair an old breach. I said, 'I don't think so. But thank you, all the same. I'll let you know what happens.'

'I don't want to know.'

I'd closed the door behind me before I remembered she hadn't told me how to locate Waterford Farm. I didn't go back.

They were waiting in the bar. Terry came to his feet. 'Oh oh! We ought to change, Chief, and I didn't bring my dinner jacket.'

'Idiot,' I said. 'Let's go and eat.'

When we'd ordered, I told them what had happened, reversing the order so that I could keep the back-hander I'd watched Jay receive until last. Terry seemed eager to meet this old dragon up at the farm. He claimed he had a way with old ladies, which I could easily accept. Then I told them about Jay's cut mouth.

'Why,' asked Oliver, who didn't miss much, 'did you leave that until last?'

'You guessed!'

'It's your sense of the dramatic, Phil. Why?'

'It's the ring. Her mother's ring. And she's wearing it. She says her father gave it to her when she was sixteen. So, how did Rowley happen to have it? If Dulcie had gone away, as he said to them first, why would she have left it behind?'

'Her engagement ring,' suggested Oliver. 'Left as a gesture of rejection. I can manage soup with my left hand. Why the hell did I order a lamb chop?'

'Aren't you missing the point?' asked Terry. We stared at him, and he smiled. 'Bella's wearing it. She knows all about her mother's reputation, she knew her mother for only four years, yet she wears her ring – and it doesn't sound as though it's very valuable, so it's not for that.'

I said nothing. Actors are actors, but even in her true self, Bella had not impressed me as possessing any deep feelings or sentimentality. Even her eventual sympathy for her father had been a backlash from her grandmother's tirade. But there was a possibility that her grandmother had accomplished two things at the same time, had given Bella an understanding of her father, and a picture of her mother that in some way pleased.

I realized that my talk with Mrs Porter, if I could bring it about, could be very interesting indeed.

After dinner we split up. From the receptionist Oliver obtained a list of the town's public houses – there were fifteen – and a sketch map indicating how he might visit them all with the least amount of effort. I noticed that the route put the closest last.

'In case, sir,' the receptionist said solemnly, 'you have difficulty getting back.'

'Thank you,' said Oliver.

Then I asked for directions to Waterford Farm.

'It's Waterford House really,' he told us. 'The farm's not been worked for years, and it's just about falling down. Mr Kemp's place, it is.'

Oh oh! I thought. I made a careful note of the directions, but already I had a good idea of the general lay of it.

I drove us out of the rear car-park, having seen Oliver on his way. Terry was silent for a minute or two. I was busy navigating out of the town. At last he said:

'I'm glad to get you alone, Phillie.'

'Oh yes?'

'He'll be quite OK, you know.'

'I'm sure he will.'

He was silent for two minutes, then, 'Has he told you how it is with him? All of it?'

'He's told me.'

'Damn it!' He thumped his knee with a fist. 'Isn't it infuriating! There was me, just got into the CID, and trying to wangle myself on to his team, and *that* had to happen. I wanted to work with him. Everybody does. You worked with him, see, not for him. He's like that. Jennie told me. And that had to happen!'

'You're losing out all ways,' I suggested.

'What?'

'Jennie too.'

'Yes.' His voice was empty. 'It's getting me down, you know. Being with the chief, I mean. Oh sure, it's easy enough to look after him. Physically, it is. He helps a lot. It's mentally. Phillie, I wasn't made for it. I try – being all cheerful and optimistic –

telling him he'll be a better inspector when it's healed. You know, jossing him a bit, to stop him getting too depressed. And him pretending he feels great! Lord, I've seen him when he didn't think I was watching. He ought to be in a hospital bed, you know. Really.'

'And you think I could perhaps persuade him to return to it?' I asked, slowing a little because we had to clear this away while we were at it.

'No. He's stubborn. Changes the subject. No,' he said carefully, pursuing his objective with delicacy. 'But Jennie said . . . told me . . .'

I glanced sideways. His fingers were clenched tightly on his knees. His voice hadn't been steady.

'It doesn't matter,' I told him quietly.

'But it *does* matter.' He also was quiet, but he spoke with intensity. 'Now it's you who won't mention Jennie. He won't. Doesn't want me to think about it, and it's all I *can* think about. Jennie! Oh, we have a grand time together, him and me, you can be sure of that. All the while he's trying to keep me from thinking about Jennie, and doing it by pretending he needs more help than he really does, and me trying to cheer him up, and pretending he's a fraud for asking for my help.'

I suggested that they were perhaps good for each other.

'You think so?'

'I'm sure of it.'

He made a tiny sound, perhaps a bitter laugh, perhaps clearing a small catch in his throat. 'You know what scares me?' he asked suddenly.

'Tell me.' For some reason it was encouraging that he could be scared.

'Sometime,' he said heavily, 'probably very soon, we're going to find out who killed Jennie, and the chief's going to go wild. You know what I mean? He's in a . . . a dangerous mood. And he's going to get himself hurt. I've got to be there, Phillie, on the spot. You understand? There to stop him – when I'm in a dangerous mood myself.'

'Then you just hang on to him, and I'll take all the action necessary. I can be dangerous too. If that'll suit you.'

Now the little sound was a genuine laugh, muted, but a laugh. 'He said you were like that. Jennie too.'

From Jennie, that would be a compliment. I was flattered. Suddenly, I felt all choked up.

'There it is,' he said suddenly. 'On the left. According to what the man said.'

I turned through the imposing entrance to Waterford House. There was an old gatehouse, no longer occupied, and huge wrought-iron gates held fully open by great tufts of grass, and with weeds that wound themselves around an old rusted padlock.

Tudor Kemp, it appeared, had risked every bit of his capital on his project.

Terry said, 'Take it easy up here, the drive looks rough.'

The headlights danced as the rutted drive threw us about. Beyond their reach was darkness, relieved only by two distant patches of light.

11

With the lights and engine switched off, we were able to stand
out on a reasonably level surface and allow our eyes to adapt.
The two patches of light we'd seen were two windows, one in
the cottage beside us, and one in the big house itself, which
stood on the same level about a hundred yards away.

It was going to be a crisp and clear October night, still and
calm, with the possibility of a mist falling at around dawn. There
was a slice of moon, but low on the horizon, and the stars were
doing most of the work. The bulk of the town was hidden from
here, but the glow of it was lurking just beyond the hill slope to
our right, and further over, to the left, the factory was in clear
view, though only as an angular block obscuring the stars. I
wondered how Tudor Kemp had managed to obtain planning
permission for it. The building would no doubt have been built
on his own ground, but no end of sweeteners would probably
have slid into welcoming bank accounts.

Below, in the trough of the valley, the motorway operation
was cloaked in darkness. In the daytime, when vehicles eventually pounded past in a steady stream, it would impose on the
sensibilities with much more force. What a strange man he must
be, to ruin his own outlook, which must have been of a green
and lush valley, for financial advancement. Certainly, the farming aspect had failed. I could see the jagged outlines of the
decrepit barns and outbuildings stretching away behind me
from the tattered hayloft at my right shoulder. But Kemp had
not simply recruited his financial position, he had thrown every
last resource into his dream, which was after all a high-risk
project that could have ruined him completely. But which, now,
was going to pay off handsomely.

We turned to examine the cottage. The lighted window was one of the bedrooms, facing sideways and overlooking, I could just tell from the light spill, a narrow cobbled yard that separated it from the run of barns. We were, in fact, standing at the end of a row of six old farm cottages, only this end one now being habitable. We moved round on to the cobbles, my ankles wobbling on the surface. The lighted window was above. I stepped back for another look, and into a rustling, prickly surface that threw up an acrid smell as it moved. Glancing behind, I saw it was a bank of ancient hay, which had flowed out when the outer wooden wall of the hayloft had rotted away. Not intending to step any further into it, I had to make the most of what I could see from there.

Terry spoke softly. 'Perhaps we're a bit late for the old dear.'

'I'm not sure. If she lives alone she probably doesn't know evening from morning, and time would be no more than darkness and light. I bet she's sitting up in bed watching the telly.'

Terry cocked his head. 'Can't hear anything. Perhaps she's still on gas.'

'No.' I could just detect the overhead wires looping in from the direction of the big house. It was clear that this end cottage was the only one of the run connected up, and when I explored along the cobbles a little way I could see that the other cottages were in a very sad state indeed, the woodwork rotting, with most of the glass missing from the ancient sash windows, and the roofs sagging dismally. In this end one the woodwork was painted, and recently, and the windows had been replaced by more modern ones, which opened sideways.

I walked back to Terry's side. 'He seems to look after the place.'

'Time's getting on, you know. Who does?'

'Kemp, of course. And it's not really late. Just after nine. Old people sleep any time, when they feel like it.'

'What do we do, then? Knock on the door, or open it and shout?' He was unsettled, anxious to get on with it.

'Open the door, I'd say. If it's unlocked.'

'It is,' said a voice behind us.

We turned. He was no more than a shadow, which moved

forward into the light spill. 'I'd need to be able to get in if anything was to happen.'

It was Tudor Kemp, who could not have failed to notice our headlights bouncing up his drive. His tone had been neutral, even friendly, but that shotgun was there again, crooked in his arm, when all he could have hoped to shoot in the darkness had to be intruders.

'It's Mr Kemp,' I said to Terry.

'So it is.'

Kemp inclined his head. 'And I believe we've met.' He waited. He wanted to hear our pedigrees.

'My name's Philipa Lowe,' I told him, 'and this is Terry Alwright.'

'And may I ask your interest in Mrs Porter?' But he was calm, polite, patient.

'We were told to see her if we wanted any more information.'

'Indeed! Information about what?'

'Her daughter, Dulcie.'

He moved forward another pace. Now the light, poor as it was, searched out his eyes. They were cold, switching from one to the other of us. I could detect that he was tense and nervous, poised. 'On that subject,' he said, 'I can give you information myself. All you'd be interested in, anyway.'

But he could not, certainly not the intimate details I'd hoped to extract from Mrs Porter.

'I'm not sure you'd know—'

A bite entered his voice as he cut in sharply. 'What is your authority to come barging in and bothering an old lady at this time . . .'

'Time is the point.'

'And who are you to be asking around? She's entitled to her peace and quiet at her age.'

'And I,' I said quietly, 'am entitled to ask questions. Not demand answers, but talk. I'm sure she'd enjoy talking. To another woman. If she's isolated like this, with only you . . .'

I left it hanging on the edge of a question.

'Come tomorrow,' he said crisply. 'I'll not have strangers prowling around after dark.'

'Nobody intends to prowl. You can be with me, if you like.'

'Hah!' he said, strangely amused. 'You don't know her. Keep me out of it. She'll tie you in knots till your brain rolls over.'

'Can I suggest you stand out here and stay on call?'

'Tomorrow—'

'Could be too late,' I cut in.

His eyebrows shot up. It had been a dramatic statement. 'Explain that.'

'My life has been in a certain amount of danger. It appears I have some resemblance to Tonia Fields. Her grandmother, I thought, might be able to help me.'

He eyed me with his head on one side, glanced at Terry, then back at me. 'There's a definite resemblance,' he admitted. 'I noticed it earlier on, at the site.'

He had weakened his attitude. I pounced in. 'So you see, I want her opinion.'

'Her sight isn't good.'

'We could perhaps manage. She would know.'

He jerked the gun. 'And him?'

'He's my minder. I need protection.'

He smiled. 'And I am Mrs Porter's minder, shall we say. She was my father's housekeeper, and more recently mine. I have a great affection for her. So . . . you will go up to her room, and I'll ask you to open that window so that I can hear if she wants help. You understand? And your friend here can mind me.' He laughed lightly. Terry touched my arm, indicating agreement.

'Thank you,' I said. 'That suits me fine.'

It occurred to me – a sudden realization that placed her in a frame of reference – that Dulcie would have lived in this cottage before she married. Kemp would have been in the same age group, perhaps a year or two older, and this was a man with a driving personality, a man who took risks, a man who had come out on top and who had to dominate. With such a man, Dulcie's coy tricks would have been useless. He might even have invoked his droit de seigneur, as had earlier robber barons. And Dulcie's mother might have known this, even approved, perhaps having dreams of promoting her standing at the big house, this time not as housekeeper but as mother of the bride. Then she would be awarded a dower house instead of a cottage. My mind drifted on . . .

'If you're coming,' he said, now impatient to get on with it.

133

He was standing by the door. I looked at Terry, who grimaced, then I took my place beside Kemp as he opened the door, put his head inside, and shouted, 'Visitor for you, Flora.'

There was an indistinct response. Kemp nodded and I moved into the tiny hall. There was a narrow staircase with a rickety handrail. The confined gap beside it clearly led into the lower rooms. Kemp snapped a switch and a light went on, illuminating a landing.

'It's up on your right,' he said.

I mounted. He called after me, 'Don't upset her.' I nodded, though he couldn't have seen it. The door on the right had a simple thumb latch. I thumbed it, pushed the door open, and thrust my head in.

'Mrs Porter?' I asked. 'I'm Philipa Lowe.'

She was not, as I'd expected, in her bed, which was a narrow single one against the wall, with a patchwork quilt over it. Mrs Porter, Flora in my mind, was seated very comfortably indeed in a large and well-padded easy chair, with her feet up on a pouffe. There was a wall-light on the wall above her head, on her lap a large-print library book, and on the end of her nose reading glasses, which apparently performed better at a distance. She must have been nudging eighty, a tiny and depleted old lady with a lace shawl over her shoulders, wearing beneath it a thick woolly cardie. Her skirt was voluminous. Her small, sharp and wrinkled face was topped by a mop of pure white hair.

I looked around. There was no other chair. I wondered how they'd got hers up there. The wall was papered in a striped pattern, perhaps to give an impression of height because the ceiling was so low, the heavy black beams robbing it of another six inches. Somebody had put in shelves on two of the walls, perhaps Kemp himself, to house her collection of china ornaments and little vases, her multiple photo frames, a wide shelf clock, and a small television set, its face blank.

'Philipa Lowe,' she said, running it round her memory. 'Come closer, my dear, so that I can see you.' I did so. The arthritic hands reached up to touch my cheeks, my hair. There was an abrupt stillness in her face, then her tiny mouth quivered. I tried to draw away, but one hand snatched at my shoulder. 'Don't go.' Her other hand removed her glasses.

But her intensity had shaken me a little. 'I've got to open the window.'

'I don't like it open. It's cold out there.'

'Mr Kemp insisted.'

'That old fool!' He was probably thirty years younger. 'I was his nanny, you know.'

I managed to open the window. It moved stiffly and creaked. 'That do?' I called out.

'Not too wide,' Kemp called. 'Flora feels the cold.'

'What's he want it open for?' she grumbled.

'So that you can shout out if I annoy you.'

She gave a sudden shriek of laughter that would've brought a regiment at the trot. It set her coughing, but she held up a palm when I tried to slap her back. In the end she recovered, sat back, took a breath, and said, 'You're not even in the running, dear.'

'Pardon?' I sat tentatively on the edge of her bed.

'They're all coming, all annoying me. What's going on, that's what I'd like to know. I bet you can tell me.'

I shook my head, but she might not have seen it. I wasn't going to tell her that they'd found a skeleton which was probably her daughter's.

'That Edith Payne, she was here. My friend. Anyway . . . she reckons she's my friend. Said she'd seen our Bella in the fish and chip shop. Fletcher's. That Arnold's been, as well, but I sent him packing.'

'It's Soo Long's now.'

She giggled. 'It's not, it's Tudor Kemp's. Don't let it get about, though. Dignity. Got to hold on to his dignity, he has. Not much sign of that, though, when he was sniffing round my Dulcie. Like a randy old dog, he was. And why do they keep coming here? That's what I can't understand. And that stupid Edith Payne! Of *course* it wasn't our Bella, or she'd have come to see me. That's why I thought for a sec' you was Tonia, but if you was, you wouldn't have come. Like Bella. Wouldn't have come to see her old gran. Well, maybe Tonia, perhaps. She might've, 'cause she *did* write, which is more'n you can say for Bella. Never even written, she hasn't. So if she'd been in town she'd have come. Save her a stamp, it would, if she don't want to write. Seems sense to me, but she hasn't come. Now you have. If you've been writing, perhaps you would. Though she

135

signed 'em Tonia. And you're Philipa. You said that, didn't you? Philipa. Pretty name. You're not Tonia, are you?'

She peered at me suspiciously. I was beginning to understand what Kemp had meant about my brain rolling over.

'I'm not Tonia,' I said quietly. She cupped a palm behind her ear. I raised my voice. 'I'm not Tonia.'

'Didn't think you was.'

'But I've been mistaken for her.'

She shook her head, pouting. 'It's not her voice.'

'But it's her face?'

'You'll have to speak louder, dear.'

'I said – but it's her face?'

'Oh yes, the face. Mostly. I suppose. Here – you can do it better than me – get me that picture. The one there by the clock. That's the one. Bring it over here and I'll show you. And the one next to it, while you're at it.'

I moved as slowly as I could without attracting her suspicions, giving myself time. She didn't seem to have much patience. My eyes ran along the row of framed photos, very old and sepia in soft focus, to the left, with the women in old-fashioned gowns, and on to colour prints, un-posed, as they got closer to the clock. Appropriate – history racing onwards, up to that minute. Or rather, it would have been up to that minute if the clock had been going. Behind it – and I almost reached for it to wind it for her, until I stopped myself – there was a wad of letters.

Her eyes were keener than I'd anticipated. Perhaps she needed help only close to. She said, noticing my hovering hand, 'No. Not those.'

When I turned back with the two photo frames, she seemed to realize her voice had been too sharp. She pouted in apology. 'I don't want to see them again.' Yet she'd kept them. 'Begging letters. Not that I mind sending money, but I hate being written to just for the money. Is that very silly of me?' she added pitifully, as though I was some sort of monitor, to pass judgement.

'Very sensible,' I said, handing her the pictures, slipping in behind her chair at her shoulder to get a good look.

'That's her,' she told me, stabbing a finger. 'Tonia.'

Two young girls stood side by side, the background a distant and unfocused Waterford House. One had her arm round the

136

other's shoulders, the shorter one had hers round her sister's waist. It had to be Bella and Tonia, at – what age? – eighteen and sixteen, perhaps. A slimmer Bella, but I was able to recognize her at once, at that time more relaxed, and certainly happier. The smile, perhaps, was only for the camera, but there was a gaiety about her, a devil-may-care expression, a lift of the head that wasn't at that time imperious. And the other . . .

'That's Tonia,' repeated Flora, stabbing a finger. 'You can see her as a dancer. You don't dance, dear? No? Ah well, we can't have everything, can we! The chin's the same.' She glanced up at me. 'But your forehead's wider. And the hair . . . what've you got there? It's all springy. You want to have something done about that, Sylvia. Sylvia? No, it was . . . now don't tell me . . . Phyllis.'

'Yes,' I murmured, not wanting to stop her.

'Lovely girl. Lovely. You've got her eyes. They went away, you know. Silly creatures. Just 'cause Rowley had left. Their father, that was. Well, he would, wouldn't he! Stands to sense. All those nasty people after him.' She giggled. 'Oh, he was a scream, was Rowley. You'd have laughed. Took their money every week, and then it came up. Took mine too. Oh yes, I gave him a pound a week, or tried to, but he always slipped it under the clock, the devil. And then it came up. I listened on the radio. I remember clapping my hands. Such fun! Only he hadn't sent in the coupon. Crafty devil. But they were all after his blood – and me laughing myself silly. You'd have laughed. Oh, you would.'

'Why would I have laughed, Flora?'

'Greed!' she cried. 'What'd I have done with all that money, anyway? I never expected anything, but the rest of 'em – oh, they were livid. Livid! So Rowley went away, and the girls thought he wasn't ever coming back, and *they* went away. No need for that, there wasn't. Left me here, all on me own. They only had to walk across the fields, you know. There's a little bridge over the brook. But they went. Not so much as a goodbye. You tell Bella she'd better come and see me. Tell her I've forgiven her. She'll come.'

'Forgiven her . . .'

'And this picture here . . . that's Dulcie, their mother. My

137

Dulcie. Now – *there* was a beauty for you, if there ever was one. Don't you think?'

She handed it up to me.

Dulcie was the May Queen. It was a professional shot, so that the whole composition was perfectly balanced, Dulcie high on a throne, crowned, glowing, and absolutely splendid. Beautiful, yes. But it wasn't Bella's wild and passionate beauty. This was a softness and a roundness, a calm smile of confidence, and about her an aura of blatant sexuality. I couldn't have pointed to any positive detail of it, but it was there in every line of her, subdued by her May Queen dress, virginal, and thus, in the setting, sexually provocative, because she was surrounded by a group of six male acolytes, each gazing at her from a different angle, and though the photographer had no doubt appealed for smiles he could not have expected such blatantly lustful ones. They centred on her like searchlights in the pall of a bleak chastity, and blunting on what was in fact an ethereal virginity, raised there, alone and unassailable.

'That's my Dulcie,' she was saying, all soft and gentle pride, no sadness yet because for her this lovely daughter of hers was still clothed in flesh.

'The others,' she said negligently, 'were her six attendants. Self-appointed. They fought everybody else off. Whittled it down to six in the end, when they got tired of fighting. She had scores! Oh, you wouldn't believe! Everywhere she went, they were after her.'

'But didn't get her,' I whispered.

But she'd misled me as to her deafness. 'I taught her to be a good girl,' she told me, slightly misunderstanding, severe.

'Rowley Fields got her,' I said, making it sound a little better.

'Yes. That's him there.' She prodded a finger. Rowley Fields was one of those on the outer edges. He was thinner and taller than I'd expected. I couldn't think where I'd got the idea of smallness. But Bella had said he used to prance – hadn't she? He had a thin, sharp face and glowing eyes, and was the only one not smiling. His was a glorious and disarming grin. Of the six, he was the only one who was clearly enjoying himself.

'Great big fool,' she said, 'Rowley was. He should've tanned her hide a bit. I told him that.'

'Did you?'

'And that . . .' She prodded the arthritic finger again. 'That's him.'

'Which him?'

'Him down below. Mr Kemp,' she explained, emphasis on the 'Mister'. 'Tudor, I call him. It annoys him.'

'Probably. But why would Dulcie—'

'A handsome devil, wasn't he?'

'Who? You mean Tudor?' To me, he didn't look all that handsome. There was a seriousness about him, even at that age, as though the weight of responsibility was already resting heavily on his shoulders. A square and positive jaw, the eyes even then hidden and remote.

'It was what she needed,' Flora was saying.

'Dulcie?'

'Yes. A good trouncing. That'd teach her.'

'You perhaps thought that Tudor would—'

But she wouldn't allow me to finish. 'But Tudor was always so thoughtful. Understanding, you know. Too big for his boots, even then, and he'd only have been twenty-five or so. Old-fashioned, like his dad. There's a word . . . courtly, that's it. Serious and slow and too patient.'

He wasn't patient now, though. His voice floated up. 'You all right, Flora?'

Flora dismissed him with a gesture. 'Tell him to go on home,' she said impatiently. 'The air's getting chill and it always settles on his chest.'

I went to the window and thrust it wide. 'She suggests that you go home, Mr Kemp.'

And Flora shouted, 'You'll be getting your wheezes, Tudor, and it'll be no good coming to me for sympathy. Somebody else can rub your chest.'

He said a rude word, which I didn't pass on to her. I turned back, half closing the window again.

'She needed a firm hand,' Flora was explaining. 'And this one's the one for that. Was. I don't know what happened to *him*. Edith tells lies.'

I leaned close. She was indicating a handsome face with a strong mouth and demanding eyes. There was a calm confidence about him and a possessiveness in his expression.

'Who's he?' I asked.

'Always dithering and dathering, our Dulcie was. Couldn't decide anything any time. You think she's settled on something . . . and pff! It's gone, and it's something else she wants.' She was speaking as though Dulcie were alive and well, sitting downstairs and reading a book. 'There's a word for her sort.'

There was indeed, a hyphened one. I didn't think she meant that.

'Something to do with sticking a needle in you,' she mused.

'Who is he?' I didn't want to get involved with her needle.

'Was, dear, was. As far as I know. That's Joey Payne. He was the one our Dulcie went away with. Poor, dear Rowley, his heart was broken. I know it. He was never the same after.'

'Went away with?' I was desperately trying to keep control of the situation.

'Not vaccination,' she mused to herself.

I sighed. 'Vacillating. That's what you meant about Dulcie.'

'That's it.' She threw back her head with delight. 'That's the very word that Arnold used.'

Oh Lord, I thought. 'You said Dulcie went away with Joey Payne,' I reminded her.

'Left the little uns.'

Payne? Wasn't that the woman in the fish and chip shop?

'Dulcie went away with him?' I persisted.

She nodded. 'Left the little uns,' she repeated, 'and Bella was only four, little Tonia two. I told Rowley, he oughta have had me over at his place, to look after 'em. But no. Talk to a brick wall you might as well.'

'Perhaps he loved them,' I suggested. 'Didn't want to share them.' But she didn't reply.

My back was aching, leaning over her shoulder. I straightened, leaving her sitting and staring down at her Dulcie and the six acolytes, and prowled the room. As Kemp had warned, she was tying my brain in knots. Yet you couldn't say it was senility. She was clear enough with her memories. All she couldn't do was organize them. And yet – if Dulcie and Joey had gone away . . .

'You said Dulcie went away with Joey?' I asked.

'Joey Payne, yes.' But her head was down and she was smiling, lost in a reverie of the day of the May Queen.

'And you never heard from either of them again?'

She said nothing, then abruptly raised her head. 'And you'll know this one.'

I had to go and look at it, if only from politeness. Her finger was indicating a more serious face than the others, the smile a token for the camera. But there was something familiar about that long chin and the wide brow.

'That's Arnold. Now . . . I'd have said she was falling for Arnie. There was a time when she never spoke about anybody else. Arnie this and Arnie that. But she was too late for that. No good mooning over a lost lover.'

'Lost?'

'When she's married, he's lost her. Stands to reason.'

Not with Dulcie it didn't. 'She was mooning, as you call it, over Arnie? Arnie who?' Then it snapped in. *That* was a very young Arnold Connaught.

'Connaught, silly. He never married, you know.'

'Never married . . .'

'I think it did something to him, when she went away with Joey Payne.'

Mooning over Arnold Connaught, then she went away with Joey Payne? This Dulcie had been playing a dangerous game. Not only the teasing and the vaccination, as Flora called it, but the playing of one man against the other. And this delicate procedure had not ended with her marriage. But perhaps, for Dulcie, marriage had been an annoying intrusion.

'But with Joey it was the grand passion. You know, dear. More important than anything else. Filled her mind and her body – and she couldn't rest.' Flora nodded wisely. She knew.

'A pity, then, she had married Rowley Fields,' I suggested, a little tartly because I was losing sympathy with this tricky and thoroughly self-centred May Queen. Perhaps that was what all the adulation had done for her. She had thought she could pick the fruit for ever, long after they had fallen from the bough.

'Oh,' said Flora. 'That was me. My doing. Put my foot down.' She tapped my arm in emphasis; I was to note this inflexibility of hers. 'She was pregnant, you see. So I got on to Rowley and Rowley's people, and we fixed it up. Rowley wasn't doing any objecting, that I can remember.'

'Nor Dulcie?'

'She spent all her time floating around in a dream.'

'Dreaming about Joey?'

'Stupid thing.' I had to believe she meant Dulcie, not me.

'Then how,' I asked, 'did you know it was Rowley's child?' We were talking here about Bella, I had to remind myself.

'A girl knows.'

A girl like Dulcie! Who could have been raped by Tudor Kemp, violently and passionately seduced by Joey Payne, and had been mooning so helplessly about Connaught's charms that she wouldn't have realized what Rowley Fields was doing with her! Or not.

'But you said,' I persisted, 'that Joey was everything to her. Passionately—'

'Oh, this wasn't physical, I'm sure. Romantic love. He wouldn't have touched her. And she . . .' Her voice failed her as she dreamed about the beauty of it.

Wouldn't let him? Some passion that must have been! Jane Austen would have loved to dissect it.

'And they went away together?'

'These others,' she said, prodding the photo vigorously, 'are nothing. You should see what they married, in the end. Plain girls. Ugly girls. Now . . . isn't that strange?'

'Perhaps not.'

She thrust her glasses up her nose so that she could get a good look at me. 'You haven't been listening,' she said accusingly.

'Oh, but I have.'

'She was beautiful. You can see that here.'

'Yes. Beautiful, Flora. I couldn't agree more.' I couldn't tell her what had probably turned them off Dulcie. 'But as the lads grow older they look for something . . . well, something deeper, hidden underneath.'

'Then they looked with their eyes shut. Those two wives are right tartars, I can tell you. But my Dulcie . . .'

'Went away with Joey Payne, for passion and eternal happiness.'

'That's just what she said.' Flora nodded.

'Dulcie discussed it with you?' I was trying to ignore the calls from below in the yard. We were getting to what I was after.

'Of course she did. Who would she come to but her mother?'

'And you helped her to pack?'

142

She took that seriously. 'No!' She pouted, nodding to herself, trying to persuade herself she approved. 'She said – a clean break. She was taking nothing from that house – from Rowley. Nothing that was his.'

Which, I was beginning to believe, would have left her free to take the two girls. But perhaps that wouldn't have suited Joey, if his love for her had been passionate but platonic. If there could be such a thing. I just didn't believe it. Flora was living in a dream world of her own romancing.

'And Joey?' I asked. 'What did *he* take?'

'How would I know that?'

'From your friend Edith Payne. His mother. You'd have heard it all.'

'We don't speak,' she said distantly – and yet she'd mentioned their speaking recently.

'Your friend—'

'Not since then.'

'You had a disagreement?'

'You could call it that. She was unpleasant.'

'In what way?'

'She called my Dulcie a rotten, conniving bitch.'

'How very unfeeling of her!' I stared across at the window. 'Oh, for God's sake!' I went over to it, flung it wide again. 'Will you please *wait*!' I shouted furiously. Then I slammed it shut completely – let Kemp worry.

But the break had been at the wrong moment. Flora sat with a tiny handkerchief in her hand, holding it to her nose and sniffing, with her tears dripping on to the May Queen. I went over and put a hand to her shoulder, but she wouldn't lift her head. I went down on my knees, trying to look up into her eyes, and reached across a finger to lift her hair away from them.

'Dulcie's never written to you, has she, Flora?' I asked gently.

There was a minimal shake of her head.

'Not one letter?'

'No,' she mumbled. Then, more clearly, 'It's him, I reckon. Joey stopping her from writing. I never did like him. Big-head, that's what he was. I hated him.'

'Oh, Flora!'

I got to my feet and reached for the two photo frames, quietly returning them to their previous positions. My hands were

143

within inches of that bundle of envelopes. Airmail envelopes! My fingers itched. Perhaps Flora had fibbed a little, as she'd been fibbing to herself all these years, and these were from Dulcie. Begging letters, she had called them. Begging for forgiveness from her mother, perhaps. But I couldn't touch them. I would hate myself, and there'd been more than enough hatred flying around here, as it was. Love and passion . . . and consequently hatred.

I bent over her and whispered, 'I'll ask Bella to come and see you. I'll tell her you've forgiven her.'

An eye, red now, peeped at me from beneath the cataract of hair. 'Bella shouted at me,' she whispered.

'She didn't understand you, perhaps,' I suggested softly.

Her lips twitched. 'People don't. They're not very bright. Most of 'em.'

I kissed her on the cheek and went down into the yard, stared at the two men, then turned and walked away. Quick footsteps followed me, and a hand clawed at my arm. I whirled round, to face Kemp's angry eyes.

'Don't *touch* me!' I said, holding my anger in check. 'I walked away because I wanted you clear of the cottage. I could just lose my temper, Mr Kemp, and start screaming at you.'

'At me?' asked Kemp blankly.

'At you, and the whole damned tribe round here. That woman in there, Flora, is waiting for Dulcie to come home. She thinks she's alive, but the odds are she's dead. It's likely the female skeleton is hers.'

'You've told her that?' His voice was not in control.

'No. You can do that. When it's certain.' I turned away from him, then back. 'But she won't believe you. Come on, Terry, let's go and find Oliver.'

We left him standing with Flora's lighted window behind his head. She was probably all he had now.

12

Brooding and silent, I allowed the car to run slowly down the rutted drive. Twice I got the impression that Terry had glanced at me, but eventually he spoke.

'Well? Get anywhere, did you?'

'Yes. No. I don't know. Dulcie went away with somebody called Joey Payne. Or was thought to have gone away. If Oliver's guess is anywhere near correct, Dulcie got no further than beneath the floor of the empty house next door.'

He gave that some consideration. Then, 'And Joey?' Another pause. 'You don't think that's him – the other skeleton?'

'I don't know. Yes I do. If one's been there fifteen or so years longer than the other—'

'That hasn't been confirmed, yet.'

'Well . . . it's hardly likely. I'm coming to the conclusion the one is Rowley Fields, and the other Dulcie.'

'Yes. That's the best bet.'

'She was a real beauty, Terry.'

'Dulcie?'

'Yes. And so was Bella, in the photos I saw. The image of her mother, at around the same age. Dulcie the softer beauty, Bella the brighter and sharper.'

'Whatever that means.'

I didn't enlarge on it, wanting to think about it before we met up with Oliver. I had to get it straight.

'There must be more than that,' Terry said. 'Aren't you going to tell me?'

'D'you mind if it keeps until Oliver's with us? Then I'll only have to say it once.'

'Sure. Please yourself.'

145

'Did Kemp say anything?' I asked.

'D'you mind if it keeps—'

'Idiot!'

We laughed. He said, 'All I got was a load of grumbles. People visiting the old lady all day.'

'Was Connaught mentioned?' I asked. No reply. 'As one of the visitors.'

'Well . . . not so much mentioned as cussed about. That'd be closer to it. They don't seem to like each other.'

'That's part of what I've got to tell you both.'

We said no more on the subject at that time, each of us wondering how best to contact Oliver. The interview with Flora Porter had taken less time than it had seemed, so we eventually decided that he hadn't had time to get really canned, and probably hadn't covered more than four of the pubs. So the best thing seemed to be to start at the beginning of his list. By the time we had decided this, we were drawing into the town.

'Can you remember that list of his?' I asked.

'Sure.' He was confident. 'Next left after the lights.' He was one of those people who can memorize maps. Very useful, that is.

We found Oliver in the noisy public bar of the Unicorn, in a corner with half a dozen other men. No women. What he was after would've been confined to men.

For two minutes we stood at his shoulder. His left arm hadn't yet become tired; it was gracefully lifting a full pint tankard. And already he seemed to be on his way to roaring drunk. His laugh was too loud, his voice blurred. Then he seemed to realize we were there, said something to the others, and they all fell about laughing. But he didn't draw us into the group, merely used us as an excuse to leave. He got to his feet and groped for Terry's arm, but once outside he steadied miraculously.

'Get anything, Phil?' he asked.

'I believe so. And you?'

'Tell you when we get back to the Crown.'

I took the car round into the rear yard, but this time the men stayed with me, taking no chances. Inside, we went no further than the lounge. It was quiet in there, and we were alone at a corner table. Terry went and fetched drinks, Oliver assuring us he was still far from drunk. My gin and lime was very welcome.

146

'You first,' I suggested to Oliver.

He laughed, setting the mood. 'It was quite a riot,' he told us, 'that pool fiddle thing of Rowley's. They all knew by the Saturday evening, of course, that they'd come up with a first dividend, and on a week when there were only eight score draws. Therefore it had to be worth cheering about. So they started celebrating on the Saturday, and by the Monday they all knew how much money it ought to be. Then the celebration really got going, and you'd never believe – the nerve of the man – Rowley was in there with 'em, laughing and fooling as he always did, and knowing! The gall of it! For some reason, they all seemed to treat him as a hero and wouldn't let him pay for a round, and there was Rowley, getting splendidly legless, and knowing the roof was going to fall in on him. And his hand went nowhere near his wallet.'

'It's in character,' I said. 'He was like that. Worry about it tomorrow. Something might turn up – that was his attitude. It would've taken something really drastic to shake him.'

'*This* was drastic,' Oliver assured me.

'Things happened for him, though. I mean, look at Dulcie. He got her, married her, and he was the least likely . . . sorry, Oliver. Go on. I'll tell you later.'

Oliver stared at me. 'That was years before. Fifteen or so.'

'It was only an example. I took it out of context. You'll understand.'

'Right.' He raised his eyebrows at Terry. They couldn't know I was trying to link everything up in my mind. 'Right,' he repeated. 'There was Rowley, just one of a riotous group, until the Thursday. That was the day when the cheque should have come. They'd expected him to be running through the streets, waving it, on his way to the bank. But no Rowley. Then somebody said perhaps he'd gone to one of those presentations where some TV or film star handed over the cheque – but there was nothing like that on the telly that evening, and still no Rowley. So half a dozen went out to the house, but the two girls said they didn't know where he was.'

'They'd be getting worried,' Terry suggested.

'Yes. Particularly as it was in the newspapers by then. There'd been two winners. Neither of them Rowley Fields.'

'His garage?' I asked.

'It was all shut up. So . . . on the Friday evening there was a big gathering. In the Unicorn. There was no denying it any more. He hadn't sent in the coupons. It was the only explanation left.'

He stopped in order to lubricate his vocal chords.

'And so . . .' I prompted.

'They got to the stage of drunkenness where they became wildly aggressive. They decided he must be hiding at the house. They decided what they were going to do with him, and then the whole group marched – no cars, it'd got to be a march, you see – marched out of town chanting slogans such as, "Death to Rowley Fields!" and, "Hang him by his goolies!" It was as close to a riot as you could get.'

'The police . . .'

'The police, in the person of Detective Sergeant Arnold Connaught, was bloody well leading them.'

'Ah!' I said. It would explain why he'd mounted only one rung in the promotion ladder in ten years. 'And what happened? The girls . . .'

'They weren't there. Maybe they'd heard 'em coming. Nobody was there, and the front door was unlocked. Strange, that.'

'I don't know about that,' said Terry. 'The girls knew Rowley hadn't been sending in the pools coupons. They must have. And they'd know there would be trouble on its way, and their father had deserted them—'

'Perhaps,' said Oliver. 'In any event, nobody was there. The girls kept out of the way, and to save the front door being smashed in they left it open.'

'Like cars in the States,' I told them. 'So what did the mob do, Oliver?'

'They rampaged through the house, searching everywhere. They tried the empty house next door. No sign of Rowley. He'd gone. There was talk of burning the house down, but apparently Connaught'd got enough sense left to put a stop to that. Then they all went home. They say.'

Terry ventured, 'You don't believe it?'

Oliver shrugged before he could stop himself, and winced. 'Suppose Rowley was there. Suppose that gang of drunken avengers went too far. Then there'd have to be a conspiracy of

148

silence about the outcome – and there was a convenient place to bury him next door.'

We thought about that until Terry suggested, 'But if they did kill him, Chief, it'd be in some violent way. Beat him to death or something. And we haven't heard anything from Forensic about broken bones.'

'There was,' I reminded him, 'mention of a cleft in the skull.'

'But we don't know which skull,' he countered. 'Hers or his.'

'Are we,' said Oliver calmly, 'talking here about Rowley and Dulcie? Yes, I suppose we are. But there's no positive evidence yet. Likelihood and no more.'

'Oh but there is. There's more.'

We had been so absorbed in each other that we hadn't noticed we'd got company. The entrance to the lounge was no more than an arched opening, and leaning in this was Detective Inspector Connaught.

'We should've gone to our room,' said Oliver gloomily.

'No, no. Perish the thought,' said Connaught, advancing on us. He hooked a chair across with one toe, no mean feat considering he had a brimming glass of beer in one hand. 'I'm just pleased to be able to set the record straight.'

'It was all false then?' asked Oliver, being polite.

'Oh no. True enough, as far as I heard it. Most of 'em were in a murderous mood. At the very least, Rowley would've finished up with a lot of broken bones. But I'd tipped him off, you see. I'd guessed the truth, and as I could make it an official police request I contacted the pools people, and they told me they had no such person as Rowland Fields on their list of subscribers. So I had to plan for contingencies.'

'You *led* them!' I burst out.

'Of course. It was the best way to control the outcome. I led them, so I had charge of events. Or there'd have been criminal damage – God knows what. The girls had made themselves scarce, obviously, so it was just a matter of saving the house and its contents.'

'And Rowley,' I asked, 'never returned?'

'That's how it was.' Connaught took a draught of his beer. 'Sensible of him.'

'But at that time,' I said, 'he had no choice. He was dead.'

'Ah!' He cocked a finger. 'You're guessing.'

149

'I'm guessing, yes. But by now you've surely heard more from Forensic.'

He grinned. He could be quite attractive when he did that. 'I have more. That's why I'm here, to tell you good people.' His eyes flicked round our three faces, not one of them eager, each of us suspicious of his approach. Then he got down to it.

'The male skeleton . . . there was a partial denture. Upper. We've traced the dentist who made it. His records show it was made for Rowland Fields. That ties that one down. Rowley disappeared ten years ago. Forensic say there was a small deterioration of the bones. The female skeleton, based on the figure of ten years for Rowley, they reckon had been in the ground somewhere between twenty and thirty years. That's as close as they'll commit themselves. Bella was four when her mother disappeared, so that fits in nicely. No special details in the female skeleton. Only one broken bone, in fact, and it's a bit of a miracle we found it, the thing's so small. The hyoid bone.'

'So she was strangled,' said Oliver quietly. He had seemed very subdued. Of course, the decision that Dulcie must be the female skeleton would be no surprise to him, but the strangling had to be.

Connaught said, 'Well . . .' He put his empty glass on the floor beside him and got to his feet. Thoughtless. Leave someone else to pick it up. 'I just wanted to tell you that. It's late. Reckon I'll get along home.'

We said nothing. No good-nights. Silently, we watched him stroll away. Connaught was beginning to assemble himself as a person in my mind, not simply a policeman. I would have liked to know where he lived, whether he was happy or disillusioned, whether he was still suffering the pangs of having lost Dulcie. Yet he had chatted casually, even callously, about the female skeleton and her broken what's-it bone.

Oliver suggested we should finish it off upstairs. Terry took the four glasses back to the bar, and we trooped up the stairs. Oliver asked, 'Your room or ours?'

'Ours,' said Terry quickly. He nodded to me. 'Bella's probably in yours, Phillie.' It made a convincing excuse.

One was needed, because Oliver had clearly over-taxed his strength. We had located him early on his tour of the pubs, but

150

if we hadn't he'd have forced himself onwards to complete his list.

Once in the room, he slumped into the fake Queen Anne chair, making no attempt now to hide his exhaustion. I asked if he'd kept up with his tablets. He said he had, and Terry suggested there was no harm in having an extra one, so that was done, and Oliver closed his eyes. When I sat on the bed to relate my interview with Flora Porter I thought he'd fallen asleep. But whenever I paused he'd open one eye and say, 'Carry on.'

Which I did, ploughing on to the end and attempting to reassemble Flora's narrative for them. At the conclusion, though, Oliver came fully awake and alert. He was a rapid recoverer.

'So what did you make of it, Phil?'

'I'd like to get hold of that Edith Payne she mentioned. Her son was the one with the grand passion – and Flora said it was the same with her Dulcie. It was Joey Payne Dulcie was going to go away with. Now it seems she didn't go anywhere, only beneath the house next door. But what happened to Joey? If I could get hold of Edith Payne . . . I'd like to hear from her whether she's kept in touch, where he is, and what he's doing.'

'We could certainly do with finding out about that,' Terry agreed, but without enthusiasm.

'And there's something I doubt we'll ever get the answer to,' I went on, 'and that is – who was Bella's real father . . .'

'Dulcie's mother pressured Rowley into marrying her,' Oliver reminded me. 'But that doesn't have to mean anything but the obvious – that he'd fathered the expected child.'

I shrugged. 'Perhaps she'd gone past the teasing stage, and it could have been . . . well, literally anybody. Flora would look around, and Rowley might well have been the only one who could've been conned into marrying her.'

Oliver stirred. 'Conned? Damn it, Phil, Dulcie was a local beauty. All the local lads would be queuing up. It was me! No, it was me!'

'You think so?' I pursed my lips, trying to work out the logic of it. 'But with all that adulation heaped on her and all those young men after her, she could choose. She could take her time.

151

And she wasn't going to surrender that perfect body of hers to anybody who—'

'Don't get all flowery, Phil,' Oliver grumbled.

'I'm trying to get her straight in my mind, Oliver. It would explain all that teasing – she was hesitating to commit herself. And when she did, it would have to be with the one she shared the grand passion with. Who was Joey Payne. And perhaps Flora, who seems to have been in complete control of Dulcie's life, grand passion or not, wouldn't want Joey Payne as a husband for her wonderful Dulcie. Perhaps she disliked him – Joey. And preferred Rowley.'

'Phil, Phil!' Oliver protested. 'This is nothing but theory. It takes all the gloss out of life. Cold and distant.'

'Analytical,' murmured Terry.

'All right. So – for you two romantics – I'll put it like this: the weight of evidence suggests that Dulcie got herself pregnant with Joey Payne, that Flora wouldn't hear of her marrying Joey, so Rowley was chosen, partly because he'd be the most compliant. I can't imagine Tudor Kemp being pressured into marriage when his father would consider it unsuitable, and Arnold Connaught . . . damn it, he's the sort who'd dig in his heels simply *because* he was being pressured, however much he might've wanted Dulcie himself. Especially if he knew he wasn't the father. No, not our Arnold. He'd want her . . . but not to marry.'

'And where's our Dulcie in all this?' demanded Oliver. 'You talk about her as though she was a tennis ball, passed to and fro across the net between the randy racquets.'

'I don't expect you to understand,' I said briskly, 'but twenty-five years ago a pregnant young woman thought herself lucky if she could marry at all. And with a mother like Flora . . . Oh, hell, I'm wasting my time. Put it like this, from what I've heard about Dulcie, she wouldn't *care* who she married. Her life was full of available men. Rowley would be the one she happened to live with.'

I was aware of my cynicism in this, aware I'd perhaps taken it too far. Oliver raised an eyebrow.

'So poor Rowley got elected.' He pondered over it, still not persuaded.

'*Poor* Rowley?' I asked. 'What about poor Joey? The evidence is that we've got a two-way passion there. Dulcie and Joey.'

'A passion that lasted five years?' Oliver wasn't intending to be convinced about anything. Perhaps that was the way he always worked, using scepticism to press his team to greater efforts. 'If that passion of his was there before Rowley married Dulcie, and we're to understand that Joey Payne was planning to go away with her at a time when Bella was four years old . . .' He stopped, frowning.

'Perhaps,' I said, because somehow I found the concept appealing, in that it lightened my assessment of Dulcie, 'it was a grand and *abiding* passion. They fought against it, tried to live without each other, then realized they couldn't go on without . . .'

'That sounds like something you've read in a sloppy book,' said Oliver, going all pragmatic on me, with not a hint of sentiment leaking out. 'These grand passions are just another bout of sex, all tarted up in fancy words. Quite simply, when she married, Joey would look elsewhere for it.'

'Oh, you great big romantic buffoon, you! People *do*—'

'I know, I know!' He sounded irritated, perhaps with himself.

'And Flora did tell me that Joey was planning to go away with Dulcie. She'd heard that from Dulcie herself. And what happened to that passionate flight? I got the impression that he was returning, in order to take her away. Perhaps he'd left the district when she married, and life wasn't showing much promise for him, either. He had to have his Dulcie with him. There's your grand passion, Oliver. Would you have done that for me? Would you return after five years to take me away from my lawfully wedded husband?'

Terry laughed, then cut it short when Oliver said, 'I'd have dragged you off by your hair, rather than lose you in the first place.'

'With only one arm, Oliver?'

Terry looked from one to the other, not understanding.

'With one arm, Phil.'

I grinned at him. 'And you couldn't strangle me with one hand, Oliver. That makes me feel very safe.'

'Don't push your luck. It can be done.'

Terry said, 'Haven't we wandered a bit from the point?'

153

'Which is?' I asked.

'Weren't we heading towards Dulcie's murder – and who strangled her?'

'Yes.' I nodded my head vigorously. 'That was where I was heading. Can you imagine that Joey did that? Did he return to Horseley Green to take away his beloved Dulcie, and change his mind and strangle her instead? Nonsense. Rowley was just about the only one it could have been. Rowley.'

'It would be one way of preventing her from leaving him,' Terry pointed out. 'But he'd be sending her away permanently. Defeats its own purpose.'

'And it doesn't sound like the Rowley Fields we're getting to know.' Oliver shook his head. 'Not the Rowley who didn't take anything seriously.'

'Except himself.' I nodded emphatically. 'Oh yes, he's the classic example of inadequacy. Inadequate sexually, mentally, socially, and living with a basic insecurity, one he had to cover with all that back-slapping and fooling about. Then for once, when married, he'd have to face the fact that he'd have nothing better to offer than his true character, based on a sexual performance he was probably uncertain about . . . and imagine *that* coming face to face – literally – with a woman who would be to him a wonder and a delight, whom he'd see as unassailable, and was known throughout the countryside as Duck-out Dulcie! Can you see any sparks flying around? Can you imagine any wild and uncontrollable passion mangling up the sheets of their marriage bed?'

They were staring at me blankly. 'Good Lord!' said Terry.

'Well . . . can you?'

'Is this,' Oliver asked, 'a cold and scientific analysis of the situation?'

'It is.'

'Hmm!' he commented. 'Heaven help us when you get emotional.'

'Which,' I told them, annoyed by their lack of reciprocal response, 'I am just about to do, unless you two make an effort to understand what I'm getting at.'

'I'm making the effort,' said Oliver seriously. 'What about you, Terry?'

'Workin' hard at it, Chief.'

'Damn it all, you two must've come across this sort of person before. Like Rowley. He's the sort who crops up in domestic killings. He exactly fits as the killer of Dulcie.' Infuriatingly, they just stared. 'In complete control of himself, even proud of that control, but it would gradually boil up inside him, he screwing the safety valve on a little notch now and then. And if he knew neither child was his – as he had to do – and suddenly Dulcie was going to leave him . . . walk out on him . . . I wouldn't imagine she'd even trouble to keep it from him. She'd pack her bags as he watched, not caring, not perhaps even aware that he was there, in the same room. And poof! The boiler would blow up.'

Oliver moved in his seat. His discomfort might not have been entirely physical. 'We get the picture, Phil. But it's all conjecture, all theory, with nothing to support it.'

'What about the ring, the one Rowley gave Bella for her sixteenth birthday? It's not vastly valuable, I'd say, but she wears it. Rowley had told her it was her mother's, so it was probably an engagement ring he'd given her. They don't do that now, I believe. They simply crawl into bed together. But at that time it was the done thing – a gift from the man. It wasn't necessarily returned if the engagement was broken off. So I can't believe Dulcie would carefully remove that ring and place it on her dressing-table. She wouldn't give it a thought. But Rowley, he had it to give to Bella twelve years later. Can't you just see him, with a body to dispose of, a dead and probably naked body, it'd be – he wouldn't leave the ring on her finger. Quite apart from the question of identification, he'd remove it as part of his fury. It would represent an ending – a total ending. And he eventually gave it to Bella! Perhaps he loved her, loved both girls. Bella was his substitute for Dulcie. Oh yes, I think we can accept that he killed Dulcie. Don't you?'

They looked at each other, nodded to each other. 'We'll accept that,' said Oliver.

'Well, thank you.' I was a little cool, because of their complete lack of enthusiasm. 'So what's the snag?'

'The snag is . . . that they were buried side by side. And that can't be explained by saying they were buried by the same person if you're going to assume that Rowley was burier number one. So . . . how come?'

I bit my lip. A poser, this was. 'Somebody *saw* him bury Dulcie, so knew exactly where her body lay.'

'Somebody who didn't do anything about it? Somebody who saw it, but waited fifteen years to kill Rowley? Heavens, how could they have *watched* that burial and not intervened, or at least fetched the police? Phil, your romantic theories involving Rowley are all very well, but everything falls down on that. Whoever buried them side by side must have killed both of them, Dulcie and Rowley. Terry? Don't you agree?'

And Terry was looking vacant and very distressed, wouldn't meet my eye, wouldn't venture a word until pushed.

'Well, Terry?' Oliver insisted, but now with a note of abrupt interest in his voice.

'Well . . . there *is* somebody.' Terry lifted his head. 'Though only Phillie, with her analytical theories, could make sense of it. But there is one person who could've watched Dulcie being buried and could not have done anything. One person who wouldn't have had the initiative to do anything until pushed into it, when her grandmother told her what a monster her father was, and as good as handed her a tacit permission to do something about him, and who still wears her mother's ring, so must have loved her very dearly . . .' He allowed it to fade away, shrugging.

'But she was only four!' I burst out. 'Only bloody well four!'

'So?' Terry delicately lifted his eyebrows. 'That would be why she couldn't have done anything at that time, and would have been too scared to say a word, not even to her sister, Tonia, later. But at nineteen she could do something – when the surrounding circumstances put a whole crowd of suspects between her and suspicion.'

'Bella!' I breathed.

13

We took it no further at that time, all three of us realizing that we needed to think about it. The concept would take a certain amount of consideration before I'd be happy with it.

So, as I now seemed to be in need of urgent words with Bella, and because Oliver was clearly aching to get into his bed, I said good-night. We agreed to get together in the morning and plan further action.

I walked along thoughtfully to my room. It was very quiet out there, with the distant rumble from the bar seeming to emphasize the silence. With my hand on the doorknob, I paused. There were voices from within.

It could be embarrassing if I walked straight in, but I have a tendency towards objecting to having to knock on my own door. Yet it could be Jay Messenger inside there, and though Bella had said they hadn't slept together for five years, the novelty of the situation could have acted as an aphrodisiac.

But at that moment Jay himself solved my difficulty. There were rapid footsteps thumping up the stairs. I turned. It was Jay.

He seemed agitated as he came hurrying up to me. 'Thank heaven you're here.' He grasped my arm. He smelt strongly of aftershave. Did he shave at night? Certainly his face was very smooth, even glistening.

'What is it?' I found myself whispering.

'It's that damned fool Inspector Connaught. She phoned me – you weren't there.'

'So why are we standing out here?' I demanded.

He thrust fingers through his hair. 'God knows.' He grimaced, gave one sharp tap on the door, and we walked in, he ushering me ahead of him.

Bella was backed up against the window, trying to look imperious and failing dismally, looking only terrified. Inspector Arnold Connaught was there, on his feet and talking, briskly efficient but with his temper hanging by a thread, and accompanied by a large and placid man, whom I assumed to be a sergeant, who was sitting on the edge of my bed, blast him, with a notebook on his knee.

The notebook was the clue. Anything you say may be put into writing and given in evidence. Oh yes, I know the Judges' Rules. Hadn't my father taught them to me, as a litany? They embody the very flesh and bones of British justice, the rights of the citizen and the duties of the police. And Rule 2 plainly states that it is after a person is cautioned that a record shall be kept . . . etc. So Bella, I could guess, had been cautioned. Not yet charged. Cautioned.

Perhaps Bella wasn't aware of these niceties. She looked as though the end of the world had arrived and she was about to be whisked off and locked away, never to see daylight again, certainly never to see a spotlight. Though it was just possible that a situation such as this had arisen in the *Colossus* series, and she knew exactly how to portray a shattered despair.

A little ashamed that I hadn't shaken myself free of cynicism, though she had only herself to blame, I went over to her.

'Bella!' I put a hand on her arm. 'I'm sorry it's come to this.'

Then I was thrust aside by Jay, who knew exactly what to do, swept her into his arms, clasped her tightly to his solid chest, and crooned to her as though she were a child, which I suppose she was.

'Who's been frightening my little girl!' When he knew damned well who'd been doing it, though, judging by the expression on her face, which was over his left shoulder and panting for air, it was Jay who was doing it at that moment.

I looked at Connaught, who raised his eyebrows at me, and it was all we could do not to laugh out loud. The sergeant looked down at his notebook.

Then Bella said, 'Put me down, you big oaf, you're stifling me.'

Jay did so, stood back with his arms hanging at his sides, and said, 'Is this an arrest, precious?' Precious! 'Have you got a lawyer? Don't say a word. Not one damned word. Leave it to Jay.'

'Don't be stupid.' She was brusque. But at least the fear had left her eyes.

'She's not been charged,' said Connaught briskly. 'Only cautioned. Please don't interfere, Mr Messenger.'

'Somebody's gotta look out for her,' Jay declared, like Perry Mason girding up his loins.

It was quite clear that this was verging on farce, though it was a little difficult to be a party to anything involving Bella without finding the dramatics going over the top.

'Relax, Jay,' I told him quietly. 'The inspector's only doing his job. Nobody needs to get all worked up. If he wants to ask questions and there's a possibility that her answers might incriminate her, then it's only correct that he'd have to caution her, and have somebody with him to get it all down in writing. It's procedure, Jay. Protection all round.'

'What the hell d'you mean, incriminate?' Jay demanded, breathing heavily and flexing his chest muscles. He was wearing old slacks and a shirt, and loafers on his feet, as though he'd come running at her phone call. Gratified, perhaps, that she'd turned to him at a time of distress.

'I don't know what she might say, do I, Jay,' I replied. 'We've only just walked in on this. Let's listen and find out.'

He glared, but I knew that a caution wouldn't have been administered unless Connaught had had 'reasonable grounds for suspecting that a person has committed an offence'. Rule 2 wording. I had the uneasy feeling that Connaught might have reached the same conclusion as Terry.

'Thank you, Miss Lowe,' said Connaught, and there was something in the lines of his mouth that indicated he was at least sincere. And something in his eyes of a sudden interest.

He clasped his hands in front of his chest. 'Now . . . where were we?'

'You walked in here,' Bella reminded him acidly, 'with your friend there, and said you'd got some questions to ask me, then you made that unpleasant suggestion that there's something to . . . to answer for.' The suppressed anger was real; she would not otherwise have tightened her lips into such an unattractive line.

'As long as you remember what I told you.'

'I've conveniently forgotten it.'

'Very well.' Connaught refused to react. 'To summarize it: that you needn't answer if you don't want to.'

She raised her chin an inch, but said nothing.

He went on: 'You came here, Mrs Messenger – Bella, I'll call you Bella. For heaven's sake, I knew you when you were a child. Right. You came here, from the States, because of a hint that the two houses were going to be knocked down.'

'I wanted to see . . . a last time . . . my old home.'

'Understandable, I'm sure. It's just the coincidence—'

'Not,' I put in, 'a coincidence if she came here only to get a last look at Ivy House before it was destroyed. Sentimental, sort of.'

Slowly he turned on his heel. 'Are you a solicitor, Miss Lowe?'

'No.'

'Have you been asked to represent her?'

'No.'

'Then please be silent.' He turned back. 'In any event, Bella, you came. I suggest you expected something. I can't accept there'd be any great thrill in seeing those two old wrecks of houses.'

'I didn't know what they might look like now,' she muttered.

'But your reaction to the first skull indicated you'd prepared yourself for it. In fact, the indications are that you believed it to be the remains of your father.'

No response. She stared past his head.

'Rowland Fields,' he enlarged, leaving no room for misunderstanding.

She said nothing.

'May I have a reply, Bella? Please.'

'You didn't ask a question.'

'Very well. Did you believe that skull might belong to your father?'

'I didn't know. I was terrified.'

'But the circumstances at the time he disappeared were such that you would've had good reason to believe it was your father.'

'Is that a question?'

'Treat it as such.'

'Then the answer's no.'

'Right. We'll now consider the second skull. When *that* appeared, didn't you believe it was the skull of Tonia, your sister, who disappeared at the same time as your father?'

At last she moved, perhaps to veil her expression. If she needed to hide it, she was not acting now. 'I didn't know what to think.'

Connaught smiled. As far as I could tell, seeing it side-on, it was intended as a smile of sympathetic understanding. 'But you did know what to think. In fact, you'd known how your thinking would be for several days, because you'd met Philipa Lowe on the QE2, and decided she was sufficiently like Tonia to be used as a substitute. Yes, you certainly knew how to handle it. You implied that the second skull could not be that of your sister because here was your sister, in this very room . . . as she is now.' Again the smile. He was being very formal and correct. The smile was of satisfaction, that he was able to be so.

'What the hell's this?' demanded Jay.

She swept a hand towards him, but now she didn't take her eyes from Connaught. 'Shut up!' she snapped, and Jay raised his eyebrows at her, his eyes to the ceiling.

'You know damn well,' she said to Connaught. 'I was scared. I had to have time to think.'

'Ah yes. I *did* understand, you know. Time – you mean – for us, the police, to come up with a proper identification. It didn't have to be that the skeleton belonged to any specific person, merely that it did not belong to your sister. And then you could breathe a dramatic sigh of relief and tell everybody you'd been so worried it might've been taken to be hers. Wasn't that your idea?'

So Connaught had worked that out for himself, and it was exactly as I'd predicted to Bella. She flashed a look at me, her eyes huge, then her attention was returned fully to Connaught. She was clearly not aware of it, but I knew he was about to spring a trap.

'Wasn't it?' he asked.

'Well . . . I *was* worried.'

'That it might well have been assumed to be your sister's skull?'

'No . . . I don't know . . . yes, I suppose. I was worried you wouldn't ever be able to tell *who* it was, and you'd assume it was Tonia, and you'd say I killed my father and my sister, when all I'd done was go away . . .' She stopped, her hand hovering, not certain how far she dared go.

'But you knew your sister was alive,' he reminded her, gently now, coaxing her. 'You said you'd kept in touch. You'd have managed to contact her—'

'It would've taken too long,' she snapped.

'What was the hurry?'

'I needed to get back to the States. In three weeks I've *got* to. And you might've taken me . . . taken . . .'

'Taken you into custody? Yes. I get your point. But all the same, you've left me with the impression you knew who that skeleton was – had been – otherwise you wouldn't have needed the distraction involving Philipa Lowe.'

'I did not. Don't know . . . damn it,' she shouted, 'how the hell could I have guessed?'

As though it might have been a genuine question, Connaught was silent for a few moments, prowling the floor with his head down, the picture of a man facing an important, even critical, decision. Then he turned on her, and his next remark was an anticlimax. Quietly, he answered her question. 'You could guess it wasn't Tonia if you knew she was alive in the States.'

'We'd kept in touch.'

'I know. Cards. Christmas and birthday. But you can't keep in touch without both of you sending cards. Therefore you'd know her address. Therefore, you could have produced her here, alive and well, if it was really necessary.'

She didn't answer. I'd anticipated it, and she did it, snatched for her cigarettes, lit one, and drew in smoke as though it was her only friend in the whole world. She was playing for time.

'May I have an answer, Bella?'

'I wasn't sure exactly where she was,' she said, not much above a whisper. 'She'd moved.'

'From where to where?'

'Does it matter?' she demanded.

'It matters.'

162

She glanced desperately at Jay, who seemed no longer ready to pounce to her defence. He stared back with what I supposed was agony for her situation. At last she spoke to Connaught, but her eyes were on the cigarette between her fingers. 'I can't answer that.'

'Then I'll help you. Was her most recent address in Pasadena?'

She whirled on Jay. 'Damn you!'

Jay lifted his shoulder high, pouting.

'Did *he* know?' asked Connaught innocently.

'No. I don't know. How else . . .'

'I've been in touch with the police in New Haven, Bella. There are more details available. Even a photograph of the woman found dead in your holiday place.' He slid a hand inside his pocket, producing a glossy five by three. 'It all came by Federal Express,' he told her. 'I have a copy of the full dossier, and in no time at all. Is this your sister, Bella?'

He held it out. She made no attempt to reach for it, merely stared at him, or just beyond his shoulder. 'You knew my sister, Arnold Connaught. You can tell me.'

'She was sixteen or seventeen when I knew her last, which was ten years ago. This woman appears to be close to forty.'

'Too old, then.'

'But *you* would know.' He stood there, the photograph held out, reversed so that she could see it, slowly raising it to her eye-level. She turned her head away, but he simply waited, smiling, aware that she would have to look at it eventually, and that the longer she hesitated the more she would be demonstrating her knowledge of what she would see.

Then slowly she forced herself to look, said, 'Argh!' in a sound of complete disgust, and turned her back to it.

Connaught stood there, still smiling, waiting.

'Let me see it,' I said, going to his side quickly, anything to break the taut silence. Without taking his eyes from her he handed it to me.

The picture showed a woman, sprawled across an expensive rug, one arm flung above her head and the other lying in front of her, one hip high, with the legs bent as though she was attempting to crawl away, and her face turned to stare up at the camera – to face her killer – as though in supplication.

She was a tatty blonde, the hair untidy and matted and

darker, almost auburn, at the roots, her face aged and torn and raddled, possibly with horror but I guessed with drugs, as Jay had implied. It was impossible to guess what she had been like before, as the bone structure of her face was not visible, the flesh in folds and pouches, her mouth a rough and inaccurately scrawled red, her eyes black with smeared eye-shadow, her eyebrows plucked to extinction and painted in higher arches. Her neck was wrinkled, down to its disappearance into the neck of her jumper, filthy and tattered, her legs clad in torn jeans, one foot bare and one foot in a broken sandal. She was staring at me with wide, dead eyes.

And I was supposed to look like that! No – I was supposed to look like the young and beautiful girl she had been, I assured myself.

Connaught snatched it back. He was suddenly furious, went over to Bella and thrust it beneath her nose. 'Tonia Felicity Fields!' he shouted into her face. 'They managed a trace. Tonia Felicity Fields, prostitute, address: the streets of Pasadena. And you kept in touch! Where did you address the cards to? Which gutter in which street? Did you send her money for her habits? A PO box? Was that it? Money to keep her a whole nation away from Roma Felucci . . .'

But by that time Jay had crossed the room, like a tiger leaping, had caught Connaught's arm and whirled him round. 'Leave her alone!' And that millstone of a fist was raised high.

Connaught was very still, his eyes on Jay's. Only one hand moved, a quick gesture to the man sitting on my bed. A restraining gesture. A bottom was lowered, a notebook was replaced on a knee, a note was noted. He had confidence in his inspector.

'Don't be stupid, Jay,' said Connaught softly. 'Assaulting an officer in the performance of his duty! How'll they manage at the studio without both of you?'

Jay relaxed with a heavy sigh. His hand fell away and he stood back. Connaught flexed his arm and massaged his muscle.

'Well, Bella?'

She turned. The incident had given her time to recover. She was calm and in control. 'We kept in touch,' she admitted softly. 'She would phone me. I would send her money. A post office box, as you said.'

'So it was she who told you the houses were coming down?'

'No! That's not so.' She took a breath. *'That's* not her. It just can't be.' She was jabbing a finger towards the photograph, as though trying to thrust it away.

'It's her. Fingerprints. They'd put her away a few times before, so they had them on file. Go on. You were saying?'

She shuddered. 'It was I who told *her.* I'd had this phone call, you see. A man . . .'

'Yes,' he said impatiently, when she hesitated. 'And?'

'And nothing. I told her. I said I would make the trip. It was possible – we'd got a break in the scheduling . . . I said I'd come here, and . . . and . . . see.'

'Because you expected at least one skeleton?'

She tried to laugh lightly, tried to act it. But it caught on something and came out as a gargle. 'We . . . we suspected something like that at the time.'

'At the time you left? Suspected?'

'You know very well what it was like at that time, Arnold.' She took a deep breath. Her brain was operating again, and this was to be a new approach, one of confidence and appeal, as to an old friend. 'We had a good idea our father had been killed, and where else . . . where else could he have been hidden except under the floor of the house next door?'

'So you did expect one skeleton to be turned up?'

'Yes.' It was terse.

'Not two?'

'No, not two.'

'Then why did you involve Philipa Lowe in this, pretending she was your sister?'

'I did not. You assumed.' She raised her chin.

'Now don't try to be clever, Bella. You were expecting two skeletons, and we got two skeletons.'

'It was not,' she said with distant contempt, 'until there *were* two skeletons that the . . . suggestion of Philipa arose.'

'I see. And this was so that you could eventually claim to me that you'd used her only to be able to say, "Oh, I was so afraid you'd think it was Tonia." Is that it?'

'No.'

'And yet you'd planned it ahead.'

'That is not so.'

165

'You recognized a similarity when you met her on the QE2.'

'Well yes, if you like. I was struck by it.'

'But with no intention of using it?'

'Of course not.'

'Because you knew that you could always, if pushed, produce the real and genuine Tonia?'

'Yes.'

'Even though Tonia was not, at this time, what one might call an arguable reproduction of the Tonia we all used to know?'

'Are you trying to be funny, Mr Connaught?' she demanded angrily.

'By that – am I to take it – you're telling me you were not aware of how much she'd changed?'

'We hadn't actually met.' She was calm again, feeling she had got through the worst. 'For years.'

'So you expected to be able to produce her if required as recognizably Tonia?'

'Exactly. Why're you picking at this?'

'Well . . . she'd be difficult to produce if she was dead.'

'How could I possibly have known—'

'She was shot with your gun in your holiday villa at New Haven, just two days before you boarded the QE2. It's logical to assume that with a crisis facing you, such as the possible uncovering of two bodies, you would send for her to meet you at New Haven, send her the money for the trip, then ask her to join you in a trip here, if only to offer a double resistance, and that you shot her—'

He was cut short by her bitter and dismissive bark of laughter. 'Tcha! Why would I do that? Because she doesn't look like the old Tonia? It's fantastic. Ridiculous. Try again, Connaught.'

'By all means. I'm suggesting she did travel east to New Haven, to meet you at the holiday villa, or whatever it is, and you realized that in the condition she was in, booze and drugs nearly destroying her, she'd be no good to you at all. In fact – a drag. She would crumble, would say anything. So she had to die.'

Jay bellowed, 'Now just you cut that out! You're not goin' to say she – '

'Shut up, Jay!' she snapped. 'Let the damn fool talk himself

166

into trouble.' Then she smiled at Connaught, a smile that ought to have buckled him to his knees. But it bounced off him.

'She had to die, Bella, because she knew the truth as well as you did. You would have had to tell her, because it was too big to carry around yourself, on your own shoulders. Oh yes, I can see it was too big to mention to anybody, and you'd be afraid to confide in any other friend. But . . . your own sister . . . in the end you would have to tell her. She would have to be told, no getting away from it. When she was old enough to understand, she would have to know.'

I had the impression he was stringing this out, wanting to watch for any dawning knowledge in Bella's eyes, any impact registered. There was shock, certainly.

'Know what? Know what?' Her voice was close to hysteria.

'Bella!' Now there was genuine sympathy in Connaught's voice, that and something else, a quiet menace he was attempting to control. 'We've finally managed to get a good identification of that second skeleton. The female one. We're certain it's that of your mother, Dulcie. Who went missing when you were only four.'

I held my breath. He was approaching what I knew to be quite horrible, and yet he was smiling softly, as though he enjoyed torturing her. Even the shorthand writer was suspended, his eyes on his inspector's face. Jay was like a tense feral animal, caught in the moment before a pounce on its prey, and the only sound was Bella's deep and throbbing intake of breath.

'Only four!' she whispered. There was no outcry of distress relating to her mother's death. But to her, her mother had been dead twenty-five years, and time had eroded the distress of it, leaving only the memory.

'At that time,' went on Connaught steadily, 'your father was involved in a complex emotional tangle. Your mother was about to run away with another man living in this town, Joey Payne. I think something went haywire in your father's head. He strangled your mother, and buried her in the soil beneath the floorboards of the house next door.'

'What the hell!' Jay breathed.

Bella raised her chin. It was not a time to fall back on Roma,

167

but she couldn't very well fall back on herself. Now, she hadn't the strength.

'I believe, Bella,' said Connaught, not completely committing himself, 'that you witnessed that burial.'

I watched her lips shaping the word, 'No!' But not a sound was made.

'A little girl!' said Jay, shocked. 'You must be mad.'

'Sometimes,' said Connaught, 'I feel I'm going mad, in this job.' But he didn't glance in Jay's direction.

It was as Terry had suggested. The ending of it had to be terrible for Bella, who at last managed to expel the word, 'No!' In a bark of fury.

'I believe you saw it,' Connaught said. 'You were possibly too young at that time to understand, to hate, to be anything but terrified, but at the age of sixteen you were given your mother's ring. Yes, the one you're wearing now.' Because she'd reached across to it with her left hand. 'You know, I can remember it. Rowley was showing it around in the pub, the ring he'd bought for Dulcie, and we all had to admire it and congratulate him, though we were all as jealous as hell. And later, of course, I could remember Dulcie wearing it. That very ring.'

His voice had become softly nostalgic; perhaps he wished to lighten the mood. He recalled to my mind the fact that he'd himself been one of Dulcie's hangers-on. There was nothing left of that adoration but a calm and persistent voice, but now I understood that steely background tone. There was a bitter anger stirring inside him.

'I think, at that time,' he went on, when it became clear she was going to make no comment, 'which would be at the age of sixteen or so, your hatred must have begun to grow. In the back of your mind the image of your mother persisted. And you'd loved your mother. I wouldn't be surprised to hear that ring's grown into a symbol, almost religious, as a memory of her.'

With which she'd cut Jay's face, and delighted in it!

'So that,' Connaught went on flatly, 'when the trouble came, when your father Rowley Fields was seen as a villain throughout the town – and stood to lose his life – at that time your grandmother sent for you. There was a distressing scene between you. I went to see her, Bella, this afternoon. She told me. You left there, she said, just before you left the district

168

altogether, genuinely hating your father, at last able to accept that hatred. Oh, I know you'd said before – you and Tonia – that you hated him, but that was different. The wrong word – too strong. It was more a distaste. Not a killing hatred. But now, that was what it became. All that emotional upset of the past years, which you'd probably never been able to straighten out in your mind, it all came together. So you went home and you killed him, probably with the spade you buried him with later, you and Tonia. Maybe even the same spade he'd used to bury your mother, lying there on the earth under the floor-boards.'

Bella had been silent a long while, looking distant, lost in shock, as his voice bored on into her brain. Now at last she reached out. 'It's not true.' Such a weak voice it was, lacking in any feeling. Bella, this was, at last resorting to a genuine emotion all her own, despair and disgust and fury inside, and emerging as three simple toneless words.

'Then how the hell did they come to be buried side by side, unless you'd seen Dulcie buried?' Connaught shouted, suddenly, frighteningly.

At last, in that second, he was emotionally involved. Then it was gone, he sagged, and said: 'Isabella June Messenger, I am charging you with the unlawful killing of your father, Rowland Fields, and with his unlawful burial. Do you wish to say anything? You are not obliged to say anything unless you wish to do so but whatever you say will be taken down in writing and may be given in evidence.'

Bella turned her back to him. We were into Rule 3.

14

I hung about feeling useless, until the WPC Connaught had had waiting in his car was brought up to advise Bella what she would need. Jay walked around muttering to himself, uncertain and suspicious about British legal proceedings, and completely confused by the possibility that this could happen without the presence of a lawyer.

Connaught said nothing. This too was sound procedure. No relevant word would be spoken until she was officially under interrogation. Jay said something to him, and Connaught nodded his agreement. But Bella, who had heard, threw over her shoulder a curt, 'I don't want you, Jay. Stay out of this.' And that was that. Jay, a born doer, was restless when he could do absolutely nothing to help.

I walked out of the room, leaving them to it, walked down the corridor, and knocked on the door of Oliver and Terry's room. There was no immediate response. I tapped again. Gently.

'Who is it?' Terry's voice was close to the door, quiet.

'It's Phil. Open up, Terry.'

He did so, standing in a restricted opening at though guarding it. 'Phillie? What on earth . . .' He glanced at his watch. 'It's after eleven.'

He was in his pyjamas, with bare feet, no dressing-gown. I eased in, forcing him to step back.

'Haven't you gone to bed?' he asked, when I'd have thought it was obvious.

I could see very little chance of sleep in the immediate future, and in fact I was never more awake. 'Things have been happening, Terry. Bella's been arrested for the murder of Rowley. Connaught came out with your own theory.'

'I'm not surprised.'

We had been speaking quietly, and I could see beyond him that Oliver was tucked in his bed, awkwardly on his left arm, and fast asleep. I was feeling out the situation, being uneasy with what I proposed to do yet uncertain whether I could drag Terry away and leave Oliver alone.

'I've got to go out,' I said.

'Out where, for heaven's sake?'

'To Waterford Farm. I must see Flora Porter again.'

'It's too late, Phillie. You can't go alone . . . can't it wait until the morning?'

I wasn't sure that it would, being terribly afraid that it might be too late tomorrow. 'No, it can't. Terry, I wondered if you could leave him. Leave a note or something in case he wakes.'

'To hell with that.' Terry threw a glance towards Oliver's bed. 'It'll keep.'

I bit my lip. It would take too long to explain that I wanted to check only one small detail with Flora, and that if my reasoning was correct she could be in danger until she'd passed it on. What I now wished to say to Terry demanded a louder and more forceful comment than I could risk. 'All right,' I whispered. 'If that's your attitude – I'll go alone. But I didn't want to . . .'

'He'd kill me if I let you.'

But apparently our voices had become raised. Oliver stirred.

'What is it?' He lifted his head. 'Phil? What's going on?'

'Oh lord!' I walked over to stand beside him. 'I didn't want to wake you, Oliver. But I *must* go up to Waterford Farm again. I need to have another word with Flora.'

'What time is it? This late? It can wait.' He seemed dazed.

'Now don't *you* start! Bella's been arrested. There was something the old dear said, and I can't tie it down in my mind. I've got to get it straight.'

He sat up, tried to smooth his hair with his hand, and groaned. Impatience, I thought, rather than pain. 'Then get it straight tomorrow, Phil. It won't hurt Bella, a night in the nick.'

How could I explain to them my niggling feeling of urgency? An intuition. They would say it was a woman's failing, intuition, and I'd be furious. Something that Flora had said . . .

171

'If I could borrow Terry—' I began.

'Borrow him? Not on your life. If he goes, I go too. Take it or leave it.'

On the face of it, this could be a touch of jealousy, but I was beginning to understand Oliver. If I needed Terry it meant I had something to fear, and Oliver wasn't going to be left out when any protecting was in the offing. A damned foolish reaction, that was what I thought. But I smiled. Mustn't upset him.

'I'll take it. Where's his trousers, Terry?'

'Terry can manage,' said Oliver austerely.

'Manage be damned. I'm in a hurry. Take it or leave it.'

He groaned. But he wouldn't expect me to object if he offered to dress me. We did it efficently, Terry and I, helped by the fact that he'd been sleeping in his vest and Y-fronts. 'There!' I said. 'That didn't hurt, did it?'

Terry said he could dress himself, thank you very much, and disappeared into the bathroom. I crouched down to tie Oliver's laces.

'What've you got in mind, Phil?' he asked, solemnly now, committed.

I told him what had happened in our room. He pursed his lips. 'And how was Bella taking it?'

'When I left, she was standing at the window. There were no hysterics, which surprised me. Just silence. It was as though all the steam had been let out of her. They'll get the shouting later.'

'You still think she didn't do it?'

'It's just a feeling. I think it matters, Oliver, this trip. I really do.'

He thought for a moment. 'Perhaps you're right. There was just one thing that worried me. But I hope we're both wrong. Lord, I hope so.'

'I didn't think,' said Terry, marching in and using some of his dry humour, 'that we need to be too formal, so I haven't put on a tie.' He was back to normal, perceptive as ever. 'What's been going on? Plotting behind my back, eh?'

'Oliver'll tell you. Come on. You two can sit in the back. I'll go and get the car round.'

But there wasn't any chance of a quiet and secret chat on the way, because Jay was waiting out in the corridor, pacing up and down, clearly aware that I'd been up to something, otherwise I'd have stayed in my own room.

'You're going somewhere.' It was a challenge rather than a question.

'So you haven't gone along to the station, Jay?' I asked, walking briskly past him, only to find him matching me pace for pace.

'You heard her. Bella says, and it is so. What's happening, Phil? Where're you going? Deserting the ship?'

I could have stopped him in his tracks. One word to Terry, one to Oliver, and they'd have discouraged him. Seriously. But I didn't want trouble. I could even feel that I might make use of Jay. If Kemp interfered with what I wanted to do, Jay was the obvious person to deal with him.

'It's just something I thought we might try,' I said lightly, not stressing its importance.

'For Bella?' He was eager.

We were walking down the stairs into a silent and dim lobby. He was too close, too intimate in his contact.

'Perhaps for Bella,' I admitted.

'Then I'll help—'

'No. Really, Jay.' One had to give it a try, but I knew he was tenacious.

'It's all right. Anything . . . I'd do anything. Tell me where, and I'll dash back to the Clarendon for my auto . . .'

'If you *must* come, Jay,' I told him, 'there'll be room in mine.' It was clearly better to keep him in sight, and prevent him from rushing in and ruining everything.

This had brought us to the lobby. I had asked Terry and Oliver to wait out in the street, but now I caught Terry's eye. He tactfully pointed Oliver in the correct direction, held the swing door for him, ushered Jay after him, then followed me quickly into the rear yard.

'We can drop him, Phillie, if you like.'

'No. He could be useful. Let him ride in front with me, you two in the back. All right? We may have to deal with Kemp.'

'I can sort him out.'

'Let Jay do it. If any shotguns are going to be discharged, let Jay stand in the way.'

'I get your point.'

That was the way we travelled to Kemp's place. The moon was down, and low cloud obscured the stars. The headlights bit into the crisp, cold air. For some reason my driving was terrible. I seemed not to be able to judge corners, and my braking was jerky. It might have been Jay's massive presence beside me, his unbroken stream of comment on the unsympathetic treatment of Bella, his frantic pumping of me for details of the British legal procedures, or his worry as to the lengths they might go in interrogation procedures. This was perhaps what he'd wanted from me, and why he'd been waiting in the corridor. But for some reason I had the impression it went deeper than that.

When the buildings came in sight as slightly blacker shapes against the black night, there was now only one window showing light. Because of the winding nature of the drive, I was quite close before I was able to confirm that it was the wrong one, as far as I was concerned. A light in the big house I did not want. A light in Flora's, which I'd hoped for, wasn't there.

I stopped the car well short of the cottages, switched off the engine and lights, and sat thinking about it for a moment. There was no need to disturb Kemp if we could help it. He had said Flora's door was left unlocked, so I could most likely manage without him. Better.

Jay unfastened his door. 'This it?'

I said, 'Don't slam it. Be as quiet as possible.' The same applied to the other two, but they didn't need to be told.

We advanced, not speaking, towards the dark and silent row of cottages. We were looking at the end of the run, Flora's end, so it was possible a light could be on at the side and we hadn't noticed it. But I'd seen it clearly enough the last time I'd called. The last time? Damn it all, it had been this same evening. Now, surrounded by sturdy men, I ought to have felt more confident. But I did not. More nervous, in fact.

We stood, the men behind me because they could see over my head, beneath Flora's dark bedroom window, closed firmly against the chill October night. I spoke softly.

'Better not talk too loudly. She's supposed to be deaf, but it's selective. I'll try the door, and if it's unlocked I can call up and warn her. She'd probably die of a heart attack if I walked into her bedroom.'

'I would, too,' murmured Terry.

174

I was about to kick back at his shin with my heel, but a sound from my left caught me in mid-kick. Night animals? But night animals don't carry electric torches. This one was suddenly switched on, with its beam directed at our feet.

'I've been waiting for you,' said Inspector Connaught from behind it. 'Wasn't that clever of me?'

He advanced towards us, his step jaunty. At his shoulder, just behind it, there was someone else, moving in unison. For a second the edge of the torchlight glinted on metal, producing a knife-edge of reflection. It served as an introduction, and it was completely in character that it should have been in that order, the barrel of the shotgun first and Tudor Kemp following it. But it was a quiet gun, a gun carried to lend self-assurance to a man I'd have said didn't need any. There was nothing aggressive in the way it swung from one hand. It might almost have been that it had become so much a part of the man that he was no longer aware it was there. Like Bella and Roma.

'And why would you be expecting us, Mr Connaught?' I asked, trying to sound calm and unrattled.

'You, Miss Lowe. Not your support group. Though I suppose . . . a woman alone . . .'

'Why expect me?'

'Because I could feel you'd detected a weakness in my argument.'

'Weakness?' I tried to sound innocent.

'Oh come on, don't play about. You know I've got to justify Bella's attack on Rowley fifteen years after there was any reason for it. All I've got is the background – that march we had on the house – which would have provided convenient cover—'

'But which could not have been Bella's motive,' I interrupted briskly.

'Exactly. Not motive, but an opportunity. But it's inconceivable she'd have waited fifteen years for this sort of opportunity. No. The motive's elsewhere – something sparked it off. All there is has to be the row she had with her grandmother, which seems to have been a day or so before Rowley disappeared. All I know is that there *was* a row. I need to know exactly what it was, and in what way it affected Bella.'

'Why not ask Mrs Porter herself?'

'I didn't get very far with her. Apparently you did better.'

Was he implying he'd been ahead of me in my thinking, and had already asked her that?

'She dislikes you?' I suggested.

'It seems so.'

'Perhaps she remembers you as one of her daughter Dulcie's camp-followers.'

There was a pause. I hadn't intended to be offensive, but I couldn't help being annoyed that he was trying to use me to tie up his case against Bella. He confirmed his uncertainty, answering quietly and persuasively.

'I suppose you could put it like that.'

'Then you could ask Bella herself.'

'Could I? No. I want to be able to put it to her as a known fact, not plead with her, or have to bully it out of her.'

If he was at all disturbed by our disagreement, it did not deflect his grip on the torch. It continued to illuminate our feet, only minimal light being thrown up to our faces. I expected, at this point, to get a violent objection from Jay, but the darkness around and behind me was not disturbed, not by so much as an indrawn breath. Connaught could not be aware that Jay was with us.

'So we have an interesting situation here, Inspector,' I said, still lightly, but using his formal title. 'We wish, both of us, to hear the same thing from Flora Porter, but we expect to put to it exactly the opposite meaning.'

'In what way?'

'You trying for proof of Bella's guilt, me looking for evidence of her innocence.'

'If you care to put it that way.'

'I do. So what's to prevent me from lying to you about what she might tell me?'

'Yourself. Saving Bella with a lie wouldn't produce the truth, and it's the truth you're after.'

I drew a deep breath. Flattery will soften me to putty. 'Let me go up and see her. I'll tell you the truth – and you could always confirm it later, anyway.'

'So I could.'

Kemp said, his tone indicating concern, 'I don't like this. I want it put on record that I strongly protest.' He was the kind of man who likes things put on record.

'Noted,' I said. 'If you'd care to help me, it would ease the situation.'

He moved forward. I thought he was smiling. 'She knows my voice. Come along. Let's get it done with.'

He moved a couple of yards away from me. I wondered why, then a movement of the torch revealed that he'd leaned his shotgun against a corner of the wall.

'You won't be long?' he asked.

'Hopefully.'

The door was unlocked, as he'd said it always was. As before, he went inside and called from the foot of the stairs.

'Flora! It's Tudor. Are you awake?'

Old people sleep often, but shallowly. But there was no response. Kemp pressed a switch at his shoulder and the light came on at the top of the stairs. He walked up to the small landing, quietly, still not wishing to startle her. I was close at his heels.

'Flora! Somebody to see you.'

There was a short pause, then lines of light appeared around the edges of the ill-fitting door. 'Who is it? Who is it?'

'It's Tudor. That young lady's come back and wants to see you again.'

'Oh – fuss, fuss, fuss. She'd better come in.'

'Go ahead,' he said softly. 'And I hope it turns out to be worth all the trouble.'

'Me too.'

Behind me his feet rattled down the bare wood staircase as I pushed open the door. I closed it quietly behind me. Her finger was still on the button switch above the bed.

'Flora. It's me again.'

She was struggling to position a pillow behind her back. I went across and helped. 'Can't a body get her rest?' she grumbled.

'I'm sorry. But it's very important.'

I sat on the foot of her bed. Her feet barely reached half-way down it. She fiddled with her hair, mumbling to herself.

'I've been talking to Bella,' I told her.

'Hmm!' She nodded. 'Did you tell her I've forgiven her?'

'Yes, I told her that.' I can lie quite freely when it's necessary.

177

'Then why doesn't she come? Did she send you? Oh, I bet she did. Secretive girl, Bella always was. Why didn't she come?'

I didn't think I could tell her it was because Bella was in the nick. 'Well . . . frankly . . . she seemed to think it was the other way round, her forgiving you. As though you owe her an apology.'

'What for? I ask you, what've I got to apologize for? I always did my best for all the girls. Ask Dulcie, she'll tell you. Always. Advice and help. Even money. Tonia wanted money. Dulcie's always been difficult, don't you think? Have you got any children of your own, dear? No? Oh, I am sorry. Mind you, they can be a disappointment. Children can. Girls especially. My Dulcie – now *there* was a difficult child, if there ever was one. But Bella and Tonia . . . it's the way they're brought up. I was much more severe with Bella and Tonia. Brought them up strict, I did.'

'Flora,' I said quietly, 'Bella and Tonia were Dulcie's children. Only Dulcie was yours.'

She stared at me emptily. 'Yes, yes,' she said at last. 'Dulcie was mine. Yes, mine. A lovely girl. Did I tell you? May Queen, she was the May Queen.'

'Yes, you told me.'

'Never a secret kept from me,' she explained.

'But Bella, she was your granddaughter, Flora. Is. Did *she* tell you her secrets?'

'Bella? Oh yes. They all did.' She frowned, pouting.

'And they came to you for advice?'

'Oh yes. Who else was there to go to?'

'And Bella – did she come to tell you when she'd decided to go away?'

'Oh yes. Leaving Rowley, her husband . . .'

'No, Flora. We're talking about Bella now.'

'A lovely man, Rowley was.'

I sighed. 'Flora . . . please . . . can we talk about Bella? Your elder grandchild, Dulcie's daughter. Didn't Bella come to you and tell you she wanted to be an actress, go on the stage, but she'd have to go away to do it?'

She brightened. She'd got it. 'Oh yes. We had ourselves a lovely natter.'

'Bella told me you had a disagreement.'

178

'Pff!' she said. 'I simply told her the truth, and she wouldn't have it. Shouted at me. Silly girl.'

'You told her the truth about her father?'

'Yes. If she was going away, how could I know if she'd be back again?'

'In order to be told the truth?'

She nodded, nodded. At last, she saw, I was understanding.

It was taking longer than I'd hoped. Half the time we seemed to be talking about different people.

'This truth,' I suggested, 'being something that you thought she ought to know? To carry with her—'

'Yes, yes,' she cut in eagerly. 'To watch out for it. The signs. Don't tell me you can't fight against it, even if it's in your blood. I've never believed that. Her father was a dangerous man, deep and tricky. Quiet with it, but it was there. Oh – he was quiet enough. Strong but quiet. But you could see it, in his eyes. Crafty, that's the word, and cruel. No love in that man, no feeling. Oh, I hated him, I can tell you . . .' She fell off to mumbling, there being so many things she could tell me, and they were falling over each other to get out. I held my breath. When it seemed she wasn't going to continue, I had to prompt her.

'But Flora, you said Rowley was a lovely man. Your own words, those are.'

But I was losing her. The weak old eyes were closing.

'Flora,' I whispered. 'Please.'

The eyes opened. 'Yes, I told her all about her father – and she didn't like to hear it. Oh no.'

'But Flora, you can't mean Rowley.'

'Rowley? Of course not. Her real father. The one who fathered her.'

I sighed. It was as I'd guessed. Bella had assumed she'd meant Rowley, which was only natural. So she'd been confused, trying not to hate Rowley. But the mistake wasn't going to assist Connaught when it came to motive. Nothing was changed there – Bella had thought Flora meant Rowley. But would Connaught have the imagination to accept that in fact it had drawn Bella and Rowley momentarily closer?

'You've got the bed too close to that fire, Flora.'

'What? No, it isn't.'

'I can smell scorching. It's dangerous.'

'The one who fathered her,' she whispered, smiling to herself.

I had to make the mental effort to seize on the lead. 'And who was that, Flora?'

'That Joey Payne, of course. You *are* slow.'

'Dulcie told you that?'

'You were talking about Bella. You *do* mix things up, dear.'

I glanced again at the tiny gas fire that was tucked into a narrow old fireplace, surely not originally intended for such fierce heat. I could still smell something singeing.

'Did your daughter – Dulcie – tell you Joey was Bella's father?' I stared at her blank face. 'Did she, Flora?'

'Well . . . she'd know, wouldn't she!'

But you couldn't be sure with Dulcie. I didn't say so. But if it were true it would explain the strange relationship between Flora and Edith Payne. They would both be grandparents of the same child.

'But Joey went away,' I reminded her softly.

'Oh yes. With my Dulcie.'

'I'd have thought they'd have taken their child with them. Bella,' I explained.

'Well . . . they didn't.'

'And what became of Joey?' I knew what had become of Dulcie. And damn it there *was* a smell of burning. I reached over to feel the edge of the bedcover. Hot, but not singeing.

'Oh – he kept in touch,' she said negligently. 'You ought to ask Edith.'

'But she'd have told *you*.'

'Yes.'

'So . . . what did become of him?'

'He got himself into this telly business. So Edith said. O' course, she was lying. Stuck-up creature, that Edith. Got me watching some silly thing on the telly. But *that* wasn't him. I'd have known. She said it was him, but it was all pretend. Pretend he'd made somethin' of his worthless life. But that wasn't him.' She nodded. Nobody was going to persuade her otherwise.

'What wasn't, Flora?' I whispered.

'It *said* it, on the screen. His name. Somebody called Jay Messenger. Nothing like our Joey Payne at all.'

Except the Jay! Oh good Lord! And there *was* a smell of

burning. There were also shouts from the yard below. Quickly, I crossed to the door, and already there was smoke seeping through the cracks around the edges. I opened it, and a great waft of black smoke poured in, choking me. I slammed the door, and Flora was screaming, 'Fire! Fire!' Oh why had Kemp allowed her to virtually live upstairs?

There were more shouts from the yard, and banging sounds from the stairs. I ran across to the window and threw it open, thrusting out my head. Oliver was standing below, caught in a flickering red light that seemed to come from the next cottage.

'Phil! Phil!'

'Where's Terry?' I shouted.

'Hunting for a tap.'

A tap, for heaven's sake!

'You'll have to jump.' The damn fool stood there, his one good arm reaching, as though he might catch me. I turned away and ran back to the door, as Flora tumbled out of her bed, nightdress tangling her legs. The inside of the door panels was smoking. I burned my fingers, opening it, and now the smoke was a dense black mass.

It was the worst thing that I could have done. The door at the foot of the stairs had probably been left open, or opened for access. I could hear somebody coughing and cursing down there. But now we had a full stream of air, drawn in by way of the door and up through my opened window. Little snatches of red and yellow flames were writhing in the smoke, like bats. In another second the full flare of the fire would reach me.

I slammed it shut. Flora was screaming in one continuous high-pitched note, dragging bedclothes off as though trying to save them. I leaned out of the window. Terry was down there, standing with his legs apart.

'You'll have to jump, Phil.'

'Oliver . . .'

'He's run to the car. Fire extinguisher! Can you jump?'

'Flora . . .'

Fingers were clawing at my shoulder. I turned. Tears and terror distorted her face, then her hands were flying around in a panic search for solidity in a dissolving world. The roar of the fire was now loud.

I took her by the shoulders and held her still, and spoke close

181

to her face, trying to keep from my voice the panic that was surging through me.

'You've got to trust me, Flora. I'm going to drop you out of the window. A man will catch you. You'll be all right. Be all right.'

'No, no.' She could barely speak.

I couldn't argue, but picked her up, suddenly whipping her from her feet with one arm behind her legs and one under her shoulders. She beat at my face with her little fists. Another stone, and I couldn't have done it. She must have been no more than five stone, but it was as much as I could do to lift her to the sill, and almost all I could manage when it came to bracing my thighs against the wall in order to lean over, thrusting her out into the night with an abrupt shot of pain in my back. I couldn't see whether Terry was below, the tears from the smoke and from Flora's blows blinding me.

'Terry!' I tried to shout, but the smoke set me coughing.

'Ready,' he called.

I tried to throw her forward, clear of the wall, but it was a feeble attempt, and I nearly went after her face down. There was a brief image of Terry taking one step forward, then she was in his arms, and he fell on to his behind with her on top of him.

I drew back, trying to breathe in the air from the window, but the door was in flames and the smoke filled the room. I couldn't rescue anything. Her treasured photos! I threw them out. The fire-roar drowned the tinkle of breaking glass. And the letters! I grabbed at the letters, but they fluttered down from my hands. No more time. One only – I crumpled it into my fist, and ran back to the window. Looked down.

Having seen Terry crumple beneath Flora's weight, I had no faith in his being able to cope with mine. There was a memory of a bank of rotting hay, right opposite, which I could now see clearly from the glare of the fire. There was a possibility that if I backed-up far enough, and could put on enough speed in the distance available, I might do one of those dives through the open window. But there was the width of the cobbled yard between me and the hay, which now looked very thin and meagre, and the yard seemed twice as wide as it had been when I last saw it. Flora was a crumpled shape at the edge of it, and

Terry was lying against the rotted wall of the hayloft, clearly unconscious. I couldn't understand that.

Sweat was pouring from me, I could barely breathe, and the heat seemed to clamp itself against my back. There was no possibility of retreating to the door to try a run. It collapsed in a blanket of flame as I glanced over my shoulder. Terror was screaming inside me.

But then he was beneath the window, legs spread as Terry had done, muscular arms held out, chest firm and strong. Jay Messenger.

'Jump, Phil, jump!' he called, and I thought there was taunting laughter in his voice.

I got my feet on the sill and hauled myself up, crouched, poised. Hot air streamed past me so forcefully it almost had me off before I was ready.

I saw his lips form the words, 'Jump! Phil . . . jump!'

There was no alternative. I jumped, my cry of fear following me. And he caught me, staggered, recovered, holding me tightly to his chest.

'What did Flora tell you, Phil?' he asked, still with that look on his face.

'That you're Joey Payne.'

'Pity.' Still he held me, talking softly close to my face, because the roar of the fire was now overwhelming. Cinders, glowing, were falling at his feet. 'I'll need your car.'

'The keys are in it.'

'Thank you.' He hesitated, then he whispered, 'I wish you *had* been Tonia.'

Behind him, I could see that Terry was stirring. Flora was raising her head, her face red, coughing fit to choke. There were running feet from the side, and Oliver's voice.

'Phil! For God's sake . . .'

There was panic in it until he saw us. Then he stopped, and Jay dropped me to free his arms. He simply loosed me, and I fell on my rump on the cobbles, yelling. Jay stepped past me. One quick sweep of his hand and he whipped the shotgun from where it was still leaning against the wall. For one second he was lost in smoke, then he was standing free with the gun in both hands.

'Stand back,' he said, and Oliver stopped dead. Terry lifted

183

his head, and from the direction of the big house I could hear Kemp shouting.

'They're coming, they're coming.' Then he burst into sight round the corner, his eyes hunting. 'Flora!' He spotted her. She was now daring to peek with one eye. 'Oh, Flora, Flora.' He made one step towards her.

'Stay where you are,' said Jay, bringing up the gun.

Kemp stopped, as though frozen, his gun looking different from that end.

'I'm taking the car,' said Jay. 'Don't anybody try to stop me.'

Connaught staggered from round one end of the house, coughing and choking. His hair was singed and his face red, his hands raw and burned and his jacket smoking. He'd been trying to get up the stairs.

'What's this?' he demanded. There was no authority in it. His voice was hoarse. Then, trying for force, 'What the hell's going on here?' It set off another bout of coughing.

With a roar, the flames burst through the roof. The fire had now spread along the complete row, and slates began to rattle down on to the cobbles. It was not a place to stand around.

Oliver was slowly advancing, his left hand held out, palm upwards. 'Just hand that over,' he said. 'You know you're not going to use it.'

Oh Oliver, you fool, you fool! I tried to scream out at him, but my throat was tight and raw. His face was slashed with vibrating red, but was gaunt with strain, an old and broken Oliver, who walked on and repeated, 'Give me that gun.'

It came up, Jay's face distorted above it. 'Stay where you are.'

Oliver still held out his arm, and kept moving, and from the shadows beneath the hayloft, pushing off from the corner post, Terry went in low, diving, and took Jay's legs from beneath him. The gun flew in the air, and with a magnificent piece of luck Oliver caught it in his extended left hand. He juggled with it, balanced it, and was ready to fire it with one hand.

Slowly Jay came to his feet, flames from the lower window reaching for his hair.

Connaught touched Oliver on the shoulder. 'I'll take charge of that, Mr Simpson, if you please. He knows you're not going to use it.'

Dumbly, not seeing, Oliver handed it over. I went to him quickly. 'Oliver . . . you must be mad.'

He distorted a grin at me. 'I can still do it, Phil. Still do it.' The joy of it was naked in his voice.

'It's all over now,' I told him. As it was, bar the shouting, as they say.

We sat in Tudor Kemp's living-room, the lights on but the curtains open. The drive outside was littered now with vehicles and support fire appliances. The fire was flickering across them, blazing as reflections in their windows. There was no danger to the big house, they had said. Kemp had told them, 'Let it all go.' But the fire chief had insisted on tackling the cottages, if only to uncover evidence as to how it had started – and possibly from that, by whom.

But we already knew who had started it, and I knew exactly why. It had been to destroy Flora's knowledge, and mine if I'd had time to extract it.

Kemp was upstairs, having carried Flora up to his own bed. 'Should still be warm,' he'd said. She had been in shock, whimpering and moaning, but we thought nothing was broken. Kemp's doctor would be along soon to check her over.

But it was to be an ambulance for Connaught, who was badly burned. He sat at my side on a pouffe, not risking any chair arms touching his red and angry flesh, me beside him in an easy chair with half a glass of brandy in one hand. Kemp had proved himself to be a calm and efficient organizer, ordering us into his house and supplying drinks all round.

All we were doing was waiting. Terry was restless, wandering round the room, trying to distract his mind by viewing the treasures Kemp possessed. Oliver was relaxed, seated to one side of Jay in another armchair, Jay being perched on a straight-backed chair in the open middle of the room, where we could all keep an eye on him.

He seemed bemused, his face expressionless, the life seeping from it so that it no longer appeared attractively rugged, but limp and false, artificial.

Connaught was sitting with his elbows on his thighs so that he could fan his hands in the air, cooling them. He was unable to handle a brandy glass, and Oliver had said that brandy wasn't a very good idea, anyway. Lying across Connaught's knees was the shotgun.

We had all been silent for some minutes. Now Connaught spoke quietly to me, though his voice would have reached the far corners of the room. 'It was the burying side by side that puzzled me. I mean . . . how? When we knew they'd been buried fifteen years apart, then all that was left was a possible witness to Dulcie's burial.'

I nodded. He wasn't looking at me, his eyes straight ahead on Jay. I said, 'And the query was: why, if Rowley was seen burying Dulcie, wasn't anything done about it? No interruption, no report to the police, not a thing.'

'It was what bogged it down.'

'I can see why you picked on Bella. Terry had already worked that out. At four years of age, that would fit. Creeping away, trying to forget the horror. But there's another explanation of why nothing could have been done at the time. Somebody tried – but failed. Rowley at that time would've had a spade in his hands. Joey went away, and Bella spoke about a motor-cycle accident to him. But I'd guess that what happened was that Rowley smashed in Jay's face when he tried to interfere.'

'But he said nothing!' Connaught's voice was strained, reaching for something he couldn't understand. 'Nothing. Not in hospital, nothing to the authorities. No action at all for fifteen years!' He just could not accept it.

'But he went to America,' I reminded him. 'The new face got him a wonderful career. It absorbed him. He didn't give another thought to Dulcie—'

'Can we stop talking about my face,' said Jay in a flat voice. My taunt had stirred him into action. He looked down at his hands, then up again, almost in defiance. 'Dulcie was going to come away with me. It was all fixed. I went . . . went along to the house. No Dulcie, not waiting outside as we'd arranged. I . . . I waited, walked around, impatient, then I saw a flicker of

187

light in the house next door. It was supposed to be empty. I went to see . . . and that bastard Rowley . . .'

He stopped, a strange light in his eyes, his face now limp and formless. Slowly he rubbed his hands over it, and when he looked up again the agony was wiped away, and all that was left was a manic and almost puzzled joy.

'I saw Bella . . . on the stage. I hadn't forgotten Dulcie, oh no. Never. It was just that I couldn't persuade myself she'd gone. Not really gone. When I saw Bella on the stage at the Alex, I thought she *was* Dulcie. Hell, Connaught, I'd been only half conscious for a month after . . . after Rowley went at me. I don't remember to this day how I got home, or to the hospital. I'd come to take Dulcie away, see – but I've told you that. Dulcie was part of a nightmare. I never really believed she could be dead. All that was left was the fact that I'd got to kill Rowley. Got to. Then the nightmare might go . . . and Dulcie . . . Dulcie would come back to me.'

It had been, after all, an abiding passion. There was no one who could replace her – until he saw Bella. 'So when you saw Bella . . .' I allowed it to tail off, a hint, awaiting his confirmation.

His eyes kindled. 'There she was,' he said softly, as though to himself, 'there on the stage, unreal, but all too real to me.' He kneaded his fists together. 'My Dulcie, just as she'd been. Dulcie.'

I said, 'But you must have realized she was Dulcie's daughter?' I asked it gently.

'Well, yes.' He'd been staring down between his spread knees. Now his eyes lifted to mine. He seemed bemused. 'I said that. She *was* Dulcie. Could never have told 'em apart.'

'But didn't she call herself Bella?'

'Her name, that's why. And she spoke about Tonia, her sister. I knew who Bella was – Dulcie's daughter.'

'Dulcie . . . come back to you,' I whispered. But he was no longer listening, so I continued softly, mainly for Connaught's benefit.

'You can just see it. He came back here, to this district, to collect Bella and take her off to a new life. And there was Rowley, after fifteen years, and Dulcie's death was not yet avenged—'

188

'It wasn't like that,' Jay cut in. His eyes were bright, his voice brittle. 'I'd sort of forgotten. In hospital, they told me it sometimes happens. An accident, and you forget the bit before. All I knew was that I'd had one – an accident – oh yes, with my face smashed in. An accident. It was seeing the house again – Rowley's house and the one next door. It all came back, sort of in a flash. Dulcie, and *him*, in the house next door . . .'

He was tense, moving restlessly. I suggested quietly, 'Later, Jay.'

But he plunged in as though I hadn't spoken. 'The house next door. It was dark. No Bella, and Rowley's place dark. I went to look, next door. Then I saw it all again, Rowley with a torch on the floor, up to his waist in an open patch he'd shifted in the floor-boards, and a spade in his hands, Dulcie lying on the floor beside him. Dulcie dead. He looked up. I went at him. Charged at him, mad to get my hands on him, but I tripped up, and he went at me with the spade . . . the spade . . .'

He stopped. No life was now in those eyes, his face dead, as his face really was, a mask. The room was rigid with silence.

'That night,' he whispered, 'the night I came for Bella, I went there again. The house next door. Empty, and the floor-boards in place. Me, I was thinking it'd all been a nightmare, but there it was – the spade – on the ground under the boards, when I got a couple up. So I took it for Rowley. Took it – and there he was, sneaking out of his own back door. Sneaking. So I got him. On the head. Dulcie's spade, it was.'

He lowered his head, and was silent. Connaught cleared his throat. 'It must've been the night we marched up from town. Lucky for him – it laid on so many extra suspects. But I expect Rowley was safely buried by the time we went through the two houses.'

'And Jay,' I said, 'went away and waited for Bella to join him in Dublin. He wouldn't have dared to hang around.'

I could almost pity him, clinging to Bella in her image as Dulcie, but finding her to be an entirely different personality. 'And Jay,' I repeated, louder in order to attract his attention, trying to drag his tattered mind from his brooding despair. 'And Jay – didn't you discover that Bella was not simply Dulcie's daughter, but also yours?' That was casually said, as though it wasn't a terrible truth for Jay. 'How did that come about?' I

189

asked him. 'From what she's said, I'd guess it happened about five years ago.'

It was then that a different emotion stirred him, his eyes lighting, his gestures suddenly violent, as though he was caught between fury and tenderness, and was fighting them off in both directions.

'I loved her – Bella. Still do. Oh Christ, I tried not to when I found out, tried to tell myself I loved her as a daughter. It's got to be different. It does, doesn't it? I didn't know. I was all confused. All I knew was that I couldn't stand it if I lost her altogether, and she'd leave me – run away from me like mad – if she ever found out. I just couldn't face that. Nothing'd changed, and it was all different. Christ, I don't know. And I didn't dare to let her find out, 'cause of the shock. She'd be . . . oh, revolted, I thought.'

When he stopped, the silence in the room was like the chill clarity of a crystal glass, still shivering from his voice, still whispering itself to stillness. At the foot of the stairs, Kemp stood, one hand on the banister, motionless, his face empty.

'It was Tonia who came along and told you, and ruined it all?' I asked softly.

'Tonia! Tonia, yes,' Jay said hollowly. 'It wouldn't have mattered if I hadn't found out. Would it?' It was an appeal.

'But how . . .' Connaught cleared his throat and wiggled his fingers experimentally. 'How could Tonia have known?'

'I think I might have something here,' I said, unclenching my left hand, which seemed to have become a rigid container for one crumpled airmail letter. I tried to smooth it out, but my fingers were stiff and awkward. 'Cancellation date five years ago,' I said, my voice a little hoarse. I drew out a single sheet of paper, quickly scanned it, and went on, 'I'll read it out.'

'Yes,' said Connaught. He was clearly now in great physical pain. Terry drew a little closer.

'Dear Nan,' I read. 'I'm not going to ask you for any more money. It was quite true, what your friend Edith told you, and I've met him. He says he'll look after me. I haven't met Bella, though. I don't think we ought to meet. Love and kisses, Tonia.'

I looked up. Jay was staring at the letter in my hand.

'It explains,' I said to the room in general, 'why Jay had to try to kill me while there was still a chance I'd then be accepted as

190

Tonia. Perhaps then the killing at New Haven wouldn't be connected up, and the woman who was shot there would've remained a mystery.' I lowered my head. 'And the truth could still be kept from Bella.' My voice was very low.

But Jay had heard. 'She was blackmailing me.' He bounced in his chair. 'Haunting me. Threatening to go to Bella. And I didn't dare to allow myself to be associated with such a tramp . . .' He lifted his head.

Connaught's back-up had taken a long while to materialize. Blue winkers now lit the sky beyond the windows, the sirens wailing. Connaught said, half turning towards the window, 'That's about it, then.'

Not quite, it wasn't. Jennie Lyons had died, and only because she'd been on her way to prove I wasn't Tonia Fields. It had all run away with him. At that time, Jay must have been operating on instinct and split-second decisions, his mind set on killing me before I proved my identity. We would no doubt find his hired Ford Fiesta parked at the Clarendon.

But still he was acting on instinct. In that moment of Connaught's lapse of attention, Jay threw himself out of the chair, diving, hands reaching towards his only possible recourse now, the shotgun that was lying across Connaught's thighs.

I still cannot decide whether Connaught had planned a deliberate trap. But how else would he have been able to react with such speed? How else manage, against the agony, to whip up the gun, swing it round, and fire full into Jay's face?

Jay fell face down, otherwise I could not have borne to stare down at him. He was dead in that second. The impact at that distance had very nearly torn off his head.

For two seconds there was silence, then chaos erupted, with Oliver roaring something, Terry running to me, and Kemp – ridiculously – grabbing for his phone to call the police.

Connaught was sitting on the carpet, tumbled there by the recoil, three yards clear of Jay and with the shotgun now lying beside him. His set expression revealed nothing, but tears ran down his smoke-blackened cheeks, carving out runnels. I crawled over to him, unable to trust my legs.

'Tonia was your daughter, wasn't she, Arnold?' I asked gently.

He said nothing, was shivering now. Trying not to hurt him,

I put my arm around his shoulders, and we swayed together in our diverse emotional agonies until the police support came and took over.

But I didn't think it had really needed both barrels for Tonia. Perhaps the second one had been for Bella.